T0208671

PAROLED

Charles Manion

iUniverse, Inc.
Bloomington

Paroled

iUniverse books may be ordered through booksellers or by contacting:

iUniverse
1663 Liberty Drive
Bloomington, IN 47403
www.iuniverse.com
1-800-Authors (1-800-288-4677)

ISBN: 978-1-4502-9133-0 (sc)
ISBN: 978-1-4502-9134-7 (hc)
ISBN: 978-1-4502-9136-1 (e)

Library of Congress Control Number: 2011901445

Printed in the United States of America

iUniverse rev. date: 4/13/2012

Forward

The story of the adventure of Stewart Vogel is complete fiction. All of the names of people in the book are not those of real people. Places named in the book, such as the Eddyville Prison, are real. The war stories that are mentioned are similar to events that really happened.

I want to thank the many Marines that told of their experiences while in uniform.

Chapter 1

August 24th, 1983, was a day that Stewart Vogel had looked forward to with apprehensive anxiety. He had had his day in court twenty-five years earlier. Now, in a small room, he would meet with five men that would review his parole request and determine if he would continue living his life, not as a person, but as a number, with no privacy, whatsoever. He was only a number, having his sense of hearing and smell constantly under attack with unpleasant annoyances. Having spent the last twenty-five years of his life in prison, the thought of spending the rest of his life behind the gray walls of Eddyville prison shattered all meaning. The experience of living behind these walls, with felons of all ages, places a serious tax on the sanity of everyone concerned.

Eddyville prison is a Kentucky State Prison, located on a site that had once been in the town of Eddyville, Kentucky. Completed in 1885, the large stone and cement structure overlooked the Cumberland River. Because of its location, "Castle on the Cumberland" has been one of its most popular nicknames for at least the last ninety years.

While the prison, with its faded gray walls, had not changed much in the twenty-five years that Stu had been an inmate, the river and the town had. In 1966, the U.S. Army Corps of Engineers completed the Barkley Dam near Grand Rivers, Kentucky. This raised the level of the Cumberland River fifty feet at the Eddyville site. In preparation for flooding the area, the small town of Eddyville was moved five miles to the west. The prison was left in its original location because it was situated high on a hill. Therefore, the prison was not flooded. So, the town left the river and the river became Lake Barkley.

Lake Barkley is named in honor of Alvin Barkley. Alvin served in both the U.S. Senate and Congress as a Kentucky representative and became the Vice President of the United States under President Truman. Today, the sight of this large castle structure at water's edge is comparable to the awesome view of Alcatraz.

Stu was up early today, preparing himself in every way possible, freshly showered, clean clothes, and the best shave he had had in years. Changes in the Kentucky State criminal code created a window through which Stu could become eligible for parole.

The warden had arranged the day so the Parole Board would not be pressed and would have as much time as they needed to interview Stu. The board room had a long oak table, at which the five board members were seated. Stu was seated on a wooden straight chair about eight feet back from the table. A window air conditioner was humming away. He had not enjoyed the comfort of an air conditioner for the last quarter of a century. Outside of the sick ward, there were very few locations where an inmate could be exposed to air conditioning. It was a real plus having the comfort of air conditioning. Stu would have had no problem making it through that warm humid day; he was used to it. For the board members, it might be another story. Without the comfort of air conditioning, they might have called the whole day short and in all fairness, Stu's day could be lost, along with his parole.

The board's five members were: Henry Mulebaur, 59, a banker from Owensboro; Robert Silver, 61, a retired judge from Paducah; Dwight Goodman, 39, an insurance agent from Louisville; Charles Russell, 67, a retired postmaster from Greenville; and the Board Chairman, Philip Gore, 54, an ex-state Senator.

The meeting opened with the chairman introducing the other board members to Stu. He went on to explain that this was not a trial, but a review to determine what Stewart Vogel was like today and to determine if there was a risk in allowing him to reenter the outside world. Because Stu had been sentenced for a homicide, while also committing a felony, pressure was added to the board's decision. The Governor was running for election. The Governor's opponent would make Stu's release a major political issue if he were to become involved in another major crime. The records showed that Stu had always maintained his innocence and had never made any admission of his guilt. Mr. Gore said they did not want to review Stu's trial, and any parole, based on Stu's innocence, would not be considered. With this simple ground rule made clear, the meeting started.

Charles Russell asked the first question. "Mr. Vogel, according to our records you served with the First Marine Division in Korea. I feel that it would be to your advantage to tell us of your service to our country during that conflict. What can you tell us about your time with the Marines?"

Stu started by thanking Mr. Russell for giving him the chance to tell of his Marine experience. "To start with, everyone joined the Marines for different reasons. My reason was to play baseball. I played first base in high school. During my senior year in high school, I joined the Navy Reserves. Several of my friends joined during the same period. It seemed like the best way to start seeing the world. We were going to get to travel and be paid in the process. That first summer, I went to the Great Lakes Naval Station for boot camp. We were given swimming lessons and trained in firefighting and the use of gas masks. Oh, there were classes on knot tying and VD films, but the things I said first are what we did the most of.

"After I returned from the Great Lakes, Lt. Sam Anderson, of the local Marine Reserves, came by my home one evening to visit. They needed a good second baseman on their Marine Reserve baseball team. He asked if I would be willing to join the Marines. The Lieutenant took care of my transfer, and I received new uniforms. Two of my good friends transferred with me. We went to training meetings all that winter.

"I was out of high school and had my first real job working for Hoosier Movers. I made $1.75 an hour and had big plans for buying a car later in the year. We were all going to summer camp during July of 1950, somewhere in Virginia. As you might remember, the North Koreans moved across the 38th parallel in June of '50. Instead of July summer camp, our outfit was called into active service. We were sent to San Diego. Here, they...I'm sorry, gentlemen, am I going into too much detail? It was such an interesting time in my life."

Chairman Gore answered, "No, Mr. Vogel. We have the whole day, if needed, and I do find it very interesting. Please continue."

"Well, in California they had a real mess. General MacArthur was in bad need of Marines. They divided us into three groups. The first group included those with prior active duty. They were all gone within a matter of days. The second group included those that had boot camp training. My record showed that I had been to boot, even though it wasn't with the Marines. I was placed in the second group, along with my two high school friends. We received a short period of training before we shipped. The third group received complete combat training.

"By the time we arrived with group two, the situation in Korea had gone from bad to worse. The first group of Marines had almost been run over by the North Koreans. When we arrived at Pusan, we became part of the defense of the Pusan Perimeter. This was an area that was seventy-five miles wide and fifty miles deep. That was all of Korea that was not in the hands of the North Koreans. Our outfit was on the move full-time. We were the backup to the perimeter defense and moved about up and down the battlefront, giving whatever we had to help hold the North Koreans back. Moving about so much in a battlefield area, we managed to trip more than our share of land mines. I remember a black kid from Chicago was the first to spring a mine. His name was Larry. Nice looking guy; had a real friendly smile.

"I guess it's not good for me to be talking about killing, but I do want to be honest with you. I would rather shoot someone face to face than trap them with a land mine. It just isn't human, but I guess there isn't anything human about war. You had to smell the dead bodies rotting to understand just how bad it really was. I'll bet they are still killing people over there with those mines.

"After about a month of chasing up and down the perimeter, we were moved back onto ships. You never really know what a rumor is, until you have been in the Marines. There are always rumors here at Eddyville, but nothing like the ones we had in Korea. The General had worked up a surprise invasion at Inchon. Inchon is a seaport on Korea's west coast. As hard of a time as those Commies had been giving us with our perimeter defense, we really expected to get the shit kicked out of us with a sea landing. It was a real surprise that it worked. All in all, the General really was a great military mastermind. After our landing, we pushed right on through to Seoul with very little resistance.

"Things were rolling and the rumor was that MacArthur was saying that we would be home for Christmas. That sure sounded good. Korea was just a hellhole. I was there fifteen months and never did see anything worth a nickel.

"After Seoul, we started north. The troops in the south had broken out of the perimeter and we were chasing a beaten Army. The North Koreans put extra pressure on the 1st and 2nd Marine Divisions, feeling that stopping us was the key to their victory. Somewhere, we ran out of North Koreans and there were a million Chinese. They had sucked us into a trap. The South Koreans that were protecting our flanks took one hell of a beating. We had twenty thousand Marines cut off in a frozen lake called the Chosin Reservoir. Air drops of food and ammo kept us going. Without the air support, we never could have made it out. I'll never forget it.

"I was sitting on an empty jerry can when Col. Tom Lavery jumped up on the back of a tank and said, 'Men, we have got the enemy. He can't get away. We have made contact with them on all sides.'

"That Tom Lavery was one hell of a Marine. If I ever had to look at another battle field I would want Col. Lavery leading me. I have heard that he likes to refer to us as the Chosin Few.

"God, it was cold at the reservoir. The winter caught us. I get cold just thinking about it; thirty below zero and living in a foxhole. The cold was our real enemy. We lost big numbers to frostbite.

"I have been asked many times if I ever killed anyone during the war. It was a real carnage. If my life depended on it, I could not make anywhere close to an accurate guess as to how many people I may have killed.

"All of my time in Korea was in combat. The guys in the Army would get sent to Japan for R&R, but not the Marines. Korea was nothing but a full-time war. As a child, I sat through all of the WW2 movies where there were pretty girls in every town that had been liberated. Well, they will never make films like that about Korea. There were always hundreds of refugees moving around us in our retreats. I don't know if they were scared or shy, but they really made themselves scarce when we entered a new town.

"It was hard to understand just why we were over there. Korea looked like a place we should have paid good money to have gotten rid of. There was nothing there. I don't get to see many new things, but I am amazed every time I see something made in Korea. I just stop and think back and wonder how they did it.

"I have read about the war in Vietnam and the problems with drugs. All the time that I was in Korea, I never managed anything stronger than a cup of coffee. I was eighteen when I was sent over and twenty when I returned to the States. I was returned to inactive after serving fifteen months of active duty.

"Two of my high school friends served in Korea with me. My one friend, Sonny Walker, was killed at Chosin. Bob Henderson, my other friend, suffered frostbite and ended up losing his left hand. That was a little unusual; most lost their feet to frostbite. I had a close call with frostbite, myself. Bob is my only contact with the outside world. He lives in St. Petersburg, Florida. Said he never wanted to be anywhere cold again. The last I heard, he lives on a sailboat and works for a local newspaper.

"The hardest part about going home was Sonny's dad. He wanted to hear how Sonny was killed. Sonny was dead, and talking about it couldn't help me or Sonny. I told his father that I just didn't want to talk about it. Mr. Walker said I had to tell him, that he had a right to know. He even put pressure on my dad. Sonny's dad had always been a great guy.

"Anyway, I guess I made a mistake, because I gave in and told him. Sonny had been caught with his pants down. He was taking an early morning crap when a sniper picked him off. It was Sonny's mistake; a bad mistake. I still come to tears when I think about it. The early morning sun would reflect off your rear end if you dropped your pants; an easy target for any sniper. Snipers would always slip through under the cover of night. Mr. Walker didn't take it very well. Somehow, the story of Sonny's death made it around Bloomington, even though Sonny's dad was the only one I ever told. We were no longer friends and he made it a point to avoid me.

"I hope that I have given you a good idea as to my service in Korea. I would not want to do it again, but I am proud that I was a Marine and that I served my country. From what little I have been able to read concerning Vietnam, it looks like a major political screw-up that took the lives of many a young Marine and left the survivors emotional wrecks."

Someone asked if he had received any medals while he was in the Marines.

"Yes, I was awarded the Purple Heart for a very minor combat injury," Stu answered. "My good friend, Bob Henderson, lost his entire right hand from frostbite. He didn't receive the medal because it wasn't a combat injury. The Silver Star and the Korean Combat medals are the ones I remember. I know there were a few other minor awards."

Mr. Russell commented that he didn't see any record of these medals and wondered why this wasn't in the records.

Stu replied, "Sir, a lot of good Marines were killed in the same battles for which I won the Silver Star. At the time of my trial, I didn't allow my lawyer to mention any of my awards. If I was convicted, I thought it would bring dishonor to these awards."

Mr. Gore, the ex-Congressman and Chairman of the Parole Board, spoke next. "Mr. Vogel, could you just continue and give us a little rundown on what you did after you returned home?"

Stu continued, "Well, sir, after I got out of uniform, I talked to Mr. Jarrett at the Hoosier Movers in Bloomington, Indiana. I had worked for him before I was called up. He said I could have my old job and offered me $2.25 an hour to start back. He really wanted me to think about what I wanted to do with myself. I remember him saying, 'Let's face it, loading and unloading furniture is hard work and you don't want to do that all of your life if you are born white.' His cousin in Louisville had a larger moving company and he said he could help me get a job there as an over-the-road driver. The thought of seeing the country from behind a steering wheel appealed to me.

"I took the job with Mr. Jarrett's cousin. He owned the Blue Arrow Moving and Storage Company. Most of my driving trips were to the East. After living in mud holes with the entire world around me blowing up on a daily basis, the life of a trucker was a real luxury. I really enjoyed that job. The travel was exciting and the money was good. The time to myself helped me recover as an individual. I met a few girls, but I didn't have what you would call a real girlfriend. You see the country, but you don't develop lasting friendships."

Mr. Silver, the auto dealer from Paducah, wanted to know if Stu would want to return to the life of a trucker.

"With not much hope of ever being released, I stopped making plans long ago," Stu replied. "Twenty-five years at Eddyville will do that to you. There has to be a limit to the type of job I'm qualified for. I am past the age of starting again as a mover. As to just being an over-the-road driver, I've done that. In my life, I have been treated both bad and good. My treatment here has been fair. My records show that I am a convicted killer. Mr. Gore explained at the start that to discuss my innocence would be a total waste of time, so I'm not touching the subject. However, I do want to mention the small circle of friends I have allowed myself here. Eddyville has all types and you have to be very careful whom you befriend. The best ones here are the lifers. The ones that made it for murder were usually higher grade, better educated and less troublesome. I have lived in the same stench of urine, combined with the aroma of a sewer. I'm not proud, but I have stood it. I have a clean record here. My cellmate is a native-born Greek that came to this country after WW2. He is my best friend here at Eddy. I'll never forget his first day. His accent was quite heavy. He said, 'Buddy, we got to stay a long time, so I might as well teach you a good Greek game.' We played backgammon daily for the last twenty years. It may sound silly, but if I am lucky enough to leave here, I would like to play some really good players."

Mr. Goodman, the young insurance man, asked, "Mr. Vogel, you have spent twenty-five years in prison, during which time you have always maintained your innocence. Now, to help me understand you, I am going to assume that you are, in fact, innocent, while you give the answer to the next question. I would like the rest of the Board to make the same assumption. My question is, how will you look at the outside world after being falsely imprisoned for twenty-five years?"

"I have thought of that many times myself," Stu said. "I cannot say that I have changed in prison, but only that I have grown older. At age forty-seven, there is a difference. Somewhere you stop thinking green and have moved to the downhill side of life. My first year in Eddy, I felt more wronged than I do now. This place is much harder on a young man. You get used to the way things are and it becomes your way of life. Hearing a fisherman's outboard motor on the lake in the early spring is one of the most resentful times, knowing that some lucky Clyde has complete freedom and is going fishing. Each spring, after the first few outboard motor sounds, there were so many that I would quit thinking about it and it would just become another noise.

"There were two young ladies working in a bank that I'm sure were scared during the robbery they witnessed. They were the only ones, out of seven, that did make a positive identification on me. They were both very nice looking. I would have been proud to have had a date with either one of them. One of the two girls gave a positive ID. Her friend seemed unsure, but she backed up the other girl anyway. Somehow, I always felt that if they had not been friends, they would not have both agreed on my identification. During the trial, I could sense that neither wanted to let the other down in their statements. The one girl was very positive about my identification. I had been in that bank a week earlier, inquiring about a car loan, so maybe it looked like I was staking the place out. Anyway, their identification certainly changed my lifestyle, but when I think of my good friend, Sonny, getting his ass shot off, I somehow feel lucky to even be here.

"Jimmy Carter's comment that life is not fair might apply to Carter. My life has been hard, but what is fair? People are born blind, without hands or legs. That's what I call not fair. If I fail in that hearing, I will spend the rest of my life here. Now assuming the same premise, that I am innocent, would mean that the taxpayers of Kentucky have paid over a quarter of a million just to keep me here. Maybe they have been cheated, too. I cannot give them their money back and there is no way to give my twenty-five years back."

Stu rubbed the back of his neck before saying, "General Bradley said the Korean War was 'The wrong war, at the wrong place, at the wrong time and with the wrong enemy.' Well, Bradley could have been describing my life. My objective, if I'm paroled, is to reverse what has happened and try to be in the right place at the right time."

It was time for their lunch break and Stu was told that they would call him back in the afternoon, after they had reviewed the morning's proceedings.

The Chairman pressed a button for the guard to return. "Guard, please see to it that Mr. Vogel has lunch. We will want him back here in the outer office by one fifteen."

Prior to Stu's morning with the Parole Board, the board members had a short interview with the warden, the librarian, the chaplain and several of the guards. They all agreed that they believed Stu would pose little or no risk outside of the prison walls. The chaplain said he knew Stu, but had not been able to interest him in attending any of the worship services.

The board had lunch with the warden in his private dining room. Prison trustees did the serving, so whenever a trustee was in the room they were careful not to discuss cases.

After they were served, the warden asked how it was going.

Charlie Russell didn't answer his question, but instead said, "Warden, how many men do you figure you have like Vogel?"

"Only one," answered the warden. "Vogel is the most unusual prisoner that I have ever had. You can tell just by looking into his eyes. He has learned to accept whatever has happened, and really doesn't give a rat's ass as to what's going on around him."

Charlie Russell then asked, "How do you think he would do on the outside?"

"I really don't know," said the warden, while wiping his chip with a napkin. "He is different. I'm not sure where he will want to go or what he will want to do. He might just make a living playing backgammon. I understand that it can be done. He and that Greek have played that game for years. Our library has several books on backgammon. Stu requested most of the books. Nick, his cellmate, never caught on. A cousin of mine who lives in Louisville travels all over the Midwest playing in backgammon tournaments. I told him about these two nuts and he came down last year to play them. He told me later that their play was exceptional and something of their own creation, i.e., they didn't follow some of the set moves. He claimed that Vogel was the better player. If Vogel is granted parole, his cellmate, Nick, is going to have to start all over again training a new player. He also commented that he thought Vogel could make a living, just by playing backgammon."

Henry Mulebaur, the banker from Owensboro, expressed his opinion, saying that as a banker he had been on the paying end of two bank robberies. Neither was a pleasant experience, but he always felt that the person holding the gun experienced more fear than the people looking down the barrel. He knew Stu's innocence was not something they needed to talk about, but from his experience someone with the combat experience that Vogel had would not have shot an unarmed teller. He could not have made it through Korea firing his weapon in panic. Mulebaur had seen combat in the Second World War and felt patience was necessary for survival. He had been in the Battle of the Bulge and commented that Stu's telling about the cold at Chosin brought back memories.

Henry said, "Christmas day we were supposed to get a real meal, but the damned krauts started their major offense. We had a precooked cereal that we were supposed to mix with hot water. I had to break the ice out of the top of my canteen just to get a little freezing water to mix. That's one Christmas I will never forget. The krauts were shelling the road we were on and we ran up a hill and took cover in a cemetery. Those tombstones made good cover, but God, what an awful way to spend Christmas. As for Vogel, I can't believe he is the type that would panic. Most of the convicts coming before us in the hearings are in a state of panic. We have heard our share of liars, and they're scared they will fail to cover all of their lies. Vogel's not afraid of us."

Ex-Congressman Gore commented that he had never thought about inmates watching the pleasure boats on the lake. The warden quickly responded that they can only hear the motors, but cannot see a thing. The windows were painted out long ago.

They were served chicken and dumplings for their lunch. Charlie Russell asked if the inmates would be getting the same that day.

"As a matter of fact, chicken and dumplings will be tonight's dinner. However, the ratio of chicken to dumplings might be different."

Chapter 2

On the way to the dining room, the guard took Stu to a small men's room that Stu didn't even know existed. Standing there, doing his thing, he wondered how many places or rooms there were at Eddy that he didn't know about.

The prisoners' dining room had emptied by the time Stu was led in. The guard explained to one of the trustees that Stewart had been having a meeting with the Parole Board, and he should be given some lunch.

The trustee, a large black man with a shining bald head, brought Stu his lunch, a baloney sandwich and a glass of milk. The trustee asked, "How is it going with the board?"

Stu said, "I really can't tell. They have kept me running my mouth off all morning. I know tonight, after it is over, I'm going to think of a million things I wish I had said."

Walking away, the trustee said, "Buddy, you go ahead and think of them now. I won't bother you none."

Stu sat there in the empty dining room. It was hollow. Three trustees were cleaning the floor. They were making a racket with the metal chairs as they pushed them in and around the tables.

Being a dining hall trustee was a good deal as far as the food was concerned. The major problem with the job is that your buddies keep the pressure on you to steal food out of the kitchen. Stu had learned long ago it wasn't worth the hassle.

A prison job offers several advantages to an inmate. It gets them out of their cell before noon. Inmates that do not have prison jobs are kept in their cell until lunchtime. Eddyville is a maximum security prison and the morning lockup helps the overall security. Working is also a source of income. An inmate can be paid from forty cents to a dollar and twenty-five cents an hour. They don't receive cash; however they do receive credit on the account. They are allowed to spend up to thirty dollars a week in the commissary.

Stu worked in the laundry. He liked it best. It was clean, warm in the winter, and had a large exhaust fan that made it one of the best summer jobs. Plus, they had a small shower room that he could use every day.

What would freedom be like? Things had changed in twenty-five years. Stu wondered if he would even be safe on the outside. Would he just end up being some pathetic country bumpkin that everyone would soon learn to take advantage of? He had read about the business recession and knew unemployment was at a high level. Stu wondered what the board members thought about his comment concerning the wasted taxpayers' money.

The guard appeared at the dining hall door and called out, "Let's go, Vogel."

On the way back, the guard asked Stu if he wanted to make another pit stop.

Stu commented that it might be a long afternoon and that just might be a good idea.

Again in the little restroom, Stu realized that it was air-conditioned, too. Damn, why hadn't he noticed that before? Had it been because he had been sitting in the cool board room most of the morning that caused him not to notice, or was he really on edge and too shook-up to notice?

While sitting in the corridor waiting to be recalled, he could hear voices, but could not make out what was being said. Inside, chairman Gore was in the process of explaining that he had received a strictly confidential letter from the Governor's office in Frankfort, instructing him to try his very best to increase the number of paroles for the remainder of the year. The state's prisons were packed beyond their limits and if they didn't start moving people fast, they were in for a real problem.

"Gentlemen, I am ready to have a vote on this case now, and I, for one, favor granting Mr. Vogel his parole. He has requested a parole without being under the watchful eye of a parole officer. This is a problem which is out of our hands; however I do feel that we can offer

Mr. Vogel freedom to roam the country and leniency in reporting to his parole officer."

Charlie Russell then moved that the board grant parole to Stewart Vogel. The motion passed, with all members voting in favor of the motion.

Now that the board had voted in favor of his parole, Phil pressed the guard buzzer. Now the rules of the board changed and only the Chairman would be asking questions.

After the long delay, the buzzer caught Stu by surprise. It set him on edge, wondering what questions were to come next. Entering the room, he sensed that the board members seemed tired. Their faces had somehow gone blank. Something had changed.

The Chairman opened the second session with Stu by saying, right off, that the board had voted in favor of his release. He could have said parole, but he knew from past experience that the inmates loved hearing that word release.

The Chairman then added, "Now my question is, do you have any family or anyone that can help you to adjust on the outside? We have halfway houses throughout the state to help parolees adjust and we can send you to one of these, if that would help."

"First, before I answer your question," Stu replied, "I want to thank the board for their faith in me. It is hard to explain, but after all these years…well, I am kind of stunned. Yes, I do have family, a younger sister. Her name is Susan Vogel Hartig. She is married and a schoolteacher in Jasper, Indiana. My going to prison was very hard on her. She was in high school when the newspapers were having a field day with my trial. Louisville is an easy drive from Bloomington, so the local paper had two reporters and a sketch artist there for my entire trial. She wanted to defend me, but was worn down by her friends. I know that she is ashamed of me today and long ago accepted my guilt. She has two daughters that believe her older brother was killed in Korea. I'm sure at this point she wishes it were true. I would like to see her and her family, but I do understand the hardships my conviction placed upon her. Her husband drives a beer truck. I guess he still has the same job. Jasper is a little German town in southern Indiana and things don't change much there. All of the businesses are locally owned and only the family members move from the bottom up.

"My father died in an auto accident a year after I was convicted. He was my true supporter. He understood. I will always feel that my being in prison diverted his thoughts from his driving. I have read that recently divorced people are considered poor driving risks. I think my being in here was kind of like the same thing for Dad.

"My mother moved down to Jasper with my sister in 1961. When she sold the family home in Bloomington, she placed six thousand dollars in a trust so she would have the income from it during her lifetime. The trust was to be turned over to me in total if I was ever freed. She died in 1975. I wrote to the bank, concerning the trust, after her death. They informed me that my mother never took a penny of the income from the trust. I guess at this point Susan really won't be too thrilled to hear of my release. The trust would have reverted to her in the event of my death."

"So, when you leave here, you will most likely go to Bloomington?" asked Chairman Gore.

"Correct," Stu answered. "Bloomington first, and Florida second. I want to look up my friend, Bob Henderson. Somewhere along the way, I want to swing thru Jasper. I would like to visit my sister. That is, if I can do that without creating a problem. When the weather cools, I would like to go fishing in that lake out there. I really would like to see how this place looks from the water. I know my friend, Nick, is going to miss me after all of these years together, but maybe someday soon he will get his papers, too."

Chapter 3

The warden handed Stu three hundred dollars in cash and had him sign a receipt. Then he handed Stu copies of the terms of his parole. Everything had moved very fast. The court had responded by return mail and now he was walking out of Eddyville.

The prison chaplain drove Stu into the Princeton bus station. It was ten thirty in the morning and the next bus to Louisville would leave at eleven and arrive in Louisville around three. Nick had managed to get word to his son to meet his cellmate.

Stu called Little Nick from Princeton and confirmed that he would be there at three. When he stepped off the bus in Louisville, he was wondering if Nick's son would look enough like him that he wouldn't have any trouble identifying him. Standing there looking the place over, he could not spot anyone that looked even a little bit like a Greek.

He tried calling Little Nick on the phone, but couldn't get an answer. Stu waited a full hour before taking a bus to Bloomington.

Stu felt down in the dumps, having been stood up by Nick Jr. He guessed that Nick Jr. just didn't want one of his father's ex-con buddies coming into his home. Being in prison for twenty-five years makes it hard enough to know what day it is, much less to remember that the State of Kentucky has two time zones. Nick Jr. had been there at three and waited almost an hour. Stu arrived at four. It never occurred to Junior that Stu would be coming in at four.

Stu wanted to get out of Louisville. He felt more like a criminal there than anyplace else. It was there that he had been arrested, tried, and convicted. As the bus crossed over the Ohio River, tears came to his eyes. Returning to Indiana after twenty-five years was very emotional. The bridge was part of a new interstate highway. He remembered the old narrow bridge and the single lane roads.

He was excited and tired. It had been a long day and he sure as hell wasn't used to traveling. The hot dog he had purchased at the bus station wasn't any better than what they would be eating back at Eddy.

The trip to Bloomington was by way of Columbus, where he had to transfer to a local bus line. It was after ten when he finally arrived in Bloomington. Arriving, he spotted a flickering red neon sign - ROOMS.

Entering the tall narrow door under the sign, he saw a small counter area located in the corner of a narrow room. There were several hand-printed signs posted on the wall behind the counter. The largest said, PRESS BUZZER FOR INNKEEPER – ONE SHORT RING PLEASE. The other signs stated that there was a two dollar towel deposit, no loud music allowed, a one dollar key deposit and no visitors in the rooms.

He pressed the buzzer, one short buzz. After waiting, he was just getting in the mood to try a much longer buzz when he heard the door behind the counter opening.

A large heavyset woman appeared from behind the door. "Yes?" is all she said, but it sounded more like, "What the hell do you want?"

Stu said, "I need a room for a night or two."

She placed a small registration card on the counter and commented that it was twelve dollars and fifty cents for the first night and eight dollars for each additional night. "We don't clean the room until after you leave," she said. "If you stay more than seven nights, we change the bed sheets on the eighth day."

She collected for the first night plus the deposits on the towel and room key.

Writing his name on the card, he came to the second line, marked "address", thought for a moment and wrote, "Cumberland Drive, Eddyville, Kentucky".

The clerk, looking at him, asked if he'd been to Bloomington before.

Stu responded that he graduated in 1949 from the local high school.

She said, "That's too far back for me. I was in the Class of '70. Wasn't born 'til '51."

As she handed him his towel and the room key to number six, she indicated that the room was upstairs and said there was a bath at the end of the hall.

While picking up the towel and room key, Stu said, "If you have a newspaper, I would appreciate reading it if you are through with it."

The girl replied that she didn't take the paper, and didn't even like to watch the local news on TV.

The room wasn't any better than his cell at Eddy, but it did have a door that he could walk out of any time he pleased. It was pretty stuffy, so it didn't take him but a few seconds to open the window. There was a transom over the door, which he also opened. The open window let in the night sounds of the city, as well as the cool air.

He had just stretched out on the bed when he was startled by blasting loud music. He jumped out of his bed and ran to the window, just in time to see some idiot peel out in an oil-burning wreck of a car.

It wasn't two minutes later that another car appeared with an even louder sound. This time, Stu didn't even bother to get up. He thought, *Hell, these kids should join the artillery if they like noise.* He went to sleep thinking about the bank and wondering if there would be any problems getting money out of the trust.

It was six in the morning when he awoke to the noise of the city and the aroma of coffee mixed with diesel exhaust. The washroom door at the end of the hall had been left open, so there was no problem going right in. Expecting someone to start pounding on the door, he hurriedly shaved and showered. After finishing dressing, he pulled out his wallet and counted his money. He had already spent sixty-four dollars.

Stu sat on the end of his bed, reading through an old newspaper that had been left by a prior tenant. The paper was ten days old, but it was still of interest to him. He paged through the grocery ads, carefully looking at the prices and checked a few of the automobile prices dealers were offering their new cars for.

At this moment, sitting on the end of a messed up bed in a flophouse hotel room, he felt really poor. It was a new feeling. He hadn't needed to worry about taking care of himself while he was in prison. Somewhere along the line, he would have to start looking for a job.

Outside of Eddyville, Bloomington would be the only place in the entire world where anyone might recognize him. It had been years.

Walking down the street, he passed a few pedestrians, none of whom looked remotely familiar.

Ducking into a small coffee shop, he seated himself at the counter. The waitress, a young skinny girl that was all skin and bones, served him a cup of coffee.

"Cream?" she asked.

"No, thank you," he answered. Stu ordered a slice of fresh melon. Indiana is famous for the melons from the southern part of the state. Stu asked the waitress if he could see their telephone book. Looking through it, he tried to look up Mr. Jarrett and Sonny Walker's father, but both names were missing.

He waited until nine fifteen before he entered the Farmers' Bank. It opened at nine, but he didn't want to be the first one through the door. He suspected that the trust department might not be in gear this early. There was a black man in uniform. He appeared to be a compromise between a guard and a janitor. The guard was in the process of picking up some dead leaves under a planter when Stu approached him.

"Excuse me, sir. Could you direct me to the Trust Department?" Stu asked.

The guard asked who Stu was looking for.

"I have no idea," Stu replied. "I'm just trying to find the department."

The guard pointed to a lady with gray hair, sitting at a desk. He said, "Her name is Catherine Lear. She and her boss are the department."

Approaching the desk, he said, "Mrs. Lear?"

Catherine Lear, a fairly attractive and very smartly dressed lady, looked up. With a very gentle voice, she responded, "Miss." She then inquired, "Can I help you?"

"Yes. My name is Stewart Vogel. My mother, Marjorie Vogel, established a trust for me at this bank in1961. I would like to talk to someone about that trust."

"Please sit down, Mr. Vogel. It shouldn't take me but a minute or two to pull the file. Mr. Elliott, the head of our Trust Department, is at a breakfast meeting." Looking at her watch, she commented that he should arrive shortly. "By the time Mr. Elliot gets in, we will have had a good look at the file."

She then rose and walked to the file room.

It was at least ten minutes before she returned. He sensed that she was a little flustered, and had most likely read the entire file before she returned.

Miss Lear said, "I'm sorry for the delay, Mr. Vogel. Just old age, I guess. I should have recognized your name. I have made entries in this account for over twenty years. I remember seeing you play baseball when I was young. Sonny Walker was my cousin, and he was on the same team as you. I guess my mind blocked out that you had aged just like everyone else. If someone had asked to see the Vogel file, I most likely would have had total recall. Somehow, seeing you and remembering you as a young person completely threw me. Well, it is good to see you. Welcome back. For the record, I need to see any identification you might have."

Reaching into a large envelope, with the Kentucky Department of Corrections' return address clearly printed in bold black, he pulled out his Social Security card, Marine discharge and a copy of his release from Eddy.

She said, "These will be just fine. If you don't mind, I would like to run a copy of these for our file."

"Would it be okay if I looked through the file?" Stu asked.

She hesitated. "I don't think Mr. Elliot would object, but please don't remove anything."

Upon opening the file, he found a large ledger card which showed the initial deposit into the account of six thousand dollars. It was dated August 28, 1961. There was a long column showing the interest earned for each year. The ledger balance was a pleasant surprise. Trust accounts for convicts, while not the everyday thing, were not too unusual. He had heard talk down through the years about banks taking advantage of trust accounts. He remembered Nick saying that he had made as much as fourteen percent on his money market account. He noted that the interest percentage had increased over the span of the trust, but it never made it to ten percent. He didn't feel he had been screwed too badly, as he looked at the balance of twenty thousand, six hundred seven dollars and twenty-six cents.

There was a series of letters clipped together from a Jasper attorney named Richard Goehausen. His client, Susan Vogel Hartig, was requesting that the trust established by her deceased mother, Marjorie

Vogel, be terminated. The letter stated that his client would receive the full benefit of the trust after the death of her brother. In the event her death preceeded his, the proceeds were to be passed on to her children. The letter further stated that Stewart Vogel was serving a life prison sentence in the State of Kentucky and would only be leaving the prison in a pine box. Based on hardship, Goehausen was preparing to go into the Monroe County Court for a judgment that would allow his client full access to the trust account. He was asking for the support of the bank trust department.

Stu was surprised to see that all of the letters were recent. There was a copy of Mr. Elliot's reply, regretting that he could not cooperate with Mr. Goehausen's request. He argued that the bank would be liable and, because of this, he said that the bank had no interest in allowing the trust to be broken. He further stated, based on the advice of their counsel, that Mrs. Hartig would be wasting her time and money in this venture.

A young, sharply-dressed man passed by Miss Lear's desk. He stopped when he noticed that Stu was studying one of their trust department files. Every department of the bank had their own file jacket colors. The trust department files had a light blue jacket.

The young man asked, "Sir, are you being helped?"

Looking up from the file, Stu said, "Yes, are you Mr. Elliot?"

"Yes, I am," replied Elliot. "Now, if you don't mind, I have to ask who you are. I'm sure you understand that we can't have strangers paging through our confidential files."

Stu stood up, while saying, "Miss Lear said she thought it would be okay with you." Holding out his hand, he told Elliot his name.

"Oh, my God! Am I happy to see you," Elliot said, while he held Stu's right arm with his left hand and shook his hand.

Then before another word was said, Catherine returned to her desk. She said, "Well, it looks like you two have already met. Mr. Vogel is the beneficiary of a trust where we serve as trustee."

Elliot said he was well aware of the Vogel trust.

Catherine returned Stu's identification papers and placed the copies in the file. Elliot then picked up the file and invited him into his office.

As Mr. Elliot was seating Stu, he said, "Mr. Vogel, you will never know just how glad I am to see you. I noticed you reading the correspondence from your sister's attorney. As trust officer, it is my job to protect and preserve the trusts of our clients. The fact that you are sitting before me now gives additional support to both the reason your mother created the trust, and our necessity in defending it. There sure would be one hell of a problem if those Jasper attorneys had their way."

Elliot assured that there would not be any problem in the trust making a total distribution to him at this time. They did, however, need to check on any tax liability. He asked if Stu had any taxable income while he was in prison. "I will need to have Miss Lear prepare a statement for you to sign. This will state that your income remained below the taxable level for the years covered by the income of the trust."

He pushed a button on his phone and asked Miss Lear to come in.

After explaining to her just what he wanted in the way of a document and as she was heading out of the office, Stu spoke up. "Miss Lear, I failed to ask if your uncle is still living."

Catherine responded, "Yes, he is. He's in a nursing home outside of Nashville. I know he would enjoy seeing you. I'm off this afternoon and could drive you out. It would be a wonderful surprise for him."

Turning to Elliot, Stu asked if they would be able to get everything taken care of this morning.

Elliot said, "I see no major hang-ups, but you will have to watch Catherine. She will have you paying to fill her gas tank before you get out of town." Elliot, in continuing, questioned Stu about his release and asked if he had been in contact with his sister.

Stu answered, "No, I haven't talked to anyone. Susan wrote after Mother died. It was the only letter I ever received from her. Eddyville was my graveyard. I'm dead as far as Susan is concerned. It is my understanding that her children have been told that I was killed in Korea. I'm not upset with this. My being branded a killer has not enhanced her life in any way. I can understand her position. Certainly she has every right to protect her daughters from any stigma."

Elliot went on to say, "I really know very little about you, Mr. Vogel, other than what I have read in the file. I'm not from Bloomington. I did attend college here. I'm thirty years old and it looks to me like you have been in prison almost my entire life. I am sure you are gratified that your mother had the foresight to establish this trust. She must have been very exceptional. The fact that you are here helps to solve a problem, and in no way created one. While we are waiting for Susan to prepare the IRS papers for the file, what say I phone that Dutch bastard of an attorney down in Jasper. I want to ruin his day."

Stu said, "Sure. Go ahead. It is as good a way as any for Susan to find out I have been released. You can explain to him I'm not upset about this. I would also like for him to call Susan and say I will call her later."

Elliot opened the file to one of the attorney's letters. He dialed the number on the letterhead. Reaching over, he pushed a button on the desk speaker. There was a ringing sound. Elliot told Stu not to say anything, as the speaker was two-way and anything he said would be heard in Jasper, too. After the third ring, a sweet voice with a Dutch accent answered, "Schmidt, Goehausen and Steinmitz."

After asking to speak to Mr. Goehausen and explaining that he was the head trust officer of the Farmers' Bank to two additional secretaries, he was finally connected to Goehausen.

"Hello, Richard! I hope you have called to say you have seen the light, or that Mr. Vogel has passed away. I'm so darn busy, I really didn't want to go to court over such a trivial amount."

Elliot laughed, saying he knew that Jasper had gone big time, but he didn't realize that it had reached the point where twenty thousand dollars was trivial. "Getting back to the reason for my call, I wanted to inform you that Mr. Vogel is not a corpse and is alive and sitting in my office at this very moment."

Silence......

Then Goehausen said, "STEWART VOGEL is in your office?"

Elliot answered, "Yes, and he would appreciate your passing on this good news to his sister. He will phone her later. He wants everyone to understand that he is not upset with the attempt to break the trust. However, I'm pretty sure he would be less than understanding if you had succeeded."

Goehausen said, "Yes, I'll report this conversation to Mrs. Hartig. Thank you for calling." *Click... buzzzz.*

Turning to Stu, Elliot said, "Now, back to you and your trust. I would like to explain that the account could have earned more money, but because of the way it was set up as a 'money on demand' account, the passbook account was the best instrument at the time. The bank has had three trust officers during that period. I checked into moving some funds into time deposits which pay higher interest rates, but this could have created a problem with a withdrawal request. Now, if you would like to move some of your funds into a high-yielding account, I would be most happy to assist you. If you haven't got any plans, maybe I can be of service to you or even offer you some free advice."

Thinking for a moment, Stu then said, "I'm kind of without plans at the moment. My release came as a surprise, as did the balance in the trust. My cellmate had funds he kept in a brokerage money market account. I expect to move around and try to find a quiet place to settle. I think having an account with a national concern would work a little better for me. Other than maybe visiting my sister and an old friend in Florida, I have no plans."

Looking at Stu, Mr. Elliot said, "Well, Mr. Vogel, if you don't mind my saying it, your clothes make you look like a person that has been released from an institution. What say we take off for an hour or so and let me help you with the start of a new wardrobe?"

Stu was surprised. He had expected to have a problem with the bank. Instead, everyone had gone out of their way to be nice to him. "Okay, I'm your man. Let's go."

As they passed Catherine's desk, Elliot mentioned that they had some outside business and would return later. He led Stu over to one of the teller windows, saying he had best pick up a little cash. "Miss Green, I would like for you to meet Mr. Stewart Vogel. Mr. Vogel would like to withdraw five hundred dollars from his account. I have made out a trust withdrawal slip and, if you will witness his signature, we will be on our merry way."

Stu signed the slip and handed it to the teller.

"In what denominations would you like this, Mr. Vogel?"

"Five Texas tens will do."

As Miss Green handed him the five hundred dollar bills, she said, while smiling, that she wanted them to stay out of trouble.

Elliot looked at Stu. "Promise, Miss Green, we will be good little boys."

The temperature had risen quite a bit since Stu had first entered the bank. Riding in Elliot's car, Stu commented that air-conditioned cars weren't all that common before he went into Eddy. As they headed east, skirting the I.U. campus, he saw that several of the older buildings had survived the tests of time. "I have never been in a sporty car like this. What is it?"

Elliot said, "It's a Datsun Z car. They are made in Japan. Not what you would call a family car, but it fits my style. Are you thinking about buying a car?"

"I just haven't any plans, but an automobile is something I can do without for the present."

They drove into the parking area of a large shopping mall. Elliot remarked that this was all new since he had first come to Bloomington.

Inside the air-conditioned mall there was the usual row after row of routine stores.

Elliot said, "I'm taking you to Henry's. He is a great guy and a customer of our bank. I promise you, he will treat you right and he knows his business."

Entering the store, they were greeted by a small, smartly dressed, gray-haired man. He greeted them, saying, "Good morning, Richard. Nice to see you again."

Elliot introduced him by saying, "Stu has lost everything and needs to start from scratch."

Henry said, "Okay, I'm ready if you are." He noticed the just-out-of-prison look of Stu's clothes, but avoided bringing up the subject.

They started with several sets of undershorts and worked their way through the store. They bought shoes, shirts, socks, a blue blazer, and a light jacket. Stu ended up with a very complete wardrobe. He even purchased a nice piece of canvas luggage that held all of his new purchases.

Before leaving the store, Stu discarded the clothes he had been wearing.

Returning to the bank, Elliot suggested that he let the bank issue him a credit card that would also work as an ATM card, and change the trust account into an interest- paying senior account. That way, he could receive money out of the ATM machines throughout the United States. The ATM's were new to Stu, so Elliot walked him through the entire process. Stu agreed that it would work for now.

Back at the bank, Catherine looked up as they approached her desk. She said, "Where did you leave Mr. Vogel? My, but clothes do make the man."

Stu felt good about his new look and the purchases he had made.

Elliot said, "Okay, Stewart, let's clean out that account and move you into the new account."

Catherine spoke up. "Hold on just a second, before you two take off again. I have a message for Mr. Vogel. While you two were on your spending spree, Stewart's sister called. Here is the number. She said she wouldn't be home until after four."

Elliot suggested that Catherine take off a little early. That way, they could be in Nashville for lunch.

Stewart withdrew another five hundred dollars before leaving the bank and thanked Elliot for all of his help.

Elliot said he enjoyed helping and mentioned that if Stu had any thoughts of moving back to Bloomington, he could help him find employment.

He loaded his canvas bag into Catherine's car.

Pulling out of the bank parking lot, she asked where he was staying.

Stu said, "I guess you would call it the local flophouse. It's about four blocks from here."

"Please don't get me wrong, but I kind of figured that," Catherine answered. "Let's pick up your things because I know we can find you better quarters."

Catherine waited in the car as Stu entered the hotel. Going directly to his room and looking through his things, he decided to discard the entire lot. He gathered up his toothbrush and shaving gear. As Stu approached the desk, the same young lady had heard him enter and came through her door.

Looking at him she said, "You don't look like you will be staying."

Stu laid his towel and key on the counter and informed her that it was a correct assumption.

"Mister, you look like you hit oil since you came in here last night."

As he entered Catherine's car, she commented that she wasn't surprised that he had come out of the hotel with so few items. She said, "It's old age, I guess. Somehow I've learned what to expect and there aren't many surprises anymore. However, I will admit that you walking into the bank this morning was one hell of a surprise."

Catherine asked him if he had anyplace special he remembered where he would like to go for lunch.

"Anywhere would be fine," answered Stu.

Catherine suggested they wait until they got to Nashville. "It has become a real tourist attraction and there are several nice restaurants in the downtown area."

The ride through the scenic hills relaxed him. It had not been a hard day at all and Stu was really starting to enjoy his freedom. Stu told her how pleased he was with all of the help that Mr. Elliot was.

She said, "Richard has been with the bank for just two years. I hate to admit it, but I'm their oldest employee. He's my third boss, and the best I have ever had. He works harder than either of his predecessors and can always find time to help others."

Stu said, "I really feel good about getting a chance to see your uncle. He kind of cut me short after I returned from Korea. I can understand his hurt. When you go through all that I have, it's easy to become understanding. We were in intense battle when Sonny was killed. I remember helping to load his body on a truck. All of the other bodies were frozen stiff. I wanted to get him on the truck, because I knew we were close to pulling out. Sonny's body wasn't frozen. It's sad the things you remember, but I hated loading him in with all of the frozen corpses. They just seemed *more* dead than Sonny. The Colonel said we were all going out together. We were all Marines, dead or alive. He was right, too. If we had left our dead, I think it would have ruined our morale. I know Sonny's corpse never made it home. Several of the trucks took direct hits and burned. There isn't anything nice about a war and it was a war, even though Washington called it a police action. The Parole Board asked me about my time in Korea. I guess it helped telling about some of my experiences. I've talked more about Korea this week than I have in the last twenty-five years.

"My father always said that if you want to learn about someone, take them for a long drive. There is just some magic in the hum of the engine. Well, I guess I about talked my fool head off. It looks like he knew what he was talking about. Tell me about yourself, Catherine. What is your world?"

She said, "Simple. Just plain, small town simple. I live by myself in a two bedroom condo out on Lake Monroe. I never married. I always tell people my husband died at birth. Had a few close calls. There are times that being by yourself is pretty darn lonely. I purchase tickets to several of the events at the university. From time to time I even manage to go out on a date. I really do get along just fine and enjoy life. I visit my sister in Chicago at least once or twice a year, mainly when I need a break. I enjoy traveling and I take a big trip every other year. The I.U. alumni usually have great trips. I rarely go alone. I can usually find a friend to travel with. Of the things I do, bike riding is number one. Weather and daylight permitting, I like to ride ten miles every day.

"My father was Dr. Preston Lear. My mother died of cancer when I was in college. After I finished school, I continued living at home. I always said it was to look after my dad. However, I think he did more looking after me, than I did of him. Dad was a wonderful man. I will always cherish those years and the great times we had together. We went everywhere and did as much as we possibly could. I moved out to the Pointe after he died."

Nashville, Indiana is located in Brown County. Brown County is famous for its beautiful virgin timber that covers the rolling hills. In the fall, tourists pack the area to see the magnificent display of color in the trees. There are several artists that live and work in the area year-round, trying to catch a small portion of the magnificence that surrounds the area. The streets of the city are lined with little craft shops.

After having some trouble finding a parking place, they finally succeeded. The restaurant they entered had a rough-sawn cedar exterior. The interior looked very much the same as the exterior. The flooring was a varnished hardwood, complimenting the rustic cedar paneling. All of the tablecloths were red and white checked. The chairs, with their straight backs and wicker seats, completed the decor. It was a charming little restaurant. This would be the first place where Stu had a real dining experience in twenty-five years.

The owner's wife was dressed in an antique costume that was typical of a rural look. She seated them near a window at the front of the building, saying, "Sally is your waitress. She will be right with you."

Sally, a young, pretty, blond-haired girl, came to their table with two mason jars filled with ice water. She asked if they would like to order a drink first, and mentioned that they had a good selection of beer and wine.

Stu asked Catherine if she would like something before they ordered.

She responded, saying she really didn't care for anything other than iced tea. Looking at Stu, she suggested that he have a beer.

He ordered iced tea, also. He suggested she do the ordering, since they were on her home court, and she should know what was best.

Without a second's delay, she ordered two Reuben sandwiches.

After the waitress had left, he asked what was in a Reuben sandwich.

Catherine answered, "Why don't we just wait and let you tell me."

Sitting there, enjoying his tasty sandwich, he realized there certainly was a lot of enjoyment in life. Having missed so much of what he never knew, he made a pledge to himself that enjoyment of the good life would be his everyday order of business.

The nursing home was located on a hillside. The building was a long single-story brick structure, not too old in appearance. The view, which overlooked a beautiful tree-lined valley, was magnificent.

Entering the building, Catherine suggested that Stu should wait in the lounge. "Uncle Eddy is most likely in a wheelchair. If he isn't sleeping I'll be back with him in two minutes. I'm not going to tell him who you are. I think he will recognize you."

Stu entered the room marked VISITORS' LOUNGE. It was empty. He had just sat down and was starting to think of all of the things that had happened in just part of a day, when Catherine popped in, pushing Uncle Eddy. Stu started to stand, but she told him to stay seated.

As Mr. Walker looked at Stu, tears came to his eyes. He reached out and grabbed Stu's hand, while saying, "Stewart Vogel. Well I'll be damned! I never thought I would see you again." Looking at Catherine, he said, "This is a wonderful surprise; even better than when you slipped in that bottle of brandy for me. I always had great respect for your father. Just loved the man. They should have sent him to jail with you. I think it would have been easier on him if he could have shared your imprisonment. We all knew your conviction was just one big mistake, but there wasn't a darn thing that we could do about it. After your father was killed, we traveled to Eddyville to visit you. It had to have been back in the early sixties. Mabel and I traveled down there in our old Buick. Spent the night right there in Eddyville at a tourist home. The next morning it was cold as all hell. We were standing in line at the visitor's entrance and I just changed my mind. Those cold gray walls had an effect on me. I remember saying how I just didn't want to see that boy behind those walls. We drove all of the way back to Bloomington without saying one word, and I'm sure you remember how Mabel liked to talk. I wanted to tell you I was sorry for the way I acted after Sonny was killed." He stopped and looked up toward the ceiling. "You hear that, Mabel? I said it. Now get back to your harp."

As they were walking back to the car, she held out her car keys, asking if he would like to drive.

Looking at her, he said, "Thanks, but I think I had better pass. I haven't obtained a driver's license and it could become a major problem if something happened."

Heading back over the same scenic highway, now being shaded by the late afternoon sun, they were both silent. After about ten miles, he spoke up, asking where she was going to find a place for him to bunk.

She said, "I want you to stay at my place. I'm not going to let you stay anywhere else, and besides, I am going to prepare you your first home-cooked meal."

Chapter 4

Her condominium was a large contemporary unit, with the living room ceiling open to the second floor. The bedrooms opened onto a balcony that also served as the upstairs hall.

Stu needed to phone Susan, and asked for permission to make the long distance call. "I can pay you later."

Catherine said, "Don't be silly. I want you to know you are welcome here and I'm in no rush to get rid of you. I kind of like having a man around from time to time. If nothing else, it helps my image. I want you to plan on staying here whenever you are in town, even if it takes another twenty-five years."

Catherine announced, while he was phoning Susan, that she was going to take a short bike ride. She would borrow her neighbor's bike and leave it outside the front door. If he wanted to join her after his call, he could just head out the drive and turn left on the road toward town. He would not catch her, but they would meet up on her way back.

She again suggested that he invite Susan to drive up tomorrow, saying she would clear out and let the two of them have a real reunion. "However, I'm flexible, and would enjoy the drive to Jasper if that would work better."

After dialing the number that Catherine had given him, he heard the voice on the other end.

"Hello."

Stu asked, "Is this Susan?"

She answered, "Stewart, I cannot believe it's you. When did you...?"

Stu was quick to answer, "Yesterday morning."

Susan asked where he was and when she could see him.

She asked, "Would tomorrow be too soon?" He explained that he was staying with Sonny Walker's cousin. "She lives out at Lake Monroe, at a place called the Pointe."

Susan said, "Yes, I know the place. Al's boss owns one of the units. We have stayed there in the past. I could make it up there tomorrow around ten if that would work."

Stu said, "I'm looking forward to seeing you and ten tomorrow will be just fine. We can talk about the past and the future. It will do us both good. I'm staying in unit 16."

Susan commented that number 16 would be one of the early units overlooking the lake.

Maybe Catherine was right. Working up a good sweat might be good. He found the bike where she had left it. He had never seen a ten-speed bike and didn't understand the first thing about how the gears worked. As he rode out the drive toward the road, it seemed he had to pedal fast for the little forward motion he was producing. He knew something was wrong. Looking down, he figured that the chain needed to be moved to a larger-sized gear on the rear sprocket. Following the cable from the chain-shifting device to the forward lever, he began to understand how it worked. By the time he had pedaled the short distance to the road, he had figured out how to shift into all of the different gears. Biking was great, and something he had never even thought that he would ever be doing again in his life. He could understand Catherine's love for biking. After about three miles, he spotted Catherine coming from the opposite direction. She was wearing a helmet, some very tight pants, and gloves. He observed how very trim she was. He couldn't remember her from when he was growing up. He knew Sonny had other family in Bloomington. He guessed she must have been at least three or four years older.

As they were parking their bikes, she suggested he retrieve his luggage from her car.

Walking in with his bag in hand, he asked Catherine where he should put it.

"There are two bedrooms upstairs; one is mine and the other is a guest room. You can put your bag wherever you would like to sleep."

Stu was a little confused. He wasn't too sure what Catherine had said, and if he had heard her correctly.

When Stu returned from the upstairs, after placing his luggage in the guest room, Catherine handed him a tall cold drink.

She said, "Drink up, and then tell me what you think it is."

Halfway through the drink, he said it had to be part lemonade, but couldn't guess what else.

Smiling, she said, "Beer. I have found it to be great after a bike ride." She added that it was two thirds lemonade and one third beer.

As she finished her drink, she remarked that it was time for a shower.

Raising his right arm while turning his nose toward his armpit, Stu said, "I guess I should too."

Catherine responded, "With me."

Things had started to move too fast. He gently took hold of her arm and guided her to the large U-shaped sofa. "Please sit down for a minute and let me tell you a little about myself."

Catherine didn't say a word. She sat down across from him, wondering what was going to be said.

Stu said, "This has already been the greatest day of my entire life. It started out with finding twenty thousand in the trust. Then, I had lunch off of a china plate instead of a plastic tray, with a real tablecloth on the table and real meat in the sandwich, which tasted great, instead of some soybean-filled baloney. I'm wearing clothes that make me feel like a real person. I didn't need to get my cell door unlocked. This has been a day of total change, really nice change, and I have enjoyed every second. Without you, this day could have turned into a loser. I have been showering with other people for the last twenty-five years, some of whom wanted to do more than just shower. My problem is that I have to change from being a number in an institution to a person in a private world. Privacy is a privilege which can only be enjoyed by a free man. Behind bars it doesn't exist. Every new inmate has trouble with constipation. They shy away from the exposed commodes until their bowels hurt. What I'm saying is, for now I need to shower and sleep alone."

He explained that it was not uncommon for men in his position to commit suicide. The change can get to be too much to handle. He wasn't the suicide type, but there were times at Eddy it would have been the easy way.

He stood and moved to where Catherine was seated. Sitting down, he placed his arm around her and kissed her on the cheek. "You are the dearest person I have ever met, but for now I'm just going to have to be your kissing cousin. Everything is so changed. I feel like a fish out of water."

Opening his bedroom door, after he had showered and dressed, he smelled the spicy aroma of the lasagna she had placed in the oven earlier.

Hearing his door open, she called, "Hey, cousin, come down and open the wine."

During dinner, Catherine informed him that it was standard procedure for her neighbor, Fred, and his wife to come over. "We drink a little sherry and play several games of backgammon. Nel is a sweet girl. To me, she is just wife number four. I have learned not to get too close to Fred's wives. It hurts too much when he moves them out. Nel will go through the sherry while we are playing. They are both harmless and I always enjoy our Friday nights. Have you ever played backgammon?"

Stu told how his cellmate, Nick, had taught him a little about the game.

Fred and Nel entered without any of the formality of knocking or ringing the doorbell. They just walked in like family. Stu jumped up and introduced himself, saying he was Catherine's cousin from Kentucky. Fred looked to be a good thirty years older than Nel.

Fred informed Catherine that he'd had a bad day and would show her no mercy tonight. "Hey, Vogel, you ever play this game?"

"Yes, but I am sure I'm not in your league."

Fred said, "Actually, there are very few in my league and I consider myself to be one of the best players in the state."

Stu said that if he was that good maybe he could learn some good moves from him.

Fred was quick to say, "If it's a lesson you want, I play for five dollars a point."

Stu had never played backgammon for money, but was very excited to have his first chance.

Fred rubbed his hands together and told Catherine he hoped she wouldn't mind if he gave her cousin a little education.

Catherine nodded her approval.

Fred advised Nel to find a good show on the tube, as it might be a longer session than usual.

Stu said he didn't want to play very late, so they should set a quitting time. It was agreed that they wouldn't start a new game after ten thirty.

Catherine warned Stu that he could easily lose several hundred dollars playing with Fred.

Stu said he understood it was a game of luck and Fred just didn't look that lucky.

Stu won the opening roll. Fred felt that Stu's first move was that of a very inexperienced player. Fred quickly turned the doubling cube.

In the game of backgammon, doubling presses the opponent into playing the game for twice the amount, or forfeiting. Once the cube has been passed, the player that accepts the double owns the cube. Only the doubled player can double again. Each time the cube passes, the ownership of the cube changes. A game starting at five dollars would change into a twenty dollar game after two doubles. Winning a game with a gammon doubles the amount again; a backgammon triples the amount.

As the evening wore on, Stu built up a commanding lead. He could tell Fred was an excellent player. Fred, however, did not understand that Stu's overall play was superior. Fred kept pushing the doubling cube and continued losing. At the ten thirty quitting time, Fred was down three hundred and thirty-five dollars.

Fred was convinced that he was the superior player and Stu had just been extremely lucky. He said, "Catherine, where did you find this lucky bastard?" Turning to Stu, he commented that he hoped Stu realized he had been very lucky. Fred told him he had several faults in his game. "Moving too fast and not studying your moves is going to make you a loser."

Stu acknowledged he had been lucky.

Fred said he needed to have a return session with Stu, so he could get his money back with interest. "We will host the dinner tomorrow." It sounded more like a command than an invitation.

Fred then excused himself, saying he needed to make a quick visit to the bathroom. To Catherine's surprise, he used one of the upstairs baths.

As Fred descended the stairs, she questioned him. She had never known him to use one of her upstairs baths before.

Fred said, "If you must know, I just wanted to see if Stewart's suitcase was in your guest room. Hell, I guess he really is your cousin." Walking out the door, he advised Stu not to spend his money because he would need it to pay off tomorrow.

After Nel and Fred had left, Catherine turned to Stu. She said the game was way too fast for her, but wanted to know if he was really lucky or had he actually outplayed Fred?

Stu said, "Yes, there was luck, but Fred was the one having it. He's lucky he didn't lose more. Fred sounds like he has known you for a long time."

Catherine said, "Yes, we have never been more than just good friends. He likes his women young. He enjoys coming over here in the evening for adult conversation. You haven't told me about Susan."

He said, "She will be here in the morning around ten."

Catherine suggested that they should have a schedule for tomorrow. They needed to bike early before the traffic picked up with the boaters coming out to the lake. Next, they would have a light breakfast while they cooled down. After breakfast, they could shower, separately, and dress for the day. She also wanted to give him a laundry lesson, before he ruined some of his new clothes.

He thought, *I've worked in a laundry and she wants to show me.*

She said she would leave before nine thirty, so he would have the whole place to himself. She would fix two chicken salad plates and leave them covered in the refrigerator. There was always the Four Winds Inn, if they needed a break and wanted to eat out. She had several errands to run and plenty to keep her busy. She guessed that she would be back home around 4 o'clock.

Stu said that if he could borrow a typewriter, he would like to send a letter to the Governor of Kentucky. He was sure he could get her some government funding if the Governor knew she was running a halfway house.

In the morning, Stu had finished shaving and was getting dressed when she knocked on his door to see if he was up. Downstairs, she handed him a large glass of orange juice.

She said, "This is all you get until we finish our ride."

He commented that he felt like he was in training.

Out on the road he started getting tired earlier than he had the day before. The seat felt harder, too. He slowed up. He would just have to go at his own pace. She didn't seem to mind and just kept pulling out further ahead. He turned around at the same point he had the day before. He was completely showered and dressed by the time she returned. He had found the coffee and had it brewing.

Catherine asked, "What happened to you?"

"Nothing," Stu replied. "I just have my limits. Don't worry. I'll be in shape when the season opens."

She said they were going to have some extra special melon a farmer brings to her at the bank. "I think he is sweet on me. He is eighty-two, going on ninety. Next week he is bringing me some of the first sweet corn of the season."

She said, "I still have last Sunday's Indianapolis Star, if you would like to look through it while I am dressing."

In the back section of the paper there was an advertisement for a cut-rate early morning flight to Tampa. The flight departed from Indianapolis three days a week, Tuesday, Wednesday and Saturday at three o'clock a.m. It was a direct flight, arriving in Tampa at five forty a.m. He called the 800 number listed in the advertisement.

The lady answering for the airline was very pleasant. She explained that their flight to Tampa was never fully booked this time of the year. When he was ready to go, there would be an empty seat ready for him. The advertisement was announcing the summer special of $99.00 to Tampa.

Stu had his dirty laundry ready for his lesson when Catherine came down. She guessed that Susan would be on her way by now and wondered if she needed to fix a third lunch, just in case she brought her husband.

He told her not to bother because they could always go to the Inn.

"Stu, about tonight…are you sure you want to go over to Fred's?" asked Catherine.

He was actually looking forward to it, but told her he didn't want to stay late. They both agreed to be home in time for the ten o'clock news.

Stu said, "There is something I would enjoy doing in the morning, if it wouldn't inconvenience you too much." Stu said he hadn't gone to church in years and had stopped going after his return from the war. He had never attended church in Louisville. The few times he returned to Bloomington he did go with his parents. Stu had checked the phone book and St. Mary's had a ten o'clock Mass in the morning.

Catherine pointed out that they could take a seven o'clock a.m. bike ride and still make it in to church. "Would you like to visit your parents' graves after church?"

Stu said he had dug too many graves and didn't want to start visiting them. His next trip to a cemetery would be one way.

She asked if he had any other plans he might be making. He said it depended on Susan. He would love to meet his two nieces and her husband. It had been a very long time, but he didn't know if he would be welcome in Jasper. If that were the case, he wanted to catch an early morning flight out of Indianapolis to Tampa. Stu said she might remember Bob Henderson since he had been the star pitcher on their high school baseball team. They were all in Korea together. Catherine remembered that Bob had returned from Korea, minus his pitching hand. Everyone talked about his hand. Somehow, Sonny's death wasn't talked about. Dismemberment doesn't go away. The dead are buried and forgotten.

Bob didn't know he was out of prison and Stu really was looking forward to surprising him. Bob had been his only friend on the outside for all of these years. "I would say he is the only one left today that is still positive I couldn't have been involved with a robbery," Stu said.

Bob, Sonny and Stu had a very special relationship. They liked to call themselves the Holy Trinity. They took care of each other and saved each other's hides several times. In the process, they had killed the enemy. They could never be too sure all of the Koreans they shot were North Koreans. They had to be careful and couldn't put trust in anyone other than another Marine. They had trouble with the Koreans stealing their supplies.

The Koreans weren't the only thieves. Sonny and Stu had done a little stealing of their own. They managed to steal a large diesel generator from the Army. "We were the only outfit without a generator and were tired of being second class citizens. Captain Hamilton didn't ask any questions when we showed up towing the U.S. Army generator. He did suggest it looked a little ragged and maybe it could use a fresh coat of paint."

Bob's testimony at his trial really hadn't helped. Although his lawyer thought the testimony of a disabled veteran could help, as it turned out, the prosecutor turned everything Bob said around. He had been a poor witness and was the turning point of the trial. Stu was never pleased with his lawyer. Stu hadn't even been in Louisville at the time of the robbery, and somehow throughout the trial, his lawyer failed to establish that fact.

Now that Stu was talking about leaving, Catherine told him how much she enjoyed having him and wanted him to feel free to come back anytime. "I would like for you to consider coming back. I have lived a fairly lonely life. Maybe we could even find a way to share some time together."

Stu said, "It's nice to know I have not worn out my welcome. I would like to come back and visit. I would also like for you to visit me wherever I settle, just as long as the place hasn't got visiting hours. I've been a kept man for years. If I moved in, I would just be a kept man again. I need to live alone for now. I also need friends. I want you to be my special friend."

Looking at her watch, she announced it was time for her to leave. Susan should be showing up anytime now.

After she left, he stood by the window, watching the sailboats on the lake. There wasn't much of a breeze, but they seemed to be moving at a good clip.

It was ten forty when the doorbell finally rang. Albert was standing next to Susan.

Both Susan and Albert squeaked with nervousness as they said, "Hello."

They certainly didn't have to fear him. Why were they so nervous?

Susan was heavier than he had expected. She had never been overweight before. Albert was not a surprise. He was pretty much the same as his mother had described him. She had referred to him as a big thick-headed Dutchman. From Stu's first observation, she was most likely correct.

Albert came right out with questions about his release, stating that they had been of the opinion that he would never be released.

Stu answered, "I guess it's just one of the benefits of the business recession. The State of Kentucky is hurting. The coal business is way off and, with everything else, their tax revenues have slowed too. Their prisons are bursting at the seams. I think they are trying to make room for new customers by turning out the old timers. I'm sure they will save on medical costs too."

Albert really wasn't going overboard at trying to be friendly. He was rather cold in the way he questioned Stu. Next, he asked Stu what his plans were.

He told him he didn't have any bank jobs lined up, if that was bothering him. "I have a friend in Florida. I'm sure Susan remembers Bob Henderson. I want to make a surprise visit to him in Florida and I would also like to meet my two nieces, if you will allow it."

Susan was content to let Albert do all of the talking. It really wasn't talking, however. It was questioning. Albert said, "This is a nice place. I didn't know you had such rich friends. Who does it belong to?"

Stu explained how he had met Sonny's cousin and how she had been very gracious in inviting him for a few days. Albert wondered what type of woman this was, inviting an ex-con to stay with her.

Albert said he had come along with Susan in order to explain a few things.

Stu felt it was just great. The son of a bitch wasn't interested in meeting him. He just wanted to set him straight.

Albert went on to say that they had not had an easy life, either. They weren't rich and the money from the trust would have helped send the girls through school. He felt Stu would never get out of prison and they would end up with the money later. Even if Stu did get out later, Albert figured he still had some of his robbery loot stashed somewhere.

Stu was enraged. "You bastard! You have the gall to assure my own sister that I am guilty so you could have no qualms about stealing the trust money. The trust was the last hope effort made by my mother. You were never shortchanged. The lawyer sent me a copy of the estate settlement after mother died. As I recall, you received a little over a hundred thousand dollars. If you're so hard-pressed, what happened to that? I sure as hell don't feel the need to attempt to prove my innocence at this late date, but I certainly do resent any implication that I am a criminal."

Albert said he was glad he had come with Susan. He knew Stu would be hard after serving all those years in prison. "I want you to understand, as far as we are concerned, you are dead and have been since Korea. We don't want you in our lives or the lives of our children." Turning to Susan he said, "Let's leave. I have said all I'm going to say."

Stu shouted, "You're goddamned right you have said all you're going to say! Now get your Dutch ass out of here so I can visit with my sister. We have matters to discuss that don't concern you." He suggested that Albert should have lunch at the Inn and handed him ten dollars. "Here, have lunch on me and then wait in the lobby until I send word for you to pick up Susan."

Albert didn't waste any time getting out of the door. Stu had actually scared him.

Susan said, "Stewart, you haven't changed in all these years." Susan was glad Stu had sent Albert away and said she was counting on it. "I was afraid you might send me packing too."

She laughed, saying, "It was close. I figured if things were that bad between us, you wouldn't need Albert to speak for you."

With a big smile on her face, Susan said, "God! It's been twenty-five years and you really haven't changed. You looked old to me then and you still look old to me."

Stu laughed, but didn't comment on her looks. He did think she had been shucking too many chocolate bars. "Here, let me give my baby sister a big hug."

Tears came to both of their eyes.

Reaching into her purse she pulled out a small box. Handing it to him, she informed him that their mother had saved this for him. Stu opened the box. It contained four military metals. He held the Silver Star in his hand, thinking back to the time Colonel Lavery pinned it on his chest. He couldn't remember why it was given to him. There were so many things to remember and he really didn't enjoy thinking about them.

During lunch, he told Susan that he knew how embarrassed she had been after his arrest. She was a young girl. He also knew that a dead uncle couldn't just rise from the dead. He said, "If you had written to me in prison and asked for some of the trust money to be released, I would have helped. I never expected to see the outside of the prison walls." Stu said he was a little scared about his future. He would have to find some way to make a living. It was for sure he couldn't live very long on twenty thousand dollars. Stu told how Mr. Elliot, the bank trust officer, had offered to help find employment in Bloomington. Stu wasn't too sure if he even wanted to live in the area, saying he would always be an ex-con here. That was the part of his life he wanted to get away from.

He suggested that Susan should inform her daughters that she had found a long lost cousin and that he would be coming to visit. "When I'm ready, I'll fly into Louisville. Maybe you and the girls could pick me up there." He went on to say he really couldn't help her with any money at this time, but he would help when he could. She and her daughters were the only family he had.

He told Susan how their mother worried about Albert's feelings toward him. "Mother understood and warned me that he would never be of any help." Albert appeared on the scene long after he was imprisoned. In all fairness, he realized that Albert knew very little about him. "I am not going to try to convert him. We can just stay out of each other's way. Tell him I'm going to give you a thousand dollars to help pay for Sally's education. Who knows, maybe Albert will look forward to seeing me."

After Susan had left, he called the airline again and booked a reservation on the three o'clock a.m. Tuesday flight. Catherine returned and inquired how his visit had been. He explained about his problem with Albert and how he had ushered him out the door. Stu had a great visit with Susan.

Catherine handed him a present, saying she had stopped at Henry's and bought him some sailing shorts for his Florida trip. Noticing the small box of medals he had placed on the coffee table, she inquired about it.

He picked up the box and showed her the medals.

Stu said, "I really don't know what to do with them."

She said it would be nice to have them framed. "This Silver Star medal, what was that for?"

"Fighting. There were thousands of Marines in the war. We were just real fighters. I guess I was one of them." He asked her if she would mind keeping them for him.

He told her of the flight reservations he had made and asked for any suggestions on the best way to get to Indianapolis.

Catherine told him there were several people from Indianapolis at the Pointe every weekend. She would call around in the morning and find him a ride.

They walked over to Fred's for their dinner. Fred's condo was the exact same layout as Catherine's. His furnishings were contemporary, too. Nel was wearing a very eye-catching outfit. She looked like a playmate out of a magazine. She looked terrific, wearing sheer white trousers with a bib top made out of the same white material. There were some white sandals on the floor where she had been sitting.

As Fred was fixing the drinks, Nel served the hors d'oeuvres. When she bent over to set a small plate in front of him, her breasts were completely exposed. Stu was having a hard time keeping his eyes off of her.

When both Fred and Nel were in the kitchen, Catherine whispered to him that he was going to get the full treatment tonight. "Even money, Nel will be hanging her tits all over the backgammon board. I'd say they have a plan to distract you."

He thanked her and said he understood. His friend Nick would have lost a thousand dollars just so he could have kept looking.

Fred called, "Come on. Let's do these steaks on the outdoor grill."

The evening had cooled and there was a soft breeze coming from across the lake. Stu remarked how pretty the lake looked at this time of the day.

Fred had raced a sailboat that morning, saying it was hot as hell out there today. He could have missed the race, but it would drop him in the overall standing for the summer championship. Fred said he had finished third out of twenty-two boats this morning. Fred asked him if he had ever done any sailing.

Stu said, "No, I haven't. It's funny. Ask me that question in a few weeks. I'm on my way to Florida on Tuesday morning to visit with an old friend who happens to live on a sailboat. But, no, I have never been sailing. I am flying out of Indy on Tuesday to visit him."

Fred asked, "Where did you learn to play backgammon?"

Stu smiled, saying he thought he was still learning. Stu told him about his Greek friend. They had never played for money. He agreed that playing the game for money made the game more exciting.

Fred told him that he had a meeting with a banker in Indianapolis Monday morning and was planning on staying Monday night at his club. He could ride up with him and then he would get a double room so Stu could get a little shut-eye before taking a taxi to the airport.

Stu said, "That would be great, thank you. Also, thanks for letting me use your bicycle. Trying to keep up with Catherine could kill you. How do the steaks look?"

Fred said, "They are ready."

Never in his entire life had he tasted a steak as tender and juicy. Most of his steak eating had been at road houses. They only seemed to know one way to fix them, regardless of how you ordered them. Well done. He thought of his friend, Nick. He wished he could have shared his steak with Nick. Nick loved food. At least he liked to talk about it.

After dinner, Fred announced that he was ready to give Stu his backgammon lesson.

Catherine was right. Nel was alongside of Fred, giving Stu an eyeful. They agreed on quitting at ten. Fred suggested that they play for twenty-five dollars a point.

Stu commented, "That's a little steep, but I can handle that if you will play me even."

Fred said he didn't understand what Stu meant when he said "playing even".

Stu smiled and said, "Nel's tits have to be on my side of the table. I want you to enjoy the view instead of me."

Fred suggested that Nel should see what was on TV. Nel stood up, leaned over and kissed Fred on the cheek, and in the process, gave Stu another eyeful.

Nel said, "Good luck, sweetie. I think I'll watch TV upstairs so I won't bother you boys."

Fred invited Catherine to play, too. She thanked him, saying twenty-five dollars a point was too rich for her blood.

Fred was never ahead all night and, even though he played with caution, he still managed to lose twelve hundred dollars. After the last game, Fred suggested that they play one last game, double or nothing.

Stu refused, saying he would have to win it back just like he lost it, at twenty-five dollars a point. "I expect to be back through here before long. Maybe we can have a rematch then."

Stu was surprised when Fred paid him in all hundred bills. He wondered what kind of guy carried that kind of money around.

Once they were back in Catherine's condo, Stu handed a thousand dollars to her, saying he would like for her to deposit the money into his account at the bank.

"No, never put winnings in any type of account," she said. "Sooner or later, the IRS will spot it and you will end up with a tax audit."

The next morning, Catherine awoke to the aroma of coffee perking. Wearing her robe, she joined him in the kitchen. He had the table set, with fresh, sliced cantaloupe awaiting her.

"You are sure nice to have around," Catherine said. "I could get spoiled very easily."

He said if she wouldn't mind him messing up her kitchen, he would enjoy making some omelets. Stu said his dad had always made them on Sundays.

The nostalgia of the day was starting to build, having omelets and thinking about going to St. Mary's. He wondered if he would see anyone he knew or if anyone would recognize him. Stu really wasn't sure just why he wanted to go to church.

When he was a student in the Catholic grade school, he was taught how the church never changed. It was called the universal church. Anywhere in the world, you could attend a Catholic Mass in the same universal language, Latin. The priest had always faced the altar, with his back to the parishioners. He was surprised to see the altar had been moved forward in the sanctuary and the priest stood behind the altar, facing the parishioners. The prayers had changed from Latin to English. Even the distribution of communion had changed. He had never seen lay people dispensing the communion hosts. All of the changes in the ritual were unexpected. He could see where it did improve the participation of the laymen.

As the parishioners returned from communion, he had a good chance to see their faces. Very few people looked even remotely familiar.

They sat near the rear of the church. He had announced, before they entered, that he wanted to be one of the first out. He just didn't want someone walking up to him asking if he was Stewart Vogel.

Before they returned to the Pointe, she took him on a driving tour of the Bloomington area. Bloomington was always a pretty town. Even with all of the growth it had experienced in the last twenty-five years, it still maintained its charm.

She suggested they have lunch at the Four Winds Inn. The Sunday brunch was always a beautiful spread.

As it turned out, the Inn dining room was packed. There were small children on the loose all over the place.

"This place is just too busy for me," Stu said. "I don't think I could relax enough to enjoy a meal."

Driving back to her condo, she commented that she couldn't imagine the number of adjustments that he was having to make. "The more I'm with you, the more conscious I am that these adjustments can be a problem. You are such a loveable, easy-going person. I just hope you are not too fragile to make the change. I want you to promise to call me anytime, day or night, when you need a friend, just to talk to."

Back in the condo, he sat by the window watching the sailboats. Catherine offered him a cold beef sandwich. He thanked her, saying he wasn't hungry at the present moment. "I just need to wind down a little."

She said, "Elliot is playing in a golf tournament here at the Pointe. I'm going to take off and watch him play. You are welcome to come, but I think you just need a little time alone."

After she left, he busied himself packing his things. He was wondering about the trip to Indianapolis and thought he had better check with Fred on what time he should be ready in the morning.

Nel answered the door. "Hi, Stu. Come in."

He told her he had come over to check with Fred on their departure time in the morning.

Nel said, "Follow me. I'll show you what he's doing."

As he followed her up the stairs, he thought to himself, *Poor Fred, stuck with some shitty Sunday project.*

Entering the master bedroom, she walked over to the window. Nel said, "See that red sailboat with the red and white spinnaker? That's

Fred! He has his racing crew out for a little spinnaker practice. They are two thirds of the way down the lake. If he turns around right now, it would still take him an hour and half to get home."

Turning to walk away, he told her to have Fred check with him later.

She said, "Wait, will you do me a favor and let me read your palm? I'm kind of into that."

He agreed, thinking her to be some sort of silly bimbo.

Nel said, "Hold your right hand palm out. It works better if you close your eyes, too."

Taking his hand in hers, she placed it on her bare breast. He froze. She reached down and was starting to unzip his trousers with her other hand. Before he realized what was happening, a pulse of excitement starting running through his entire body. Knowing he was losing control of the situation, he retreated toward the door.

Stu mumbled, "Damn, why me?"

Nel said, "If I need a reason, I can give you several. Like, I'm physically attracted to you. I know you're leaving and won't be sneaking around for seconds and getting me into trouble. My sex life with that sixty-six year old goat is practically nil. He just likes me around to show off. I'm just another damned trophy. I hate to beg, but I will, if that's what it takes to get you in bed."

Stu told her, "It's something I really can't explain. I am starting to work my way out of a horrible experience. To jump into bed, with the wife of someone I've just met, isn't what I need."

Back in the sanctuary of Catherine's condo, he sat there thinking about what almost happened. He was actually trying to remember how Nel's breast felt. One thing was for sure. Stu knew he couldn't fend off any more of Nel's advances. As a matter of fact, if he stayed another day…well…he just wasn't sure.

Suddenly his Indianapolis trip changed. Before, he was looking forward to the ride with Fred. Now, Fred had become a different person in his mind. He never really cared all that much, but now he felt like he hated him. What was it? Was he just jealous of him? He thought about it. Fred seemed to have everything he didn't: money, Nel, and a playful lifestyle. His feelings weren't much better toward Nel. He didn't like to think he was being taken advantage of. He was glad he was leaving.

Stu was taking a nap when the doorbell rang. It was Fred. He announced that they needed to get away early in the morning. His bank meeting was at ten, so they would go directly there. Stu could wait in the banker's outer office, while Fred had his meeting. They should be checked into his club in time for lunch.

Fred said, "You might just be sitting next to the Governor at lunch. The club has these large round tables in the Men's Grill. They just fill the tables one at a time, so you are seated in the order you walk in. It's really kind of nice. Monday afternoons are big at the club. Most of the country clubs are closed on Mondays. Bridge and backgammon are the two main games played in the card room on Mondays. On other days, when there are very few players, gin rummy is about the only game played." Fred said members just floated in and out of the card room. Some players would go directly from the Grill Room, others might drop in later. He guessed that there were many clients being billed for the hours their lawyers were in the card room.

Catherine and Elliot walked in shortly after Fred had left. Elliot had just stopped in to say goodbye and to wish him well. Elliot commented that he hadn't done well in the golf tournament, saying his putting had failed him all day.

Stu mentioned that they just missed Fred and they were planning on leaving early in the morning. "Fred has a bank meeting in the morning and would you believe we are going to play backgammon at his club in the afternoon?"

Elliot said, "I hope you are not playing him for money. He has the reputation of being a real pro at that game."

Catherine told about Stu's success in beating Fred.

After Elliot departed, she suggested they have a little talk. She said, "If I know Fred, he is going to try and pump as much information out of you as he possibly can. He's very intent on finding out more about you. I would like to suggest you tell him you have been with the government and you have retired from your position. You might add that it was of a very sensitive nature, so you won't be discussing it."

He thanked her for the advice and promised he would keep in touch with her. "I'm coming back to visit my sister and will not leave the area without reporting in."

Fred did try to get information from Stu, but seemed satisfied with his answers. He did ask if he had traveled abroad for the government. Stu reminded him that he would not be talking about any facet of his time with the government.

Fred said, "Well, I'll tell you what I think! I think you have been in some Arab country in the Middle East and that's where you learned to play backgammon. I have played with Arabs before and they all move fast too."

The trip was interesting. Stu saw so many old farmhouses and other buildings that he remembered from his past. Fred had quieted down after his initial question session and Stu even managed a short nap.

Downtown Indianapolis still looked somewhat familiar. There were dozens of new modern office buildings, but everything still centered around Monument Circle. He remembered going up in the monument as a child. It was an eighth grade trip. He remembered that Sonny was the first one to make it to the top.

As they entered the bank, Stu asked Fred why he came to Indianapolis to do his banking.

Fred said that he had sold his business six years ago and turned everything over to the Star Bank Trust Department to manage for him. He had manufactured automotive brakes and had reached an age where he wanted to retire. A German company made him a very good offer for his business and he took it. He mentioned that Star Bank had almost doubled his net worth in the past six years.

As they walked up to the check-in desk at Fred's club, the clerk said, "Good morning, Mr. Wertz. Nice to have you back again."

This was the first time Stu had heard Fred's last name. He felt stupid that he had never even asked.

After checking in, they went to their rooms to freshen up before lunch. The Grill Room was a large room on the sixth floor. The game room was on the same floor. Fred showed him the game room first. It was a beautiful wood-paneled room. All of the card tables had green leather tops surrounded by a wood trim. The game chairs also had matching green leather cushions. There was a small bar area on one end of the room.

The Grill Room had tile walls and flooring. All of the tables were large and round with large, white oak captain's chairs. They were the last two to be seated at the table. Fred knew everyone and introduced Stu to each one. Once they ordered, the food arrived within minutes.

They entered the game room after lunch. Fred explained that it was a rule of the club that all gambling debts needed to be paid in full and in cash before leaving. As his guest, he would be responsible for Stu's debts if he couldn't or didn't pay. Fred said that he and several of the other members kept money in safe-deposit type lockers in the club office. "I try to keep twenty or thirty thousand here at the club. I have never lost that much, but I have lost as much as ten thousand, at times.

Fred said, "We have six or seven players in one game. It's pretty standard that we play twenty-five dollars a point. To start the game, everyone rolls two dice. The highest player is in the box and is playing all of the other players. If you are in the box, you are starting at twenty-five dollars times the number of players playing against you. You stay in the box as long as you win. When you lose, you're sent to the end of the line. There are some players who will decline their turn in the box. Each player will have their own doubling cube. The player in the box will also have a doubling cube. As the player in the box, you may have some players accept the double and other players drop out. You may also have some of your opponents double you, independently of the others." He went on to explain that as the day wore on, some players would go back to their offices and other players would join them later in the afternoon. Every game ended in a cash payment. The six or so players could discuss their moves only after there had been a double. Prior to that, only the team captain could make the moves. Fred said it speeded up the game not to have a discussion on every move. If a player ended up being the only one in the game against the man in the box and he wins, then he moves into the box next.

"Well Stu, do you have any questions, and do you feel up to the challenge?"

"I will give it a try. As you said, a player can always drop out of the game." He realized most of the time he would have other players making moves for him. He would only get ahead when he was in the box, making his own moves at one hundred and fifty dollars a game.

Fred introduced Stu to the other players, announcing that Stu was his guest. As the game started, Fred was actually in the box and won the first game. In the second game, he felt he held a very favorable position and doubled all of the players. Everyone folded but Stu. Stu went on to win the game, thereby placing himself in the box. In the first game they all doubled him. Without hesitation, he doubled them back and later gammoned them. He had won twelve hundred dollars in the first game. He won six games in a row before being defeated. He had also picked up over five thousand dollars in the process.

As Fred had said, players would come and go throughout the afternoon. No one seemed to be upset if they dropped a couple thousand in the game. Fred left the game later in the afternoon to raid his lockbox. When they finally called it quits, Stu had no idea how much money he had stuffed in his pockets during the afternoon. Leaving the game room, all of the players invited him back, saying they enjoyed playing with him.

They had dinner in the club dining room. It was on the club's first floor, which was very formal. Stu wore his new blue blazer. Fred asked Stu how much he had won.

Stu answered that he hadn't had time to count it out and had just dumped it in his travel bag. He told Fred that he felt a little bad winning as much as he did.

Fred said, "You might find it hard to believe that it was just pocket change for those guys. Everyone in the game is worth millions and they will be back playing again. Tomorrow. They sell small gym bags at the front desk. You might consider picking up one of those to carry your loot in. I wouldn't want to leave it in my checked in luggage, if I were you."

Stu said he would follow Fred's advice. He sure as hell didn't want to walk around with hundred dollar bills hanging out of his pockets.

The taxi was waiting at the front door when he came down. The driver placed his luggage on the other side of the front seat.

The driver said, "I have a problem with the trunk lid. One of the day drivers backed this crate into something and jammed the damned thing." He went on to complain about the young drivers on the day shift and how they tore the hell of the equipment.

The airport was like a tomb. Most of the airline ticket counters were closed. Actually, only the Star Air counter was open. There were a few people checking in ahead of him. Stu paid cash for his ticket. The Star

Air clerk asked if he would like to sign up for a Star Air credit card. Shaking his head, he thanked her and told her no.

When he returned from Korea, it was on a troop ship all the way to California. The remainder of the trip was by a commercial airline. This was to be his first trip on a jet.

After he reached the boarding area, he was informed that he could go ahead and board the plane. Walking down the empty boarding ramp, he was thinking there wouldn't be many passengers on the plane. As he entered the plane, the stewardess looked at his boarding pass and informed him that his seat was in the last row. The plane was larger than any he had seen in the past. It surprised him to find that eighty percent of the seats were already occupied. A good many of the passengers were already asleep and the rest looked like they would be joining the others soon.

As the pilot announced their descent into Atlanta, he was confident he was faced with a sleepless night, but while the plane was on the ground and boarding the Atlanta passengers, he fell asleep. He missed the aerial view of Tampa Bay as his flight landed. The sound of the wheels touching down and the braking roar of the jets awoke him.

After picking up his luggage, he checked on the limo serviced to St. Pete. There were two other passengers in the limo. They dropped off the first passenger, an elderly gentleman, at a small apartment complex. Stu told the driver he would like to be dropped off at a hotel near the marina.

The Bay View Hotel had a Spanish exterior and looked like it might have been built in the twenties. It was in mint condition.

The desk clerk greeted him with a pleasant, "Good morning."

He hadn't heard a New York accent in so many years, he had forgotten they existed. He signed the registration card and informed the clerk that he would be staying only one night. The clerk wanted to imprint his credit card, but Stu told her that he would be paying in cash.

He slept until noon. After a shower and shave, he felt like a new man. Surprising Bob was next on his agenda. Bob had divorced his wife and later remarried. Bob's first wife was from Bloomington. He knew her, but that was about all.

The hotel coffee shop was very busy when he entered. Luckily, there was a small table open and he was quickly seated.

The Yacht Club's dock was less than a two block walk from the hotel. The weather was cooler than it had been in Indiana. There was a nice breeze coming in off the bay and the short walk was refreshing. As he approached the pier gate he read, PRIVATE PROPERTY-ST. PETERSBURG YACHT CLUB-MEMBERS AND THEIR GUESTS ONLY. Guests were required to register with the dock master upon entering. There was a small office right past the gate. The sign on the door identified it as the dock master's office.

Upon entering the office, Stu was greeted by a young man wearing khaki shorts and a white Yacht Club shirt, sitting with his rear end half on and half off the desk. He was talking on the phone and held up his index finger to acknowledge Stu's presence. It was easy to detect that the young man was trying to line up a date with someone he had just met.

Finally he put the phone down, after asking the person on the other end to hold for a minute. He asked, "What can I do for you, captain?"

Stu said, "I'm trying to find Bob Henderson. Do you know him?"

"Sure. Everyone knows Captain Bob, but you are out of luck. He pulled out of here yesterday morning. I'm pretty sure he will be staying at the Venice Yacht Club tonight."

Returning to the hotel, Stu was wondering what would be the best way for him to get to Venice. He entered a small shop off of the hotel lobby in order to purchase some badly needed sunglasses. The clerk mentioned that the crowd in the lobby was an AARP tour group. They book these tours during the off-season, when the rates are down.

Stu asked if the clerk knew where they were headed next.

She said, "I'm not sure, but I think to Fort Myers."

He hurried out and held up a twenty dollar bill so the bus driver could see it, saying, "What're the chances of catching a ride to Venice?"

Reaching out and taking the twenty, he commented that they always made a stop in Venice. It was part of the tour. "If you have any luggage, get it out here quick. We are pulling out in ten minutes." The driver explained he would be splitting the twenty with the tour guide, and he would be riding up front with her.

Hurrying, Stu checked out of the hotel and loaded his luggage onto the bus and handed the driver another twenty. He also handed another twenty to the tour guide. She thanked him, saying it wasn't necessary, as she stuffed the money into her purse.

As the bus drove out of St. Petersburg, the tour hostess was speaking over a small microphone, announcing the different points of interest and their planned schedule for the rest of the day. "We will shortly be crossing over the famous Sunshine Skyway Bridge. The bridge extends over the entrance into Tampa Bay. It is the highest bridge in Florida. You will see the Bay on the left side and the Gulf of Mexico on the right. There is no stopping on the bridge, so any picture taking will have to be through the bus windows. Please do not get out of your seats to take pictures."

After the hostess finally sat down, she greeted Stu in a friendly manner and explained that the tour was a twelve day trip out of Atlanta.

As the bus pulled into the Old Town area of Venice, the hostess announced that they would be stopping for an hour. The area was loaded with little shops and fine restaurants. She said they would be stopping for lunch in Punta Gorda, so they shouldn't have an early lunch here. She did suggest they might like to have a cup of coffee and split a piece of homemade pie at Hilda's Pie Shop.

After retrieving his luggage from the driver, he crossed the street where there was a taxi parked in front of a small hotel. When Stu asked to be taken to the Yacht Club, the driver announced he was waiting for someone who had called from the hotel. "Wait here just a minute."

The driver entered the hotel and informed the desk clerk that he would be back in a few minutes. The taxi driver was actually early for his pickup at the hotel. The ride to the Yacht Club couldn't have even been two minutes. The driver did comment that he thought the Yacht Club was closed on Wednesdays during the summer. Stu let him know he was meeting someone on a boat.

Chapter 5

Stu found a bench in the shade next to the building. He knew he was early, but he did worry about what he would do if the boat didn't show. His thoughts took him back to Eddyville. It must be hot and humid there. He had several hours to wait and his mind kept him busy, wondering. *What type of cellmate would Nick end up with? What about Catherine?* In a way, he wished he hadn't met someone as nice as Catherine. He certainly didn't have any plans. As nice as Bloomington was, he just didn't want to settle there. Stu looked forward to seeing Bob, his only real friend outside of prison. Bob was someone from his past, although the past was no longer important to him. The future was what excited him: being a private individual with the freedom to do as he damn well pleased. He wasn't really too sure what he wanted and he didn't have the faintest idea what he would do after he visited Susan.

Winning money at backgammon was different than playing with Nick. It wasn't as much fun as he had had playing Nick. He knew he didn't want to end up just being a hustler.

Sitting there pondering his thoughts of the last few days allowed a large sailboat to slip up to the dock unnoticed. The noise of the skipper reversing his engine alerted the arrival.

A trim young woman jumped down onto the dock and secured the forward mooring line and raced to the rear of the vessel to secure another line. Her hair was jet black and braided into a long pigtail. She was very tan. White shorts and a long-sleeved white shirt flattered her tan skin.

Stu was having a hard time getting a view of the skipper. The Bimini top made the area where the skipper was sitting extra dark. The girl was still fussing with the lines when Stu walked over to her. She was a beautiful Chinese woman, prettier than any Oriental he had seen in Korea. By the time Stu was in talking distance, the skipper had already disappeared below.

Stu asked, "Hello, is this Bob Henderson's boat?"

The woman replied, "Yes. Do you want to see him?"

Stu said, "No. Just tell him he can't tie up here tonight."

The woman replied, "Why not tie up here? We tie up here every time we come to Venice."

Bob could hear the voices and came up asking what the problem was? Stu knew he had him going. It was just like the old days.

Stu said, "You know damn good and well what the problem is."

Bob was miffed. This wasn't the dock master. What's going on here? He was still in the cockpit of his boat and hadn't had a good look at Stu's face.

"Who are you, mister? I don't believe I have encountered you down here before."

"I'll tell you who I am. I'm the guy that said you're going to have to get your boat the hell out of here."

At this point, Bob realized he was being had and the man standing on the dock was Stu Vogel. Bob also knew it was his turn to be the jokester. If Stu wanted to surprise him, then why couldn't he have a little fun, too? Bob reached down and pressed the engine starter button.

The girl called to Bob, "What you doing? You leaving?"

Bob said, "Yes. Untie the dock lines."

The girl moved quickly at the task of untying the lines and throwing them on the boat's deck. Stu walked over and placed his foot over the cleat to which the bow line was secured. As the girl approached the cleat, she detected she was not going to be allowed to untie the line. Somewhat frustrated, and more than a little perturbed, she asked what the problem was.

Stu said, "You folks trying to slip out of here without paying any dockage?" asked Stu.

She yelled back to Bob, "This crazy man say we owe him dockage."

Bob shouted back, "We only have Korean money! Would he take that?"

She was even more confused. They didn't have Korean money on their boat.

Before she could say anything, Stu asked, "Is the money from North Korea or South Korea?"

Bob heard the question and yelled out, "This money is only good on the thirty-eighth parallel."

Stu replied, "Okay, tell that cheap bastard of a captain that I will settle for a free beer and supper."

The woman turned to Bob and said, "Now this crazy man wants...."

"I heard. Tell him we only have fish heads and bilge water," Bob quickly shot back.

With that comment, the woman realized that she was in the middle of a couple of jokers. She said, "Okay, one of you round-eyed bastards better tell me what is going on here or I'm going to turn the hose on both of you."

Bob jumped off the boat and gave Stu a big Russian bear hug, then introduced his wife Lu Sue. Stu proceeded to help Lu Sue moor the boat. After loading his gear on the boat, he commented that the newspaper advertising business must really be great. Bob explained that the boat was all they owned. Between Lu Sue's travel agency job and his government check, things had worked out well for them.

Later, he explained that a second marriage wasn't in his plans. "Two years after Ruth and I divorced, I sold everything and went to Hong Kong to buy a boat. It turned out to be kind of a package deal. Lu Sue worked for the company that made the boat. We have been married six years and it has worked out great."

Stu said, "Are you telling me you two nuts sailed this thing all of the way from Hong Kong?"

Bob explained that they had shipped the boat back on the deck of a freighter to New Orleans. Bob said, "Enough of this boat talk. Tell me all about yourself and how you found us here. My mind is full of unanswered questions."

Stu ran through an update, telling about his parole, receiving the trust money, meeting Catherine, visiting with Sonny's father, and of his backgammon winnings.

Bob said if he didn't want to eat fish heads, there was a great little seafood restaurant just down the street. He said they serve a great grilled grouper. He suggested that they walk there and then turn in early after dinner. "Tomorrow we can leave out early. There is a weak low pressure system working its way through and we should have a favorable wind throughout the day. We can make it back to St. Pete before dark."

While dining at the restaurant, Bob told of the circumstances surrounding his divorce. Ruth had gone to high school a few years behind them. Bob said he had no hard feelings about the divorce. It had changed his life for the better and he and Lu Sue were much happier together. Bob had the feeling Ruth had married him somewhat out of sympathy. They really hadn't known each other that well in high school. When he finally returned from the war, he was kind of a local one-armed hero. She had wanted to move to Florida after they were married. Bob said, "I have enjoyed my job with the newspaper, selling promotional advertising for all of the special shows. There are two boat shows, one home show and nine other shows I promote. It gets easier every year."

Bob went on to say that Ruth wasn't satisfied with being a full time mother and had become a real estate agent. She actually had become very successful at selling condominiums out on the beach. One of her customers was Tony Luci, a wealthy banker from Oklahoma City. Tony's money seemed to work out well for her and their boys. Bob missed the boys and would love for them to look up their old dad someday. Bob Jr. was in college and Eddy still had two years of high school.

It was five thirty in the morning when Bob woke Stu and said, "Come with me. I have a key to the Club's shower room. We can shave and shower while Lu Sue is fixing the fish heads."

As they climbed down onto the dock, the sky was just beginning to show the first signs of light. A heavy collection of dew had accumulated overnight.

Bob said, "We will need to hose down the boat before we leave."

The coffee aroma perked Stu up more than the shower. Lu Sue had fixed some scrambled eggs with some kind of oriental noodle. Stu would have preferred toast. The noodles had an unknown taste. It really wasn't what one would consider a rewarding experience.

After they broke clear of the dock, Bob made a sharp left turn as he cleared the end of the Yacht Club dockage. He didn't follow the markers out to the channel. Instead, he ran a shorter course to the inlet. Now Stu understood how Bob had managed to slip in yesterday, undetected.

The entrance from the inland waterway to the Gulf of Mexico must have been less than a half mile from the club. They waved to the early morning fishermen who were fishing from the jetties.

He felt lucky to be heading out on his first sail. Bob's boat was a real beauty and Stu was very excited. The breeze was quite cool. Clearing the jetty, the boat started picking up the motion of the waves. The fresh salt air was great, but he wasn't too sure about the motion of the boat. Maybe he shouldn't have eaten the noodles. Bob could see he was turning a little green and instructed him to sit next to him, telling him he would feel better once they were under sail.

Stu watched as Bob unfurled the sails and trimmed them to where the boat heeled over and began picking up speed. The boat was now plowing through the waves and spraying sea water over the forward deck. Bob was doing a great job of sailing the boat by himself. He showed Stu how the autopilot worked, saying it was like having an extra deck hand.

Bob said, "I have it running now. We should be able to sail on this course all the way to the entrance to Tampa Bay. Sit here behind the wheel and get the feeling of how the boat sails."

After a few minutes he announced that he was turning off the autopilot. He wanted to see if Stu could comfortably sail on course. Bob talked about the many sailing trips he had made with Lu Sue. The Bahama Islands were his favorite. They were looking forward to his retirement years and were planning on following the sun, north in the summers and south in the winters. Bob said there were hundreds of sailors living as full-time transients. The cost of living almost gets down to the grocery bill and an occasional diesel purchase. Lu Sue would be a real help too, as she liked to fish and could dive for lobsters as well.

The entire day was spent with Bob schooling Stu on the operation of the boat. He pulled out navigation charts, explaining their use and putting him through a one day cram course on the operation of the boat.

Later in the day, after they had secured the boat in Bob's slip at the Yacht Club, Lu Sue poured Bob a large gin drink. The drink was nothing but pure gin over ice. She turned toward Stu and said, "Okay, sailor boy, what you like to drink?"

Stu wasn't into sailor drinking, but told her how to make the biker's drink that Catherine had made out of lemonade and beer.

"Damn, Stu, what kind of drink is that?" Bob asked.

Stu said he wasn't much of a hard liquor man and it was probably the only mixed drink he could handle.

Bob said, "You know, Stu, you're going to feel damned silly someday when you're old and dying and not have any vice to blame it on."

Bob was busy making plans for tomorrow. He checked the weather reports over the marine radio. The forecast called for a mild pleasant day, with light winds out of the northwest. After opening his chart book and showing their present location, he told Stu he wanted him to solo tomorrow. Bob said, "Lu Sue and I both have some work to do. I want you to run the boat down to Longboat Key. Lu Sue and I will meet you there before dinner time." He said it would be a piece of cake as long as he stayed between the markers. He would call the restaurant in the morning and reserve a slip at their dock.

The next morning, as he motored Bob's pride and joy out of the marina, he thought they were all nuts. Him for trying it, and Bob for suggesting it. After he unfurled the sails, the wind shifted more to the north. He was having a fairly easy time. Being alone didn't bother him. He actually enjoyed the loneliness. It was his first day to himself. He hooked up the autopilot, went below and pulled a cold beer out of the refrigerator. It was a wonderful feeling, sitting in the cockpit, with the boat sailing itself. Columbus never had it this good.

Later in the afternoon, he entered the Intracoastal Waterway. He could see on the chart two bridges he would need to have opened before he could pass. The first bridge opened every hour and half hour. The second bridge was fifteen minutes later or earlier, depending on which way you were headed. He had taken the sails in and was now running under power. When the first bridge opened in response to his horn signal, he was thrilled.

His arrival at the restaurant dock was a full two hours ahead of Lu Sue and Bob. He used the time to give the deck a good scrubbing before showering and dressing for dinner. While waiting, he pulled the money from his Indianapolis backgammon games out of his bag. He had never taken the time to count it until now. It came to just a little over twenty-one thousand dollars.

When the Hendersons arrived, they both seemed pleased to see the boat in one piece. They were most anxious to hear about his day of sailing. Lu Sue busied herself with fixing Bob his gin on the rocks. She asked Stu if he still wanted a bicycle cocktail or was he ready to drink like a sailor. He said he would stick with the bicycle drink for now.

Stu said, "You seem to be on a real high today, Bob. You must have swung a big deal."

Bob replied, "You're pretty sharp to notice. Here, read this letter."

Bob pulled an envelope out of his pocket and handed it to him. The postmark was from Oklahoma City.

> *Dear Bob,*
>
> *I don't know if you have kept up on what has happened in our end of the country, but I want to let you know what is going on.*
>
> *Tony's bank has been in the national limelight these past few weeks. It has been a frightful experience. We have lost everything, including our home. Bob Jr. is arranging a student loan, in order to help pay his way through college. Eddy has been attending a private high school, which we can no longer afford. For now, Tony Luci's name is scarred in Oklahoma City. All of Tony's close friends had heavy losses in the bank. He hasn't got anyone to turn to for help. It's bad for Eddy. I would like to send him to you. He is a fine boy. I know that bringing the two of you together, after all of these years, will be good for both of you.*
>
> *Tony said he has been busted before and he will put it all together again.*
>
> *I'm beginning to think it is part of the way of life here in Oklahoma. Tony isn't a young man. This has really hit him hard. He is smart. I hope he will have the endurance to survive.*
>
> *Please let me know if you are willing to have Eddy live with you.*
>
> *Sincerely,*
> *Ruth*

Stu said, "Well, it looks like you're going to have a new crew member. I'm happy for you. I know what this must mean to you."

Bob responded that Stu knew him better than his own wife, or even his ex. Lu Sue had to ask Bob what he was going to do. Stu didn't, because he knew.

During dinner, Bob said he had talked to Ruth and said that they are in the process of making arrangements. Eddy wanted a few days to say his goodbyes. His guess was that Eddy wouldn't show up for at least a week or two.

When they had returned to the boat after dinner, Bob asked him if he would like to play skipper again the next day. He pulled out the charts and showed him the location of the Bradenton Yacht Club. It really was very close to where they were, but if he would run down the Intracoastal to Sarasota and enter the Gulf there, he could end up with a good day of sailing.

It was after nine in the morning when Lu Sue and Bob departed. They helped Stu with his lines before they left. Motoring the boat down to Sarasota was his first real Intracoastal run. He only had to open one drawbridge before entering the Gulf.

Sailing alone was very enjoyable. It was just what he needed. The porpoise joined and escorted him for several miles. He set the autopilot and went forward on the leeward side, trying to touch them as they swam by. He talked to them and then laughed at himself. Here he was, in the Gulf, with nothing to do but talk to the fish and pelicans. He was enjoying the hell out of it. The pelicans put on a very impressive air show, skimming over the water and then later diving for fish from a higher altitude.

Entering the Manatee River from Tampa Bay, he managed to run the boat hard aground. Bob had warned him the bottom would catch him sooner or later. His words were, "If you ever meet a sailor down here who says he hasn't been aground, you will know you have just met a liar."

Following Bob's instructions, he set an anchor out in the deeper part of the channel. Bob had told him that if he happened to have the misfortune of running aground at high tide he would have to radio for help. A rising tide can either help him off the bottom or get him into more trouble. That is why it is important to set an anchor, first thing.

He checked the tide clock over the chart table. It showed that there was a rising tide. After he was topside again, he noted that the water was, in fact, running into the river rather than out. This helped to confirm the tide clock's reading. He observed that the breeze would likely help to move him away from the shallow area.

As he sat there waiting for the forces of nature to free him from the shoal, he read the Waterway Guide. It made interesting reading. Desoto Point was directly across the channel from where he was aground. Hernando Desoto had landed there in 1539. He wondered how many times these early explorers must have gone aground. Suddenly, the boat was floating. He hurried and pulled in the anchor and was underway again.

He docked at the Bradenton Yacht Club. After he had showered and dressed for dinner, he sat in the boat's cockpit reading a newspaper he had borrowed from the Club's bartender. There was a detailed story about an Oklahoma City bank closing. He was deep into the article and didn't notice someone standing on the dock.

"Where's Bob?"

He hadn't heard the person approach, and was surprised to see how close the fellow had managed to get without him detecting his presence.

"Bob? Oh, he isn't here, but I expect him anytime now. You're welcome to come aboard and wait if you want to see him."

The man introduced himself as Art Cooke, saying that he and his wife lived on a boat here at the Club. However, his wife was away on a trip and he was tired of talking to himself, so he welcomed the chance to sit and visit.

Stu learned that Art was a retired Army officer and had seen combat in WW2 and Korea. His wife was in Iowa to help her daughter, who was now two days late having a baby. Art was a talker and didn't ask any questions. Sailing was his thing now. He and his wife had crossed over to the Mediterranean twice on their boat and had visited most of the islands in the Caribbean.

As Lu Sue and Bob were walking down from the Club House, they spotted Art on their boat.

Bob said, "Well, I'll be damned. Here I am, looking all over this place trying to find you so I can introduce you to my friend."

Art explained that he had seen the boat come in. It had surprised the hell out of him when he hadn't seen Bob on the boat. He said, "Truthfully I've been working my jaws overtime waiting to see if you were going to show up. I've never seen this friend of yours. To the very best of my recollection, you have never even allowed anyone to get behind the wheel of the beauty, much less take it out without you aboard. I wasn't going to let this boat leave the dock if you hadn't shown."

"You're right," Bob said. "There isn't anyone I would trust with my boat, but Stu here was a Marine, not Army. Actually, we have been friends since high school. He saved my ass more than a dozen times in Korea. Of course, I saved him two dozen times. He was always screwing up."

Art asked Lu Sue what she thought.

It was a no-win situation and she refused to comment.

Art said, "Wait a minute. There is something wrong here. Bob, are you sure this is your boat? I have been aboard over thirty minutes and haven't been offered a drink."

Bob said, "Lu Sue, look at the trouble you get me in with my friends. Let's be a little nicer to my friends, or I'm going to have to take you back and trade you in for one of your cousins."

Lu Sue yelled, "My cousins no like round-eyed sailor after I castrate him, so best keep Lu Sue."

At that remark, Bob told her she won and he would even fix the drinks.

The next morning they were awakened by the splash of Stu diving into the pool. It didn't take Lu Sue but a few seconds to join him. She swam laps for twenty minutes and then pulled herself out of the pool next to Stu.

He told her that she was a great swimmer and wondered if she had learned as a child.

"Thank you. Bob teach me everything. I just poor dumb Chinese when Bob marry me."

He seriously doubted there were any dumb Chinese.

Stu said, "Tell me about yourself."

"Very simple life. I born in Canton, China, in 1952. My family escape China when I three years old. We escape by boat in dense night fog and float down river. I told we almost hit the patrol boat. All children bound and gagged so we not make sound. I really not remember any of this. My older sisters do. I learn to speak English at the boatyard. The manager there speak very good English and French. Sammy my best friend in all Hong Kong. I his mistress. All Chinese big shot businessmen had mistress. It honor to be mistress to such important man. Sammy, his English name, wonderful to me. He treat me very nice and teach me many thing. When Bob come to Hong Kong to buy boat from Sammy, I meet him. Sammy know Bob want me. He say I should marry Bob and go to States. My cousin take my place with Sammy, and here I am. My father work in furniture factory as wood carver. My two sister work in textile mill in Kowloon. I write family every month. I hear from them and Sammy. Sammy keep promising to come to Annapolis Boat Show. So far, he never make it. Bob very happy Eddy coming to live with us. I know it make big change in our lives, but I happy too. This morning, driving back to St. Petersburg, he said we are going to take Eddy to Hong Kong for Christmas. Bob very nice man. I lucky Chinese girl to marry him. Maybe you like to come with us and I get you cousin to marry."

Jokingly, Stu asked, "Couldn't I just order a cousin by mail from Sammy?"

Lu Sue said, "Sammy no send cousin to marry stranger."

Returning to the boat, they found breakfast ready and on the galley table. Bob had fixed hash-browned potatoes, fried eggs and bacon. The aroma of the coffee blended in with that of the country breakfast. He was pulling the biscuits out of the oven as they seated themselves.

During breakfast, Stu took the occasion to talk about his friend, Nick, and his backgammon playing. He told about winning money from Fred and his friends in Indianapolis. Bob wanted to know what kind of money he was talking about.

"Well, I guess in the few days since I have been out of Eddyville, I have picked up twenty-four thousand, give or take a few hundred," Stu replied.

Bob said, "WOW! What you're saying is you have more than doubled the money your mother left in the trust. If you are that good, I know someone in Sarasota that you need to meet. He is really loaded and owns half of the real estate down there. Would you be willing to play him if I could arrange a game for this afternoon?"

Stu replied, "Sure, why not."

Bob wanted to know if he could have half of the action, win or lose. Stu commented that he didn't have any idea what kind of money they would play for and warned Bob that he could lose a few thousand dollars. It was a dice game and sometimes the dice could be very cruel. He would prefer to share the winnings with Bob, but wanted it agreed that he would handle all of the losses. That being agreed upon, Bob called his friend through the marine operator.

Stu could hear the conversation over the two-way radio. Bob explained that he had a friend from Kentucky staying with him on his boat. The weather outlook wasn't good for this afternoon and they were trying to find something to do. Bob went on to say that his friend was a backgammon player and wondered if they played at any of the area clubs. He knew Larry was a big time backgammon player and was hoping he could help entertain his friend this afternoon.

Larry, the voice on the other end of the radio call, responded that things were pretty dead for him this time of the year and he certainly would enjoy playing, too. He commented that all of the hotshots had pulled out for the summer. While they were talking, Larry mentioned that his normal game was for twenty-five dollars a point, but he would be willing to drop it to any level his friend would be comfortable playing for.

Stu said, "Before we go, I need to write a couple of short letters and I need to get them mailed today."

Stu hadn't written Catherine and felt he had already delayed too long in expressing his thanks for her gracious hospitality. He also wanted to write a short report to his old cellmate, Nick.

Lu Sue drove them down to the Sarasota Yacht Club. She had some shopping that needed to be done and said she would be back to pick them up around four thirty.

Larry was seated in the dining room when they arrived. Someone was sitting with him. When he spotted Bob, he waved them over to his table. Larry introduced the other person as his lawyer. "I just need to get a few papers signed today, and Chet here was nice enough to run them by."

Chet picked up the file of papers, saying he was sorry he couldn't stay for lunch.

After lunch, they moved into the game room. There were four men, who must have been in their eighties, playing gin at one of the tables. Larry said the gin game was an everyday event, except on Mondays, when the club was closed. On Mondays they move the game to the Bird Key Club.

The first game was a real sparring match. Larry turned the doubling cube first and then lost his momentum. Stu turned the cube back to Larry, and before the game ended, they were playing for four hundred dollars. Larry won the game with a backgammon, which meant that Stu had lost twelve hundred dollars. It took Stu the entire afternoon to improve his position.

When Lu Sue arrived at four thirty, they were flat even in the standing. Larry suggested that they play one more game so one of them could leave as a winner. Early in the game, Larry turned the doubling cube. Stu accepted the double and then proceeded to lose the game. Reaching across the table, he shook hands with Larry and said he enjoyed the afternoon. Larry commented that he would be available most anytime if he wanted a rematch.

As they were getting into Bob's car, Stu told Lu Sue that Bob had just learned he didn't win at backgammon all of the time.

Lu Sue said, "Well, I hope you saved enough to buy dinner? I have a great seafood restaurant in mind. We shouldn't have any trouble getting seated this early."

As Bob drove, Lu Sue started opening packages from her day's purchases. Stu was surprised when she produced fuel and oil filters. She even had some packing compound for the shaft. She announced to Bob that there were two cases of oil in the trunk. It was a special kind that she had been trying to purchase for months.

Bob explained that Lu Sue did most of the engine maintenance. "She's a wiz with that Perkins diesel."

She also mentioned that she had purchased some interesting reading material. She had stopped by a bookstore in the mall and spotted a business magazine with a cover story of an Oklahoma bank failure. The article mentioned Tony Luci and how he had gone from riches to rags overnight.

After they enjoyed a seafood dinner, they returned to the boat. Bob asked Stu what his plans were and where he would be heading next.

Stu said, "Well I need to check in with a parole officer in Louisville. Next, I want to go fishing and then make a short trip to Jasper."

Bob said, "You're in a fishing paradise and you haven't said a thing about fishing."

Stu replied, "I spent twenty-five years living on Barkley Lake. Really I just want to see what Eddy looks like from a fishing boat. While I am in the area I might pay a visit to my old cellmate. I'm not too sure I want to walk inside of those walls again. I will have to think about it for awhile."

The idea of living on a boat like Bob and his friend, Art, seemed like a great life. Sooner or later, Stu knew he was going to have to find some kind of work.

Bob commented that there were always great buys on sailboats at the end of the summer season up the East Coast. Stu might be surprised what he could pick up for thirty or forty thousand dollars.

With Eddy soon to arrive, Stu knew the time had come for him to start making his exit plans. Lu Sue suggested that he should fly out of Sarasota. She mentioned that there was a good connection to Louisville. The flight departed three times a week at six thirty p.m. His thoughts turned back to Larry and getting in another backgammon game before he departed. He asked Lu Sue to check if there was a flight departing the next day. If so, he asked if she could try to get him on the flight.

After the flight arrangements were made, he asked Bob to see if he could arrange another backgammon session with Larry.

Stu said, "Tell him I'm flying out tomorrow evening from Sarasota, but I could play right up to four in the afternoon."

Bob had no trouble arranging another game with Larry. Stu had suggested that they start their game in the morning because Bob wanted to head back to St. Pete with the boat. It was agreed that Stu would again meet Larry at ten in the morning. Lu Sue had made his flight reservations.

The next morning they helped Bob break loose from the dock and then Lu Sue drove Stu to Sarasota Yacht Club. Larry was there waiting for him with the same lawyer he had met yesterday. As he approached their table, he heard Larry say, "Tell them that is my final offer and if they turn me down, they have just bought it back at that price."

The lawyer laughed and commented that Larry always said that, and it usually worked. Picking up his papers, the lawyer wished them both "good luck" in their game.

They moved back into the game room and the game started again. This time Stu won the first game and proceeded to have several winning streaks before lunch. He was ahead twenty-seven hundred dollars as they sat down to lunch. During lunch, Larry suggested that they double the amount they were playing for.

Stu shook his head, saying that Larry was an excellent player and he just wanted to see if Larry could win his money back at the same price he lost it.

Larry had been in the Navy during WW2 and enjoyed talking about it. When he arrived in San Diego, he had held the rank of seaman. He was due to ship out in a few days, but happened to see a posted notice for a sailing instructor. He picked up a book on sailing at the base library and applied for the position. He got the job and, as it turned out, his only students were nurses. The personnel officer who gave him the job said he would be giving him a temporary move up in rank and grade. He explained that, as an instructor, Larry would need respect and the rank of Navy Chief, but it would only last as long as his job. Needless to say, the job lasted until he was discharged after the war. He asked Stu if he had been in the military.

Stu said both he and Bob had been in the Marines, but nothing as exciting as Larry's experiences had happened to them.

"Is that where Bob lost his arm?"

Stu nodded, yes.

During the afternoon game, Larry kept passing the doubling cube. He was behind and was trying to play catch up. An early double works in the favor of the other player, most of the time. Knowing they would be quitting at four o'clock, Larry excused himself, saying he had to make a phone call.

Twenty minutes later, his lawyer reappeared carrying a briefcase. He was the bag man, bringing the money to pay off Larry's losses.

As four o'clock approached, the lawyer counted out seventy-three hundred dollars to pay off Larry's loss. Chet, the lawyer, went on to explain that he had succeeded in making a very large real estate deal for Larry this afternoon, but he knew Larry would rather win a hundred dollars playing backgammon than a million on a business deal.

Bob had said he didn't want any part of Stu's game with Larry, so there wasn't anything to split. The amount of cash he was carrying kept getting bigger and he knew he had to get a safe-deposit box somewhere soon.

Chapter 6

The ticket line was fairly long. He wondered what things might be like in their busy season. A young, well-dressed man in his early twenties, tried cutting into the line ahead of him and an elderly lady. Stu reached out and caught him on the shoulder. He pointed to the rear of the line. Somewhat embarrassed, the young man commented that he didn't notice the line. Stu told him that besides being ill-mannered, he was also a liar, and it was time for him to grow up.

The lady in front asked the clerk for assistance in getting to the plane. The clerk said he would get her someone with a wheelchair. The lady complained, saying that she could walk just fine, but she just could not see well enough to walk to the plane on her own. Stu told the clerk he would be more than happy to assist the lady.

The lady, Mrs. Meier, must have been at least eighty-five years of age, quite spry and very well-dressed. As it turned out, her seat on the plane was next to Stu's. She was on her way to Louisville to visit her daughter. She visited her daughter each summer and her daughter always visited her in Florida one or two times in the winter months. This would probably be her last Louisville visit. She had lived in Louisville all of her married life and always enjoyed visiting with old friends when in Louisville. Most of her old friends now were either in cemeteries or nursing homes. She had stopped visiting nursing homes some time ago. She didn't like the way they smelled and most of the people she visited didn't know who she was.

Her husband had died twenty years ago. He had always wanted to move to Florida after he retired, but she didn't. She said, "It's a funny thing. I moved down here two months after my husband died."

Stu just sat there and listened. Finally, when she was through talking about herself, she asked him how old he was.

He replied that he was forty-seven.

She went on to say that she had a son who would be just a couple of years older than he was, but was killed in Korea. He had graduated from Annapolis and was an officer in the Marines. It was just after his graduation that the war broke out. He was sent to California for what he thought would be a period of advanced training. They had bought him a new car to drive to California, thinking he would be there for an extended period. He had only been in California three days before they shipped him out.

She was starting to get tears in her eyes, talking about her loss. Stu mentioned that he had been there as a Marine, too, and how hard it had been with all of the young lives being lost. He knew she was very proud of her son.

The flight to Louisville was uneventful, and after helping Mrs. Meier meet her daughter, he took a taxi down to the Brown Hotel. He wanted to be downtown and The Brown was the only hotel name he remembered. After checking in, he arranged to deposit his bag with most of the money in one of the hotel's lock boxes.

The next morning, he called the Kentucky parole officer he had been assigned. They talked on the phone and the officer said he had received a very exceptional report from the Eddyville Parole Board. The officer said they should have at least one meeting and also asked if there was anything he could do for Stu.

Stu told him he needed to get a driver's license and wondered if he could help.

Bruce, the parole officer, agreed to pick Stu up at his hotel at eleven. Stu still had his old Kentucky commercial driver's license with the papers his mother had saved. With his old license and with Bruce's help, it was unbelievable how simple it was.

Bruce wanted to know if he was interested in purchasing a car.

Stu hadn't given it much thought. Yes, he sooner or later would want to have a car.

Bruce said his wife's mother had died recently and they had her old Volvo. "It's old, but in great shape. If you would like to have it, we could let you have it at a bargain."

Bruce drove to his home and showed Stu the car.

"How much of a bargain?" Stu asked.

Three thousand dollars was all it took to make the purchase. Bruce then helped him with the title work and the insurance.

After they had finished up their business, Stu commented on how much help Bruce had been, saying that in prison he hadn't heard anything good about parole officers. Bruce went on to explain that he tried to know as much as he could about the parolees assigned to him. He had read all of the minutes from his parole hearing and had visited with the Eddyville warden. As it turned out, Bruce was an ex-Marine and had been in Korea, too.

Bruce said, "You are the only parolee I have even met that was awarded the Silver Star."

Bruce told him he was actually saving the Volvo for him. Several people had wanted to purchase it, but after reading through Stu's records, he wanted him to have the car.

Later in the day, Stu called Susan and said he would like to visit Jasper and meet her girls. He told her that he had some banking business in Bloomington and would like to be there in a few days, but said he'd call her again later. Stu told her he now had a fifteen year old Volvo that he had purchased from a friend in Louisville. He also wanted to get on better terms with Al, so he told Susan to tell Al he was bringing enough money to help pay for Sally's first year at I.U.

Next, Stu called Catherine, asking if she could put her cousin up for a night or two. He explained that he had been lucky playing backgammon and wanted to have a safe-deposit box at the bank. She knew he had won pretty much at the Indianapolis Club, because Fred couldn't wait to tell her. She wanted to know where she could pick him up and he informed her of his recent purchase.

The next morning he checked out of the hotel, taking his money bag from the hotel's lock box. He enjoyed driving. The Volvo ran like a top for the first fifty miles and then steam started coming out from under the hood. His luck was holding out, though, because there was a service station with a garage mechanic on duty.

After looking the car over, the mechanic explained that all of the hoses and belts needed to be replaced. With less than forty thousand miles on the car, he could tell it hadn't been driven much. The mechanic said, "If it was my car I would put new tires on it, too. Those are the original tires and they are dry-rotted. I'm not looking to sell you a lot of unnecessary stuff."

Stu told him that he had just purchased the car from an elderly lady's estate. The mechanic told him he had a hell of a nice car and suggested that he allow him to change all of the fluids, too. He put the car up on the rack and looked for leaks. Stu agreed to have everything done and he was back on the road in three hours. He was surprised to find the car's air conditioner worked as well as it did.

Arriving in Bloomington, he went straight to the bank. Catherine was at her desk and saw him come through the door. She had already made out the paperwork for the deposit box. Stu suggested that she place her name on the box, too. Stu said, "I might be off somewhere and need for you to express some cash to me."

Catherine really didn't like the idea, but agreed to do it. She commented that she had expected him earlier. He went on to tell about his fifteen year old Volvo and the work that he had needed to have done.

It was still an hour before the bank closed, so she handed him a key to her condo, suggesting he go ahead to the lake.

As he pulled the Volvo up in front of Catherine's place, Fred spotted him and came over. He said, "I didn't expect to see you back so soon."

Stu told Fred about his trip to Florida and how he had managed to leave from there with a little extra cash.

Fred commented about his car, saying that if he didn't know his automobiles, he would think it was a new car.

Stu lied and told him he had kept it in storage most of the time. Stu said that he was just in town for a day and then he was going to drive down to Jasper to visit with his sister and her family for a few days.

Fred said, "Hey, I've got an idea! There are a couple of hotshot backgammon players in Jasper. They like to play for big money, mainly mine. I sure would like to have you team up with me against them. These guys are so proud of their game, they will drop everything to play. One guy is a lawyer and the other runs a funeral home."

Stu asked their names and was surprised to hear that the lawyer's name was Goehausen. Hartmetz was the other name. Stu explained that his sister had had some dealings with Goehausen in the past, and it would be better if Goehausen didn't know his real name. Stu's middle name was Robert, so he suggested his new name be Robert Stewart. That way, he could still call him Stu.

Stu said, "Yes, I would be more than willing to play Mr. Goehausen and his friend."

Goehausen and Hartmetz had traveled up to Bloomington more than once to play Fred, and he knew they wouldn't pass up a chance to play in Jasper. He told Stu that Goehausen wouldn't be willing to walk away from his office to play for nickels and dimes. He was sure they would want to play for fifty to a hundred dollars a point and wanted to know if Stu would be comfortable with that amount.

Stu told him he would only be willing to play if he was calling the moves. Seventy percent of the time Fred would make the same move he would, but it was the other thirty percent Stu wanted to control. It was agreed that when Fred was playing, Stu would tap his shoulder when he didn't agree with the more.

Fred called his friends in Jasper and arranged to meet at their country club for lunch. Both Hartmetz and Goehausen had played in some of the major backgammon tournaments in Vegas and were very confident. They knew the names of most of the big-time players and had never heard of a Robert Stewart before. It was almost a joke to them.

Stu said that he wanted to go down a little early and check into a motel. He had no idea how late the game would go and he didn't want to show up at his sister's late in the evening.

Fred said he thought that was a good idea and he would book a room, too. "If it's late I sure don't want to be driving back in the dark."

Stu called Susan and informed her that he was back in Indiana and would like to visit her and her family in Jasper two days from now. Stu offered, "I can stay in a motel."

She said, "No, we have a big old house and you could stay in the room that Mom used. Al has softened up quite a bit, since he heard you are going to help with some of Sally's college expenses."

Catherine was a little miffed when she found out that Stu was leaving so soon. He told her about his plans to visit Susan and said that Fred had worked up a backgammon game with some high rollers in Jasper. She asked if Fred would be coming over to play backgammon later. Stu informed her that he wanted to take her to dinner and that they would drive in his new Volvo. He was actually proud of his purchase and enjoyed showing it off.

He left it up to Catherine to pick the restaurant.

She didn't think twice before coming out with her favorite Italian restaurant. It was a charming place, with rustic brick walls and candles at every table. Catherine had called ahead and made a reservation. They were customers of the bank and had saved a special table for her. After they were seated, Stu order a bottle of their best Italian wine.

During dinner, he told about his visit with Bob and his new wife. She had heard about the bank failure in Oklahoma City and had no idea that Ruth was married to Tony. She asked if he had any plans beyond Jasper.

He told her of his desire to go fishing down by the Eddyville prison. He mentioned Bruce and how helpful he had been. "I know I'm going to have to find a job sooner or later, but for now I just don't have any plans."

She commented on all of the cash he placed in the deposit box.

Stu explained about his winning streak and wondered if it might end tomorrow. Stu couldn't wait to tell her about his upcoming backgammon game in Jasper, asking her to guess who one of the players would be.

Catherine said, "Don't tell me it's a lawyer named Goehausen."

Smiling, with a grin from cheek to cheek, he told her, "Yes." He went on to explain how he had worked it out with Fred for him to use another name.

She thought the fishing trip was a great idea. Since he had been on a pretty fast track the last two weeks, she thought a little quiet time would be good for him.

Fred and Stu departed the next morning for Jasper. Fred had booked two rooms for them at the Jasper Inn. Following Fred down to Jasper was like a fast roller coaster ride. Fred either had a heavy foot or a death wish. Stu didn't want to risk getting stopped by the police, so he just slowed down and enjoyed the drive.

Fred arrived well ahead of Stu and had them both checked into the hotel by the time Stu arrived. Their arrival in Jasper gave them a little time to spare, so they rested for thirty minutes before heading out to the country club.

They drove to the Club in Fred's car. When he was introduced to Walt Goehausen and Don Hartmetz, Goehausen commented that Stu's face was new to him. Walt felt he had met most of the serious tournament players in the country.

Stu told Walt he had never been to a tournament.

Through lunch, Goehausen tried his best to pull information from Stu.

Fred explained that Stu had been in a government position, and as well as he knew him, he still had no idea what he did. Goehausen was wasting his time to even try.

The club's game room had a special backgammon table, very much like the one they had played on in Indianapolis. The table, apparently, had far less use and still looked new.

Walt was anxious to get started. He hadn't walked away from a busy law practice just to be sociable. He was thinking, *tax free money and a lot of it.* It was agreed that they would be playing for one hundred dollars a point and it would be a team game. Two against two. They would stop for dinner at six, and resume the game after dinner if everyone was willing. Prior to dinner, all losses to that point would be paid in cash.

They rolled the dice to see which players would start the game. Fred rolled a high number and was the leadoff man for their team. After the first three moves, the Jasper boys had an excellent position. When the time came for their fourth turn, they turned the doubling cube. Fred looked at Stu and asked what he thought. Stu said he didn't want it, so they lost the first game.

Stu took over the play for the second game. Again the Jasper boys gained an early lead and turned the doubling cube. Stu felt the position was somewhat risky, but could see the Jasper boys running out of good rolls in one turn. Turning to Fred, he commented that sooner or later they were going to have to bite the bullet. They accepted the double. Walt rolled a double six, which completely destroyed Goehausen's advantage.

Stu turned to Fred and said, "Let's see what they are made of."

He turned the cube to four, feeling it wasn't a good take. Losing their advantage so fast caused them to take a cube they most likely wouldn't have taken had their position developed more slowly.

Stu's game continued to improve and they ended up winning the game with a gammon, for an eight point victory. Once Walt and Don were down six thousand dollars they started playing a catch-up game. They took more chances and lost money faster. Fred was starting to wonder if the Jasper boys would be up to playing after dinner. They had lost twenty-one thousand, six hundred dollars before dinner.

Walt excused himself, saying he had to make a money run down to his office safe. He was back in less than fifteen minutes. That was one advantage of living in a small town. Nothing was more than five minutes away. Walt handed each of them an envelope with ten thousand, three hundred dollars.

During dinner, Walt said he felt they had played poorly once they were a few thousand dollars down.

Walt said, "You beat us to death with the doubling cube. Our cube management is what killed us."

Stu said, "Don't feel bad. That same type of situation occurred in Paris in 1972, during a World Championship match between Jesse Simpson and Peter Lynn."

Walt asked if Stu had been at the match.

Stu answered, "No, but Dallas Irving was and wrote a book, telling every move made in the entire match. It may surprise you gentlemen to know I really haven't played much backgammon. Most of what I know about the game I have learned from books."

"You can bet your sweet ass it's going to be different after dinner," said Walt.

Walt and Don had talked over their loss and wanted to recover as much as possible before they quit for the night. They suggested that they start the play at two hundred dollars a point and said Walt would be sitting against them in every game.

Stu said, "I normally feel the losers should try to win it back at the same rate as they lost it, but we will agree to the two hundred dollar a point game. However, let's establish a quitting time of nine o'clock."

Stu, of course, was years younger than Fred and it had been a long day, so he would be the full-time head of their team.

By eight o'clock, Walt and Don were down another thirty-six hundred dollars. Things just hadn't gone well for them. Walt suggested they quit early because he had to be in Federal Court in Evansville the next morning.

They all agreed. Don pulled an envelope out of his pocket and paid them both eighteen hundred.

Fred said he would invite them up to the Pointe the next time Stu was in Bloomington. They shook hands and were out the door.

As they arrived back at the Inn, Fred suggested that they go into the bar and have a small glass of Port. They needed to relax and just get the game out of their mind. Fred said, "I'll be seeing dice and making moves all night if I don't relax and have a drink."

Sitting in the bar, Stu handed Fred the envelope Don had given him. He wanted him to pass it on to Catherine, so she could put it in his safe-deposit box.

Fred was interested in knowing what Stu's plans were.

Stu told Fred that he had a fishing trip planned down in the Barkley Lake area, and said that he had an old friend who had also been with the government that he wanted to visit.

Fred asked, "At your age are you subject to recall by the government?"

"Let's put it this way. I keep in touch, but at my age I hope to hell they don't call me back. Even with them paying all of my expenses, I'm still making more money than what they paid me. I don't want to end up being a backgammon hustler, but I do enjoy the game from time to time. I'm sure I told you I had never played for money prior to meeting you." Stu went on to say he wasn't sure where he wanted to live or what he wanted to do next.

They had breakfast together the next morning at the Inn's dining room. Fred told him how much he had enjoyed winning yesterday. Goehausen had been his nemesis and he thanked Stu for helping to defeat him.

It was still a little early and Stu had told Susan that he would show up in time to take her and the girls to lunch. He wanted to make a few purchases for his next venture. There was a nice little men's store right on the public square. They were having their end-of-the-season sale, so everything had a big markdown. As it turned out, the store owner was the only one working in the store. He was very helpful.

Now that he had an automobile trunk for a closet, Stu was able to increase the size of the wardrobe. He paid over five hundred dollars in cash for his purchases. The owner asked if he needed a receipt.

Stu thought for a moment and said, "Yes." He just didn't want to get stopped with a trunk full of new clothing and not have any proof of purchase. Bruce had told him to be very careful.

Susan's home was in an older neighborhood. All of the houses we large, mainly built of brick. The yards all were well-kept, too.

Susan saw him parking his car and came out the front door to greet him. "The girls can't wait to meet you. I have told them who you are and they were very understanding about why I had told them you were dead."

Stu was glad to hear he could be himself instead of some imposter. Both of the girls resembled Susan. They were excited to meet him and handled it well. Susan had warned them not to ask questions, but just to let him do the asking. Sally, the eldest of the two, was a freshman at Indiana University, in Bloomington. She had come home for a long weekend.

Susan said, "I think it's great she could be here, too. Tomorrow, I thought you might enjoy spending the day with Albert. You could ride on the beer truck with him and see what's going on in Jasper."

It sounded like a good idea and he agreed it might even be fun. He suggested they go out to lunch.

Susan was quick to accept his invitation.

They rode in his Volvo. The girls had never ridden in a stick shift car before. They did ask questions about the car and where he bought it. It was a two-door model and they commented that it looked like no one had ever been in the back seat.

Susan said the car looked like it belonged to a little old lady who only drove it to church on Sundays.

After lunch Susan said she needed to do a little shopping with the girls and then pick up a few things from the grocery store for supper. Stu was welcome to tag along or just take it easy.

Stu had noticed several bikes in their garage and asked if he could borrow one for the afternoon.

After moving his overnight bag into what had been his mother's room, he dressed for biking. He spent a good part of the afternoon exploring Jasper.

When he returned to the house, Albert had returned from work and had already freshened up for the evening. He greeted Stu and said he was glad to see him. Stu sat down and had a beer with him before he showered. They talked a little about Stu riding on the truck with him tomorrow.

Albert said Stu might get a kick out of seeing how the little business operated. There were only three employees in the business. Frank drove the over-the-road truck to the breweries and unloaded the trailers with the lift truck. Judy took care of the office and sometimes helped to run the lift truck. He and Judy took care of the ordering from the breweries. The business was owned by a local furniture manufacturer who rarely came by the business. He might go as much as six months without even stopping by.

At dinner that evening, Susan commented that Mrs. Goehausen had gone out and purchased a new car today. The word around town was that Walt had lost a healthy sum of money playing backgammon with some out-of-town players at the country club.

Stu said it seemed more likely that she would buy a new car if he had won, not lost.

Susan said that he had a lot to learn about women.

Albert said he was making a delivery at the country club yesterday and heard that Walt and Don had a big time backgammon game going on in the game room. He wanted to look in, but didn't.

The next day, the men had an early breakfast and were off to the beer warehouse. Albert loaded the route truck with the fork lift. His first stops were all grocery stores. He explained to Stu that the taverns, clubs and restaurants didn't open up until a little later in the day. Albert said, "We're going to have lunch at our biggest account. They have the best lunch in town and the owner is a great guy."

After Albert finished his delivery at Gus's Tavern, they found a seat at the bar. When Gus paid the invoice, he asked Albert if business was so good that Mr. Benedict had hired him a helper.

Albert said, "Oh! This is my brother-in-law, Stewart Vogel. He's from Bloomington."

Gus grabbed the bar, as if to steady himself. Without saying anything, he reached out and took a rosary down from a picture that was hanging behind the bar and asked, "Vogel, do you recognize this rosary?"

Albert didn't know what was going on, and he sure as hell hoped Stu wasn't getting him messed up with his best customer.

Stu answered that it looked like one he carried in Korea, but he didn't remember where he had lost it.

Gus said, "Well, I sure as hell remember it. Your outfit was moving up to help cover our retreat at Chosin. We were under heavy fire when my leg was almost completely blown off. You stopped your advance, just long enough to use your web belt as a tourniquet to stop my bleeding. I wouldn't have lasted two minutes without that tourniquet. You handed me this rosary, saying if I was going to make it out, I was going to need God's help."

It took Gus over a year before he received his artificial leg and was able to walk again. Upon his return to Jasper, it was a few years before he tried to locate Stu.

Stu laughed, saying, "How could you find me? My name isn't on the rosary and our only meeting wasn't what you would call a social affair. With the entire area under fire, I don't recall introducing myself."

Gus opened a drawer behind the bar and pulled out a stained web belt with the name "Stewart Vogel" stenciled on it.

Stu commented that he did remember, but truthfully, he was surprised to find that Gus had survived. Stu said, "I guess you helped to save my life, too. If I remember correctly, I was low on ammo and I took yours."

Gus went on to explain that he did try to locate Stu a few years later, but figured he had gotten himself killed. The Marine Corps wouldn't help. However, he did see that he been awarded the Silver Star, but didn't know if it had been awarded posthumously or not.

Gus wanted his family to meet Stu and they talked about getting together later. They decided they would meet for dinner at the K of C Club the next evening. That sounded okay to Stu. He just knew he didn't want to go back to the Jasper Country Club anytime soon.

All of a sudden, Albert became impressed with his brother-in-law and started looking at him in a different light. When the word got around town that it was his brother-in-law who had save Gus's life in Korea, he would have a little family pride to share.

Back in the truck, Albert said it sounded like he had saved Gus's ass.

Stu said, "COLD."

Albert asked, "What did you say?"

Stu said, "Cold. It was so darn cold, we were all sick from shivering. I never thought Gus would make it. His leg was a bloody mess."

During dinner that evening Albert told Susan and the girls how Stu had saved Gus Opperman's life in Korea. Susan said she didn't recall ever hearing Stu say anything about his time in Korea.

Stu said what he remembered about Korea wasn't pretty and not a good subject. He was sure Gus would have plenty to say tomorrow when they all had dinner with his family.

The next day, Stu borrowed Albert's pickup truck. He and the girls loaded the bikes in the back and drove about eight miles to an old railroad roadbed that had been converted into a bike path. There was a little roadside tavern where they had lunch. The owner thought he recognized the girls and asked if they were the Hartig girls. After confirming who they were, he reached out his hand toward Stu. He just wanted to shake the hand of the man that had saved Gus Opperman in Korea.

Well, here they were eight miles outside of Jasper and the word had already spread about Al's brother-in-law. Stu did look forward to meeting Gus's family, but he didn't want to have to shake hands with everyone at the K. of C. Club.

When they returned from the bike ride, Susan informed Stu that a reporter from the local newspaper had called and wanted to interview him.

Oh shit! thought Stu. Stu was doing his best to keep a low profile, and now this. He guessed there would be a photographer present also, so his picture would be all over the area. He really didn't like the idea of Don and Walt finding out his real name. He knew that if he objected to anything with the reporter, the reporter would start digging into his past.

In the evening during the interview, which took place at the K of C Club, the reporter said he wanted them to pose for a picture. Stu held out his hand and suggested that everyone from both families should be in the picture. Gus had two sons and a daughter, all married, with their spouses, and six small grandchildren. Stu stood in the rear, with Albert and his family in front of him.

The next morning's newspaper carried the story along with the picture. The picture wasn't all that big, and with so many in the picture the faces were rather small. Someone would have to study the picture with a magnifying glass in order to recognize Stu.

He gave Susan three thousand dollars in cash before departing the next day, and promised to be back before another twenty-five years.

Chapter 7

Driving out of Jasper, Stu picked up the interstate highway. The interstate highways were new to him, and probably to his Volvo, too. It only took him a little over an hour to reach Evansville. He was interested in purchasing a bike and a rack that would fit on the rear of this Volvo. Sally had given him directions to the bike store, saying they would be able to take care of all of his needs.

Stu was in and out of the store in less than fifteen minutes and was headed south with a new bike strapped to the rear of his car.

When he reached the lake area, he followed signs to Kentucky Dam Village Lodge. He lucked out in getting a room at the Lodge. They were in their fall season and most of the rooms had been booked a year in advance. The desk clerk told him that they had just had a cancellation. The clerk said he could promise him the room for a week, but after that he would have to move out.

The clerk had given him a map of the area and after he had stowed his gear, he changed into biking clothes. It was time to road test his new bike. The bike was a very good color match with his tan Volvo.

There was a large marina just a short distance from the lodge. The ride down to the marina was almost all downhill, so he ended up coasting most of the way.

He made arrangements to rent a fishing boat for the next day and purchased a Kentucky fishing license. The marina sold cheap cane fishing poles, which came ready to use with line, bobber and hook. He could wait until tomorrow to make his purchase.

As he was walking out of the marina store, a sailing ketch was pulling into the fuel dock. Stu ran over and helped the skipper with his lines. Bob had talked about a Howell 36 foot ketch, saying it would be a perfect live-aboard for Stu, if he could ever afford it.

Stu asked, "Is this a Howell 36?"

Like every boat owner, the skipper was proud of his boat and invited Stu to come aboard. He introduced himself, saying his name was Henry Hutchinson and that he lived in Evansville.

Stu asked, "Isn't this a pretty large-sized boat for this lake?"

Henry said it was actually a perfect boat. He told Stu how much he and his wife had enjoyed the boat. Henry explained that the predominant wind was out of the west and, with the lake running north and south, it made for easy sailing. There were days that he had actually sailed all of the way to Paris, Tennessee, sixty miles away, without having to change the setting of his sails. Henry went on to say that he was planning on taking the boat down the Mississippi. "My friend and I are leaving out in two days on the trip and we could sure use an extra hand aboard. Stu, would you like to come along?" asked Henry.

Rubbing the back of his head, Stu said, "That sounds like some trip. I just came up from Florida a few days ago and need to spend a little time in the area to visit an old friend. If you were pulling out later, I might give it some consideration." Stu thanked him for the invitation, but said he just couldn't move that fast.

Henry went on talking about the trip. Henry told Stu he thought the first leg of the trip would take about ten days. The weather was always a factor. Henry didn't expect to have any problems with the boat itself, but the unexpected can always happen. Henry said, "I would be happy to leave later, but my friend is taking off from his job in order to make the trip. So I don't have an option."

Henry asked Stu if he had any dinner plans. "I'll buy if you drive." He was without his car. His wife had gone back to Evansville and would be bringing his friend back, along with all of the provisions for the trip.

Stu accepted the dinner invitation and said he would be back to pick him up later.

Henry handed him a small two-way radio. Henry said, "Just leave this on channel 62 and call me when you are leaving the lodge. I'll be waiting right up there."

The ride back to the Lodge was almost too much. It was all uphill. Stu had to stop more than once and ended up walking his bike a third of the way.

Back at the Lodge, an attractive middle-aged woman spoke to him as he was walking his bike to his room. She said, "I haven't seen you before. Are you with our group?"

Stu asked, "What group is that?"

She replied, "The Kentucky Fun Bike Tour. We go to different state park lodges and bike the areas. You would be more than welcome to join in any day. The only bad part of the trip is that all of the lodge foods are the same and not that great."

Stu surprised himself by saying that he was going to dinner with a friend and she would be welcome to join them.

She said, "Well, that's the best offer I've had all week, but I don't even know your name."

"Stewart Vogel. My friends call me Stu. And you are?"

She said, "Vickie White. I'm from Memphis. I work as a secretary in a cotton brokerage office and would sure as hell like to have dinner somewhere else."

They agreed to meet in the Lodge lobby at six.

Stu called Henry on the hand-held ship to shore radio he had lent him. "I don't know if this is good or bad, but we have a third party going to dinner with us." Stu went on to explain the best that he could and said he wanted to pick up the dinner check.

Vickie was waiting in the lobby as he entered. She was wearing blue jeans, a white silk blouse and shiny, white high-heeled shoes. As they walked toward the car, she held onto his arm. After twenty-five years in prison, it felt good to have a woman holding onto him. As they reached his car, he called Henry on the two-way radio.

Driving to the marina, she asked what business he was in.

Stu said, "I'm not in business. I'm retired."

She asked, "From what?"

He said, "I was with the government for twenty-five years and it's something I don't talk about."

She then asked, "Are you married?"

Stu went on to explain that he had never been married and that his position with the government was too demanding of his time.

Henry was waiting at the appointed spot. Stu's Volvo, a two door, meant that Henry would be sitting in the rear. Henry had a bottle of wine that he handed to Vickie, as he worked his way into the rear seat. Introductions were made once he was seated.

Henry gave the directions and they were in Grand Rivers is less than ten minutes. The restaurant was very rustic and, in a way, reminded him of the one in Brown County, where Catherine had taken him.

Vickie said she was glad Henry had thought to bring a bottle of wine.

Henry said, "I just cannot understand Kentucky. They are the largest producer of bourbon whiskey in the world and yet it leads the nation in dry counties."

Vickie was a fun person and added to their enjoyment of the evening.

Henry talked about his upcoming trip and how he felt a little like Tom Sawyer.

Upon returning to the marina, Henry invited them to join him aboard his boat for an after-dinner drink. The evening was still early and it seemed like a great idea. Vickie was enjoying their company and being on the boat. She didn't talk much about herself, but was very interested in asking questions about the boat.

Stu had a small glass of port, while Vickie downed a scotch and water. She was just a little cuddly as they walked back to the car.

Back at the Lodge, he walked her to her room. She handed him her room key. As he opened the door, she gave him a little push. Once in the room, she said she couldn't wait to get her shoes off. As she stood there barefooted, she put her arms around his neck and kissed him like he had never been kissed before. They were both very responsive.

He started unbuttoning her blouse and she said, "Wait. Let me do it." She proceeded to take her bra off, too. Next she slipped out of her jeans. She was wearing a very brief style black panty.

She kissed Stu again as he felt her breasts. Her nipples had turned hard. She had started unbuttoning his trousers. Kicking off his shoes and throwing his shirt on the floor, he moved with her to the bed. Little did she know she was about to have sex with a virgin. She was a wonderful teacher, even though she had no idea.

She fell asleep shortly after their love-making. Stu lay there awake, not knowing if he should leave or stay. He decided to stay, thinking it might be rude to leave. He slept surprisingly well.

It must have been shortly before sunrise when he awoke. She was awake and had actually awakened him. She kissed him very gently. It was the first time in his entire life he had awoken in bed with a woman.

She suggested they shower together. He was used to showering with other inmates. Needless to say, this made for an exciting change.

At breakfast they both ordered the country breakfast, with ham and eggs, hash-browned potatoes and biscuits with gravy. Several of the other bikers were in the Lodge dining room and stopped to say good morning.

Vickie said, "Our bike group starts biking at ten this morning. Why don't you ride with us?"

He explained that he had a fishing boat rented for the day. "There is a special spot on Barkley Lake where I want to fish." Then he suggested they go out to dinner again that night.

Walking back toward their room, she said she hoped he was not in a hurry to go fishing. They were both back in her bed and he was again aroused. Entering her was even more enjoyable than the first time. She told him how great he was, and he really didn't know what to answer, other than that she was terrific, too.

When he returned to his room after breakfast, there was a red light blinking on the room phone. There was a message. Henry had called and said he needed to talk to him.   Stu had already returned his two-way radio, so he decided to just stop by his boat. He drove down to the marina, remembering the difficult uphill ride he had the day before.

Henry reported that his wife had called him after he and Vickie had left. She said his crewmember for his trip had fallen and had broken his arm. His arm was in a cast and there just wasn't any way he could make the trip. Henry was really looking forward to the trip and, unless he could find some help, he just couldn't do it. Henry asked if there was any chance he could talk him into making the trip.

Stu thought about it for awhile. There were things he would need to do, like store the Volvo, get some extra cash from Catherine and pick up some foul-weather boating gear. "I'm fishing today and tomorrow I need to visit with an old friend who lives in the area. If I could meet you in Evansville in three days, we could find a place to store my Volvo and maybe you could help me find some gear that I would need for the trip. I also need to get ahold of my banker and have her send me some cash."

Henry was elated that he could still make his trip. He had looked forward to this trip for years and he was afraid that he wasn't going to get make it. He wanted Stu to understand that the trip wouldn't cost him a dime. He would be paying for everything, including the plane ticket back to Evansville.

That being the case, Stu realized that he wouldn't need to contact Richard, at the bank, for money.

Henry gave Stu his business card, with his address and phone number. He then said, "Don't worry about your car. I have a spare garage. My wife is driving down to pick me up today. She will be delighted to hear I can still make the trip."

They shook hands and agreed to meet in Evansville in three days.

Back in the marina office, Stu purchased a cheap cooler, ice, bottled water, straw hat, and a cane fishing pole with a hook and line attached. He also purchased a three day fishing permit and, last but not least, a small container of worms.

There was a large map of both lakes on the wall. He studied it for some time before leaving. He had never operated an outboard motor before, so it was imperative that the dockhand provide him with complete instructions.

Stu already knew about the channel markers and how to read them because Bob had done a good job of instructing him. It was a great day; cool, with no wind. The trees along the shoreline had started changing color.

He found the entrance to the canal, which joined the two lakes. There was a large towboat pushing several large barges, loaded with coal, in the main channel of the canal. He eased past and waved to the crew members.

Once in Barkley Lake, he followed the markers south. He must have motored ten miles before he caught sight of the prison. It was a majestic site from a distance, but as he grew closer it became the ugly place he had called home for twenty-five years. Seeing it again, he wasn't so sure he wanted to visit Nick.

He anchored on the opposite side of the channel from the prison. He hadn't even been at anchor for ten minutes before a game warden pulled alongside of his boat asking to see his fishing license. Stu recognized the game warden. He had been a prison guard at Eddyville and wasn't too well-liked by the inmates. He was what you would call a hard-ass. He hadn't recognized Stu, but once he saw his name on the license, he knew him.

The game warden said, "I thought you were a lifer. How did you get out?"

Stu answered, "Paroled last month."

He asked, "What the hell you doing out here?"

Stu replied, "Fishing."

Standing up, the officer said, "Don't get smart with me."

After saying that, the ex-guard pulled out his pistol and set it so Stu could see it. He said he needed to check Stu out, telling him to stand up and empty his pockets. He had him open the cooler and hold it so he could see its contents. He next called the prison security on his radio. "I've got one of your cons out here in a fishing boat. It's Vogel. Did he make parole?"

Hearing that he had indeed been paroled, he commented that he thought Vogel was up to something. Bruce had warned him to be very careful in any dealing with law enforcement officers.

He said, "You're not real welcome in these waters, Vogel, and I will be keeping an eye on you." He gave Stu back his fishing license and pulled away.

Well, the ex-guard had just ruined the hell out of his day. Stu pulled up anchor and headed back toward Kentucky Lake. The ex-guard followed his boat for about five miles, almost to the canal.

By the time he made it back to the marina, Henry had already departed. Stu dumped his bait overboard, thinking the fish might enjoy it better without a hook attached. Returning the fishing boat he had rented for the day before noon might have looked a little stupid, but he more or less had been run out of Dodge. He left the fishing pole in the boat and took the other items with him. When he reached the parking lot, he threw the cooler and its contents into the trash dumpster. This was the first time since his release that he had experienced a mood swing. He needed to forget about this morning and think about the trip with Henry.

When he arrived back at the lodge, he decided to load his bike on the bike rack and go back to the Grand Rivers area. He had a sandwich for lunch at a little ice cream shop. After parking his Volvo, he unloaded his bike and headed south. In less than a mile he crossed over a bridge. The bridge was the same bridge he had passed under in the fishing boat. It was over the canal that connected the two lakes. He stopped for a few minutes, watching the boat traffic. Henry had told him there would be quite a few pleasure vessels moving south from northern marinas for the winter season. He said that some days, as many as ten transient boats could dock overnight. It wasn't uncommon for some of the boats to cruise in the lake area a week or two before continuing on south.

As he continued south, he met up with the Kentucky Fun Bikers. Vickie was surprised to see him. She said, "I thought you were fishing."

He said the fish weren't biting and he had changed his mind. Then Stu rode back to Grand Rivers with the group. They moved at a little faster pace than what he had been riding, but he was able to keep up with them. He left the group at Grand Rivers, telling Vickie he would see her back at the lodge.

Later, when they were making their dinner plans, she suggested they drive into Paducah. It was just a twenty mile drive and it wasn't in a dry county. One of the other bikers had suggested a nice restaurant overlooking the Ohio River.

They were able to get a table with a great view. The river traffic is fairly heavy on the Ohio, along with extra traffic from the Tennessee River, which flows into the Ohio at Paducah. Both of them ordered a beer as they looked over the menu. Stu asked the waiter if there was anything they were famous for.

"Fiddlers. You're in catfish country and ours are the best you will ever put in your mouth."

The fiddler dinner included hush puppies, slaw and fried potatoes. They both opted for the fiddlers.

When the waiter arrived with their dinner he gave them a lesson in how to eat fiddlers. "Most people pick at them with a fork, but that's not the way to do it. It looks messy, but try this." He showed them how to pull the fins out of the back of the fish and then repeat the process at the bottom. "Now pick up the fish and eat it like you would an ear of corn."

Vickie was amazed how simple it was. Being from Memphis, she had eaten her share of fiddlers, but this way was entirely new to her.

Driving back to the lodge, she asked what his plans were for the next day.

He said he wanted to visit with a friend and then he would be driving on to Evansville. He hadn't told her about the planned trip with Henry.

At the lodge they sat out on a large deck, overlooking the lake. While sitting there, he told her about his planned trip with Henry and how it had come up.

She said, "Great, you will have to stop at Memphis on the way down the Mississippi. I'll take you two sailors to dinner."

Vickie said she wanted to tell him about herself. She had been married eighteen years to a homosexual. "I knew things were never right between us, but I always blamed myself. Three years ago, he divorced me and moved in with his real partner. After the fact, I found out they had been seeing each other for over ten years. I have been having a really hard time getting over his rejection and the fact that he had cheated on me all of these years."

She went on to tell that she still loved her former husband and said that he had always been very nice to her. She said that they no longer see each other now. They never had children. Shortly after the divorce, she started seeing a psychiatrist. She loved Chet and had always felt inadequate in the sexual part of their marriage. She said that it had been three years and it had taken until now for her to turn loose. She knew when she first met Stu that he might be the one to release her from the past. The psychiatrist had told her she may never really ever love anyone the way she had loved Chet, and to go slowly in any new relationship. With a wide grin on her face, she asked Stu if she had gone too slowly.

They sat out on the deck until the mosquitoes were starting to bother them.

Stu said, "If you'd be willing to miss your bike ride in the morning and come with me tomorrow, I will tell you a little of my life story."

She agreed. He actually had said very little about himself. All she knew was he wasn't married.

He invited her to spend the night in his room, saying he might be getting a phone call.

She agreed, feeling this might be their last night together.

They both were asleep shortly after hitting the sheets. There wasn't even a kiss goodnight. In the morning they both showered separately.

He suggested they try to find someplace away from the lodge for breakfast. He wasn't very sure how to find the Eddyville prison by car. He remembered the prison chaplain driving him to Princeton to catch the bus and he felt he could find the way, once he got to Princeton. They found a nice little restaurant right off the interstate just as they exited at Princeton. There must have been a dozen pickup trucks parked in front. It was a short order place, with the grill located in the rear of the breakfast bar. It was entertaining, just watching the cook. He was a master short-order cook.

After breakfast, the drive to the prison only took five minutes. The parking area was located forty or fifty steps below the main gate. There was a guard tower above the gate. As they sat in the car, Stu reviewed the last twenty-five years of his life and even went into detail how she was his first real date.

As he was speaking, a loud speaker announced that they were on state property and needed to do as told. They were instructed to get out of the car and place both hands on the car's hood. It wasn't a minute before a prison security car pulled up behind where they were parked. Three guards jumped out of the car. One yelled at Stu, "Vogel, what the hell do you think you are doing?"

Stu said, "I thought I was visiting."

The guard said, "We don't like ex-con visitors."

Another car pulled up with the warden. The warden walked over and instructed the guards to back off. He told Vickie to get back in the Volvo. Turning to Stu, he said it would be best if he left and never came back.

The warden said, "The guards get very jumpy when they encounter an ex-inmate. You were never a problem, but down through the years there have been several occasions when guards have been harmed. I want you to leave now and never return."

Back in the car, Vickie said, "Well that certainly scared the pee right out of me."

Stu said, "I'm sorry. It looks like I made a foolish mistake. I had no idea there would be a problem. I can't tell you how sorry I am to have put you through the guard's harassment."

Vickie didn't say another word during the drive back to the Lodge. As she got out of the car, she turned toward him, crying, and said, "Fuck you!"

That was it. No goodbyes. She hurried away toward her room.

After loading his bike on the rack and packing his gear in the Volvo, Stu checked out of the Lodge.

Chapter 8

The drive to Evansville was uneventful. He had never driven a car with cruise control before. Actually, automatic cruise control didn't come into existence until after he was imprisoned. He had studied the Volvo's manual and found the operation of the control to be very simple.

He had so many things to think about. He wasn't too sure if he should even tell Henry about his past. The trip would be interesting and he couldn't go through life telling everyone about the last twenty-five years. It certainly didn't endear him with Vickie. He certainly didn't want Henry to say, "Fuck you, and don't call me."

He didn't know just how he felt about his sexual encounter. Something was missing and he knew he was in no hurry to repeat the experience.

As he drove into Evansville, he had no idea where he would be staying. He had passed several motels in Henderson, but didn't see any when he arrived in Evansville. Driving toward the business center, he spotted a large high-rise motel. Well, large for Evansville. They had a room available. After checking in, he parked in the parking garage that was attached to the hotel.

It was still early and once he had freshened himself with a shower, he walked down to the hotel bar. He had thought he heard the familiar sound of dice. Entering the area, he saw two men sitting at the corner of the bar playing backgammon. He ordered a beer and sat down next to them to watch. The younger of the two asked Stu if he played backgammon. He explained that it was an open game and the winner could keep playing until he lost. There would be additional players showing up, but most of the time they only had one game going on, with everyone else watching.

Stu ended up playing the winner of the game that he was watching. There were other players starting to show up. The game was a ten dollar a point game, with the loser paying off in cash before the next game started. Most of the players were extremely bad players and lacked experience with the doubling cube. He felt like he was taking candy from babies. He played for over two hours, without a break. He never lost a game, only players. After two hours, most of the players had gone home and the others had quit playing. He had been stuffing money in his pockets all evening and had no idea how much he had won.

He dined in the hotel dining room. One of the players told him that it wasn't entirely safe to walk in the area of the hotel after dark, so the dining room was an easy choice. One of the original players joined him for dinner. Vic was more interested in talking about himself and asked Stu very few questions. He was a wildcat oil producer and had recently found a new major strike. Stu guessed that he was in his early thirties. Vic mentioned that he had never been married and at the present didn't have a girlfriend.

Vic said, "When the word gets around town about my wildcat well hitting oil, I don't expect to be lonely much longer."

Later, Stu called Henry to report his arrival. Henry said he would meet him for breakfast and then they could shop for the gear he would need afterwards. The hotel had a little laundry room for its customers, so Stu used the rest of the evening doing laundry.

During breakfast, Henry mentioned that his friends called him Hutch. He said he never really liked the name Henry.

The store that Hutch took him to was just two city blocks away, but they drove anyway. Entering the store, they were greeted by an elderly man. Stu guessed him to be in his late eighties. Hutch called him by name, mentioning to Stu that he was a friend of the owner's son, Jerry.

Hutch said, loudly, "Jerry always gives me special prices."

The truth was that Jerry was never in the store because he spent most of his time making real estate deals. The family was worth millions and made money at every turn. Hutch was just playing with the old gentleman.

Hutch said, "We will come back later. What time will Jerry be in?"

Ben, the old man, said, "You no need Jerry to get bargain, I can give you best deal. What you looking for?"

Hutch said wool or flannel shirts for starters.

Ben said, "We have some new ones in the back room that haven't made it to the shelf yet. You're a large size. Let me bring a few out."

Hutch told Stu that the old man was bull-shitting them. They haven't had a new shipment of anything in years.

It wasn't long before Ben, returned carrying three black wool Navy surplus shirts. "These are fifty dollar shirts. I can let you have them for twenty each."

They bought surplus khaki trousers, a warm jacket, rubber boots, white t-shirts, navy watch cap, gloves, rain gear, and the three wool shirts. Stu paid the bill in cash which more than delighted Ben.

They drove to the country club where they were meeting Hutch's wife for lunch. She was in the grill room, a very up-scale wood paneled room. His wife, Patrish, a very attractive woman, most likely in her early sixties, had already been seated and had been served a glass of wine. She was dressed very smartly in slacks that were a small black and white check pattern. Her blouse was black knit material. Her hand had a very large diamond on it. She was also wearing a diamond bracelet. She was the most attractive gray-haired lady Stu had ever seen. Hutch introduced Stu as they were being seated.

Patrish commented on how happy she was that Hutch had found him.

She did have her worries about the trip and wanted to make sure Stu wouldn't jump ship somewhere along the route.

Patrish said, "We talked this over last night and we both want you to know Hutch will be giving you two thousand dollars, plus the plane ticket back to Evansville." It was their guess the trip would take two weeks, but could easily take a month if there were problems.

They had ordered their lunch, when Vic stopped at their table and said hello to Stu, calling him by name.

Then Vic said, "Hutch, where did you meet up with this guy? You should have been at the bar last night. Stu, here, held down the winner's seat for two hours. Nobody can be that good or even that lucky."

Hutch said he wasn't aware Stu even played backgammon. "He is going to be the only crewmember on my trip to Florida."

Vic said he hoped Stu would give the boys another shot at him tonight. Patrish spoke up, saying that wouldn't be possible because they were having him as their guest for dinner that evening. She didn't even have to suggest it, because she knew they would end up playing in the card room most of the afternoon. Most of the time they played bridge six days a week, but there was an occasional backgammon game as well.

Patrish started laughing. "Boys, was this a plan? I can't believe it was anything else."

Hutch shook his head. Actually he didn't have any plans for the afternoon. He had already made all of his arrangements to be out of pocket for a few weeks.

Hutch told Patrish that the items Stu had purchased from Ben's store really could use cleaning. He asked if she would mind dropping a few of the things off at Jeff's One Hour Dry Cleaning on her way home.

As they were visiting, he noticed Walt Goehausen entering the room, along with a group of men, all in business suits.

Walt also spotted him, walked over to the table, and said, "Hello."

Stu was concerned. He jumped up from his seat to shake hands with Walt. Stu started to introduce him to the other people at the table.

Goehausen said he already knew everyone. Walt commented about Stu's backgammon skills, saying he still hadn't figured out if he was just lucky, or a truly great player. Walt said it was nice seeing him, as he moved to sit with his friends.

After he had left, Hutch explained that they were on the opposite sides of the table in a lawsuit a few years ago. "We won our case, but it was still pretty expensive. We were in Federal Court three days."

Stu had been lucky. The Vogel name never came out. He also knew he didn't want to hang around the country club if Goehausen was there.

Stu asked Patrish if there was a good place where he could pick up a few canvas bags to take on the trip.

She said, "Well, if Hutch can give you up for part of the afternoon, I know of a great factory outlet."

Patrish drove Hutch in her car to the outlet store after lunch. It was a large company that mainly made tents and other canvas items. He had no trouble finding three nice-sized bags. As they departed, Stu asked if there was a department store in the area because he felt that he needed to purchase an extra supply of socks and underwear.

She answered, "Well, we are not real close, but I'm more than happy to take you there." She said how happy she was that Hutch was getting to make his trip. He had been wanting to make this trip for years. She also mentioned that he had a heath condition that might make any future trips unlikely.

At the department store, Stu purchased an additional dozen white t-shirts, additional undershorts and socks.

As they were getting back into the car after leaving the department store, her car phone rang. It was Hutch, checking on them. He said that Goehausen had told everyone that Stu was the best backgammon player he had ever come up against. Goehausen had left, but there were several members that wanted to take a shot at him.

As they drove toward the club, she said those good old boys were a bunch of vultures and he didn't have to go in the club when they got back.

Stu said it might be his last chance to play much backgammon in the next few weeks, so he would give it a shot. He certainly didn't want to disappoint anyone.

As she dropped him off at the club, she made him leave his purchases with her, saying she would run them through the washing machine. She also took the items that needed to be dry-cleaned.

He told her he hated putting her to all of this trouble.

She said he could thank Mona, their maid, that evening.

Entering the club car room, he found Hutch and his friends playing bridge. They had a backgammon board set up on another table. There was one member sitting at the table. Hutch laid down his bridge hand long enough to introduce Stu to everyone, saying John gets to play him first.

Stu asked John what kind of stakes he played for, saying it made no difference to him.

John settled on a five dollar a point game. They played three games before the bridge game broke up. All the bridge players wanted to get a try at Stu. He agreed he would play each player three games and then leave. John had lost all three games he had played against Stu.

Vic was next and said he wanted to play for twenty-five a point.

Vic lost one hundred dollars in three games.

Not wanting to look cheap, the other two players played him for twenty-five a point too.

Stu had pocketed over two hundred dollars by the time they left the club. Hutch didn't play him, but had a great time watching his new friend take his country club buddies.

Stu drove Hutch to his home and agreed to return for dinner around six. He stayed out of the hotel bar when he returned, as he had had his fill of backgammon for the day. He settled down for a short nap before he showered and dressed for dinner.

A ringing phone awoke him from his nap. It was Patrish, suggesting that he check out of the hotel and spend the night at their house.

He thanked her, but declined. He had a little time to kill so he phoned Catherine and Susan. They were both excited to hear about his boat trip.

The dinner went well that evening. Hutch served only the finest red wine and assured Stu that there would be two cases on the boat. Patrish said the freezer on the boat had enough frozen food to last them a month. The only additional thing they would need on the trip would be fuel and water. Mona told him he would have to wait until tomorrow morning for his laundry. She wanted to iron his t-shirts and just hadn't had time.

Chapter 9

The drive to the lake was uneventful and they worked right up to lunch time, loading everything aboard. While Patrish fixed them sandwiches, they radioed the lock to see when they could lock down into the river. The lockmaster suggested that they use the Barkley Lake lock because it wasn't busy and it would be at least five hours before he could lock them through.

They radioed the Barkley Lock. The lockmaster had heard his call to the Kentucky Lake Lock. The lockmaster said he would have the lock ready when they arrived.

Hutch said they would be on their way and should arrive at the Barkley Lock in thirty minutes.

Patrish kissed them both goodbye and then helped untie the dock lines.

Backing away from the dock was a onetime thrill for both of them. They were starting on a real venture that would be entirely new to both of them. Hutch asked Stu if he could handle the boat while he stored some of their gear below and got everything shipshape. Stu had been through the canal before and he knew how to read the markers, so he had no problem taking over.

Hutch radioed the lockmaster as they approached the lock. The lockmaster reported that he was ready for them and to come on into the chamber. He also advised them that they needed to wear their life jackets and told them to secure their starboard side to one of the floating bollards.

As they entered the lock, Hutch was busy tying fenders on the starboard side. Stu eased the boat to one of the floating bollards and Hutch secured a line to it. He radioed the lockmaster to report that they were secure. Hutch handed Stu a boat hook and instructed him to stand at the stern of the boat and hold the boat off the chamber wall. Stu was amazed at how they were lowered so smoothly and so quickly. Hutch pointed out the wet water mark on the chamber wall where they had started from. They had dropped 49 feet. It made them feel like they were floating in a deep hole.

When the lock gates slowly opened, Hutch did not untie until the lockmaster blew a blasting horn signal. As Hutch untied from the bollard and pushed the boat away from the chamber wall, it was only then that they noticed Patrish waving from a visitor's section above the lock chamber. They only had time for one quick wave before they were in the river and on their way.

As soon as their boat began to move into the river, it started to drizzle. Hutch went below to put on his foul-weather gear and returned topside, instructing Stu to do the same.

Hutch had hooked up the autopilot, which took over the steering of the boat. Hutch showed him how to change the heading five degrees at a time to maneuver the turns in the river.

The drizzle stopped as fast as it had started and the sun reappeared. They were both quick to remove their rain suits. Hutch suggested they continue to wear their life jackets. They were not bulky or uncomfortable, so there wasn't a problem with taking the extra safety precaution.

They spent their first night anchored between two dikes at the mouth of the Cumberland River. Hutch explained that the dikes were built to control the flow of the river.

Hutch mounted a charcoal grill off the stern rail. After he had the charcoal burning, he went below and came up with two rather strong whiskey sours. Hutch said, "Here, I only fix one of these a night. Believe me, one of these is enough to get everyone in the sack early."

The evening was very pleasant. Hutch tossed two steaks on the grill and told Stu he was in charge. Hutch wanted his steak cooked rare. Hutch worked down below getting the rest of the meal dished up.

It was a quiet time. Stu thought about the current of the river and how all of this mass of water had passed in front of the prison. It was almost as if they were in a race with the water. They had passed through this water earlier and now it was passing them. The river water would be moving all night and there was no telling when they would pass the same flowing water again. They had heard that the Mississippi current was running at about three and a half miles an hour. Stu guessed that they would be running the boat somewhere between ten or twelve hours a day. So, in a day's time, they should cover about one hundred and thirty miles a day. While at the same time, the river water would travel about a hundred miles in twenty-four hours.

When Hutch reappeared, topside, Stu told Hutch about his thought of racing the river. He said that that was an interesting thought, but they would be the loser once they made it to Memphis, because the Mississippi River wasn't going to wait.

After dinner, while Stu washed the dishes, Hutch called the Paducah Marine Operator. He placed a call to Patrish. The connection was terrific and he could hear the excitement in her voice. She was so happy to hear that his first day of travel had gone so well. When Hutch had finished his call, he asked Stu if he wanted to report to Vickie that they would be in Memphis in three days.

Stu said, "What, lose our race with some muddy river water?"

Hutch understood.

Hutch was up early, the next morning. It was still dark and Hutch had the coffee going on the stove. Stu asked if he had time to take a quick shower.

"No problem, but use as little water as you can."

By the time Stu was showered and dressed, Hutch had a plate of steaming pancakes ready for him.

After breakfast, they watched to see the first glimmer of light from the east. Hutch suggested that they raise anchor and get underway, as it would be daylight soon.

Entering the Ohio River, they were surprised to see so many barges and towboats. The towboat pilots were surprised to see them, too. One by one, they flashed their large spotlights on Hutch's vessel. Hutch and Stu had entered the Ohio just a short distance below a lock and dam. There were three tows waiting their turn to lock upstream and one coming downstream, which had just cleared the lock. The downstream tow flashed his spotlight too.

Once they were in the center of the river, Hutch pushed the throttle down to attain the rpm level that he wanted for the diesel motor. This gave them a hull speed considerably faster than the tow that was following them.

They had full daylight by the time they passed Paducah and the spot where the Tennessee River joined the Ohio. As they passed Paducah, they noticed several large tows waiting to move downstream. It was a real pile-up and Hutch said it might be several days before things could clear up at the next lock.

Hutch radioed the lockmaster to see what the prospects were.

He said they should come ahead and tie up against his outer lock wall. Their smaller lock was in use at the present time, but he could most likely get them through in an hour.

As it turned out, it took two hours. It was very different than the Barkley Lock. There were no floating bollards and they only made a ten foot drop before the gates were opened and the horn sounded. They were informed that the wickets were down at the next lock and they would be able to pass without locking.

By bypassing the last Ohio River lock, Hutch pointed out that they had regained some of their travel time.

The wind was fairly brisk and had just enough coolness in it that both men continued to wear their heavy warm shirts through the noon hour.

It was after three in the afternoon when they passed Cairo, Illinois and entered the Mississippi River. As the water of the two rivers joined, the Ohio River was very muddy, and the Mississippi was fairly clear, so it was easy to see that there was more water coming from the Ohio River. The flow of the current from the combined rivers also gained a little additional speed.

It was after dark when they reached Hickman, Kentucky. Hutch had a friend who had made the same trip a few years before, so he had brought his trip log along to compare notes. There was a decent harbor at Hickman. They tied onto an old rusted out river barge for the night. The U.S. Coast Guard had a station there, but things were quiet and they didn't see anyone.

Once everything was secure, Hutch opened a bottle of red wine. They sat down below because the evening had turned quite cool. Hutch had also set out some cheese and crackers. After lighting the oven, which ran on propane, he placed their dinner in the oven and sat down to enjoy the wine with Stu.

Hutch was able to get a good marine radio connection and was reporting their progress to Patrish. After completing his call, he commented to Stu that neither of them knew anything about their shipmate.

As it turned out, they both were in the Korean War. Hutch had been a naval officer aboard a minesweeper. He had never put a foot on the Korean mainland, but had worked on the Inchon invasion. Hutch told him that the Navy had lost two minesweepers at that time. Hutch was a young officer at the time, a recent graduate from Annapolis. The ship he was on was hit by shore fire and he received an injury. Of all places to be hit, he was hit in the foot. That took him out of the war and got him a Purple Heart. After being returned to the United States, he spent a month in rehab and then returned to active duty aboard a ship in the Mediterranean. He was moved up in rank to Lieutenant JG.

Hutch said, "I don't want to say I was having a great time there, but I almost reenlisted. After spending most of my time as a commissioned officer aboard ship, I knew I wanted a different life. Kind of funny, but here I am back on a boat, and not even getting paid."

Stu went through the whole story of his life, including the twenty-five years at Eddyville. He laughed when he told about Vickie and their Eddyville experience and how her parting words were, "Fuck You." He failed to mention that he, too, had been awarded a Purple Heart and that he had also won a Silver Star. He was concerned how Hutch would handle the ex-con news. Regardless, he was glad it was out in the open. After hearing about his backgammon years with Nick, Hutch suggested that he should write a book on backgammon.

They talked all through dinner. Hutch again lit the furnace as they prepared for bed and suggested that they start an hour later in the morning than they had today.

The next day was uneventful. There weren't any locks on the Mississippi River, below Cairo. With the distance they made, they thought they might even be ahead of their race with the Cumberland water flow. They anchored again between two dikes, well out of the channel. Hutch fixed pork chops on the grill. Patrish had every meal planned, including what side dishes should be served with them. She had even suggested a white wine. From time to time, their boat would get rocked by the river tows. The downstream towboat's wake rocked them the most, but they were rocked with every passing tow.

After dinner, Hutch was looking at the river charts and pointed out that they should make it to Memphis around noon. They would need to stop there for fuel. They could even invite Vickie to come down to the marina and have lunch.

Stu said that if he had any say in the matter, he might want to think about it awhile.

In the morning, as they were raising the anchor, Hutch noticed that the generator wasn't working. He called out to Stu to reset the anchor. Hutch said, "I'm afraid we broke a fan belt, and the bad news is we haven't got a spare."

They found the engine manual and figured out what size they needed. Hutch made a radio call to any vessel that could assist them with that size belt. They were surprised to hear from the Delta Queen, a large paddle wheeler. Their engineer had located the belt size they needed.

Hutch reported their position. The Delta Queen was coming downstream and estimated that they would be there in thirty minutes. When they looked upriver, they could actually see it in the distance.

There was a light drizzle when they again pulled anchor and moved their boat out into the channel. Stu piloted the boat as Hutch held out a boat hook for one of the Delta Queen's crewmen. The paddle wheeler must have made an announcement onboard, because the decks of the Delta Queen were lined with passengers who were taking their picture. After that event, they both commented that they would like to have one of those pictures.

Stu had a good knowledge of replacing fan belts from his days as a trucker. With that job done, they were again on their way, racing the Cumberland water.

It was a little after three in the afternoon when they arrived at the fuel dock in Memphis. Hutch commented that they used to call this place Mud Island. He didn't know if it still went by that name or not. Mud Island is right down on the Memphis waterfront.

Hutch left Stu with the fueling job, saying he wanted to make some land-based calls. Stu also refilled the water tank. They had decided they would spend the night in the Mud Island Marina. Hutch had made the arrangements for a dock space before he returned, so when he returned they moved the boat to the space.

No sooner had they secured the boat, than the dock master approached, saying that Hutch had a phone call in the office.

Just as he was returning from the dock master's office, Vickie appeared. She had noticed their boat coming down the Mississippi from her office window. Hutch invited her aboard for a drink. She didn't seem to be in a real social mood. She did, however, get on the boat. She said, "I just felt it my duty to tell you about your travel companion."

Hutch spoke right up. "Before you say anything, let me say that there is nothing you could possibly say that would be news to me. But for your information, let me tell you what I know. First, Mr. Vogel is a highly decorated war veteran, holding the Silver Star and many other awards. He also served twenty-five years in prison, while always proclaiming his innocence. Now, on top of all of that, he is also the best backgammon player you will ever meet." Turning toward Vickie he said if she had anything to add to what he already knew, he was all ears.

She was embarrassed and feeling very self-conscious. She said, "I was just very concerned."

She got up and left and that was the last they ever expected to hear from her.

After Vickie had departed, they agreed they would have dinner ashore. The dock master had given Hutch the name of a great Italian restaurant. There was a tram that ran from the marina to Front Street. From there, they could take a taxi. He recommended that they not walk the streets after dark.

During dinner, Stu asked Hutch how he had managed to come up with so much additional information on him. Stu said, "I know you were telling Vickie things I hadn't told you."

Hutch said, "Actually, it was pretty easy once I was put in contact with Bruce. You have a real friend and believer in Bruce."

Chapter 10

The river was very busy the next morning. The size of the tows had increased ever since they had entered the Mississippi. Hutch pointed out the fuel barges and how they sat very low in the water. These towboats moved faster because they always pushed a smaller load of barges, for safety reasons.

Hutch & Stu kept their river charts in the boat's cockpit next to the steering station. Following their progress mile by mile, they always knew their position. They had set up a system where the person running the boat could get his partner topside, on the double, without calling. With engine noise down below, a call might not be heard. The system was simple. They would just slow the engine for a short period.

Hutch was down below preparing lunch when Stu slowed the engine. As Hutch climbed topside, he asked what the problem was.

Stu pointed out how narrow the channel was in the turn they were approaching. Stu said, "Here, look through these binoculars and tell me if you think that tow that's headed upstream is moving."

Hutch reported that the tow was pushed all the way over to the shore, and besides that, it looked like another tow further downriver had done the same thing.

They proceeded through the turn without a problem. They did notice the current was very strong throughout the turn. Once they had made their passage, they radioed the first tow to ask why they had pushed ashore.

The captain explained that the tows running downstream had the right-of-way, because they had less control. The captain said, "I have been waiting for over a day to get through the turn. It will take me close to three hours to make it through the turn, so I'm waiting for a three hour clearance from tows headed downstream."

Hutch thanked the captain for the information and switched the radio back to the call channel.

Just as he switched back to the call channel, Hutch heard someone call the same tow he had just talked to and requested they switch to channel 82. Hutch switched to 82 also, saying maybe they might pick up some information.

"Hello, Captain Bob. Is that you?"

"Yes, who have I got here?"

"This is Captain Stanley Marshall. I just heard you talking to that pleasure vessel that just passed you. I don't know why they call them pleasure vessels. They look more like kamikazes to me."

"Ten-four on that."

The reason he had called Captain Bob was because he wanted to tell him about a problem he had. He said, "We were coming out of Greenville. I had stopped there to pick up some empties. The crew chief had the men working on the running lights of the forward barges, when he noticed a cable had broken just as we were making the turn. The crew chief called the new man and told him to drop what he was doing and come help him. Well, that son-of-a-bitch threw the wiring down and proceeded to cuss the hell out of my crew chief. Later, the chief reported to me, saying he wanted the bastard put off at Memphis. I agreed. I don't know where the company finds these people. We had picked him up in New Orleans. This guy was so dirty and stunk so bad that the crew couldn't even eat with him in the galley. I passed the word that he needed to take a shower. Then the bastard walked down the companionway buck naked. In following the crew chief's request, I had him come up to the pilot house, so I could tell him that he would be put off at Memphis. I started to ask him what the problem was, but before I could even get the word "what" out of my mouth, he was cussing at me. I told him we were putting him off at Memphis and to get the hell out of the pilothouse.

"Well, he stood there shaking his fist, saying I would have to pay him for the entire trip to St. Louis. I had to put my hand in my pocket to get him to back off. I told him to get his gear because I was going to put him off before Memphis."

The other captain said, "That sure is some story. I'm glad I heard it firsthand. I want to comment to all the other river pilots that were listening. It's best that we keep this story on the river. What happens on the river needs to stay on the river."

There were six radio calls that came in with a ten-four response.

Stu asked Hutch what type of trouble the captain would be in if he had shot the bastard.

Hutch said, "My guess is that it would be excusable to shoot someone in the pilothouse if they were a threat to the safety of the vessel. My thought is that all of these river boat captains carry a gun."

Stu said, "That sure was interesting. I guess there are thousands of interesting things happening out here on the river that nobody ever hears about."

Hutch said, "If you thought that was interesting, wait until tonight." He explained that when he made a call through a marine operator, everybody and his brother could be listening. "It really isn't legal, but it can be very entertaining."

Later in the day, Hutch found a good anchorage behind a sandbar. There was another sailboat already anchored there. The skipper of the other sailboat called them on the radio and advised them to head in, closer to shore. They followed his instructions and anchored about thirty yards from the other boat.

Hutch was busy going over his checklist, checking the engine oil, fuel level and water tank. The skipper in the other sailboat motored over in his dingy. He was young, most likely in his late twenties.

Stu invited him aboard.

Les was from Milwaukee and had sold a business that he had inherited from his father. He had also inherited a couple of apartment buildings. He had purchased his sailboat and was planning on sailing for several years. He had met a girl in Chicago and she agreed to make the trip with him. He said that like all good plans, the relationship wasn't working out and he was going to dump her in New Orleans.

They offered Les a beer. The three of them sat in the cockpit of Hutch's boat, enjoying the beer and listening to Les brag about everything he had ever done. He even mentioned how he had won a backgammon tournament in Milwaukee and was hoping to pick up a little extra cash playing backgammon in the islands. Hutch glanced at Stu with a "should we or shouldn't we?" look. Stu told him they didn't have a backgammon board onboard, but if he wanted to bring his board over later, he would give him a try. He could always tell his friends he had been a Mississippi River gambler.

Les returned with his backgammon set after dinner. Stu had explained to Hutch his game plan for playing, prior to Les's arrival. "The trick is not to beat the other fellow as bad as you can. It's important to let him win, but just don't let him win the big games."

Les wanted to play for ten dollars a point.

Stu said, "Those stakes are too high."

They settled on a five dollar-a-point game. Les was very quick to turn the cube, thereby doubling the bet. Stu played him like a cat played with a mouse. They hadn't set a stopping time.

When they reached the point where Les was over eight hundred dollars in the hole, Stu suggested they quit for the night.

Les wanted to play one more game, double or nothing.

Stu said he would agree, but only if the cube could still be used. He advised Les to think about it, since he could lose another sixteen hundred dollars.

Les was quick to agree and, as they played, turned the cube on Stu. Les lost again.

Les said, "I'll come over early in the morning before we leave and pay you."

Stu just nodded, saying it would be okay.

After he left, Hutch asked Stu if he thought Les would try to skip out without paying.

Stu laughed, saying it would kind of go with the tradition of Mississippi River gamblers. "He sure as hell won't be the first." Stu didn't seem worried and said he was hitting the sack.

Hutch was up at five. Stu was still pounding the pillow. Hutch looked out to see if there was any movement on Les's boat. Then he went up on deck for a better view. Les's boat was not in sight.

Hutch woke Stu, saying, "That bastard is gone."

Stu looked at him and smiled. "Do you think he forgot?"

"Get the hell up. If we get going, we might catch the bastard. I'll bet he's already four hours ahead of us. We might catch him in three days, if we are lucky."

Stu asked what was for breakfast and wondered if he would have time for a shower.

Hutch said, "Shower? Breakfast? Shit, man. We have to get going!"

Stu calmly responded, "It's still dark. When did you start wanting to run in the dark?"

Hutch said, "Since the bastard took off without paying you. That's when."

Stu went on to say, "I don't think Les is any dummy. Les has a boat that is smaller and slower and a girl crewmember who can't even help steer. There is no way Les could have enough stamina to stay ahead of us."

"What are you trying to say?" asked Hutch.

Stu responded, "It's a trick, and in real Mississippi fashion. Actually, I'm proud of the bastard for trying it."

Hutch said, "Trying what?"

Stu pulled out their river chart and pointed out an anchorage a little over a mile upstream. "Suppose Les left out in the middle of the night and ran to this cut. Using his radar, he could see his way in the dark, and run without any lights."

Hutch laughed. "Damn, you're right. He's up there laughing at us, thinking we are busting our ass trying to catch him. Like a fool dog, chasing its tail. Go ahead, take your shower. There's no hurry."

Later, as they entered the narrow cut into the anchorage, they could see Les's boat. Hutch suggested that they pull alongside of it.

Stu said, "No, he might get scared and start shooting."

Stu suggested that they anchor right in the mouth of the cut and block him. It was apparent that they hadn't been heard.

After they anchored, they sat and watched.

Hutch said, "You know, I think the bastard is asleep. No reason to lose the entire day just because Les got up too early."

Hutch picked up his hand-held air horn and gave two long blasts.

Hutch was right. Les was asleep. He heard the two blasts and thought that a river tow was moving into the cut. Les jumped to his feet and looked out of the companionway, expecting to see some large barges. Instead, he had a double shock to his system.

Les shouted, "Goddamnit, goddamnit!"

The girl asked, "Goddamn what, Les?"

Les said, "It didn't work. The son-of-a bitch not only beat me at backgammon, he figured out where we are. Get the hell out of bed. I'm sending you over there with the money."

Millie, the girl, told him to take it himself. He was the smart-ass that lost it.

He slapped her hard across the face and yelled, "I said get up!"

Millie slowly got up and pulled a light cotton sweater over her bare chest and slipped into some faded jeans.

"Okay, where's the money?"

She started to leave the boat without wearing her shoes, but the cool weather changed her mind.

When Millie pulled alongside Hutch's boat in the dingy, Stu greeted her, calling her name. She was somewhat surprised to be receiving a friendly greeting.

Stu said, "Here, let me help you aboard."

Millie said, "Les told me to pay you and come right back."

"Well, Millie, at this point, I really don't give a damn about old Les."

He invited her aboard for a cup of coffee. She handed him the money, but he didn't bother to count it.

Stu said, "Millie, whether you know it or not, your friend, Les, is a louse. Sooner or later Les is going to take off and leave you, just like he left us this morning."

He told her their next stop on the river would be Greenville. They could take her there and put her on a plane back to Chicago. "I'll give you all the money you need to get back to your family."

She said, "Mister, I sure don't understand you, but I'll certainly take you up on that deal." She was so overjoyed that she was crying.

They untied Les's dingy and anchored it in the cut. Stu radioed Les and informed him that they were sending his mate back to her family, and better luck next time.

Before they reached Greenville, Hutch had checked, through the marine operator, on flights out of Greenville to Chicago. The best they could come up with was a connection through Memphis. They would need to get Millie to the Greenville Airport by four in the afternoon. She would arrive in Chicago aboard a Delta flight at eight thirty in the evening. Hutch had estimated they could be in Greenville by twelve noon, so four o'clock wouldn't be a problem.

They asked Millie if she had anyone who could meet her in Chicago.

She said she would call her father when she got to Chicago and he would come.

Hutch suggested that they call him now.

She explained that her father was the head buyer for a large fish wholesaler in Chicago. She didn't have the number, but the name of the business was Fresh Catch, Inc.

With the help of the marine operator, they were able to get the call through. Hutch had placed the call person to person. Her father's name was Valmar Kurshski.

A lady with a very heavy Polish accent answered the Fresh Catch phone. Hearing the call was for Valmar, she asked him to please hold. After two rings, Valmar answered. The operator reported she had a marine call for Valmar Kurshski.

"This is Kurshski. Go ahead."

Hutch handed the microphone over to Millie.

"Dad, this is Millie. Can you hear me okay."

He acknowledged and wanted to know where she was.

She said it was a long story, but for now she needed him to pick her up at O'Hare. She would be coming in on Delta flight 623, arriving in Chicago at eight thirty that evening.

Her father was very happy to hear from her and would be waiting at the gate. It was easy to tell the excitement in both of their voices.

After they docked in Greenville, Stu suggested that he take Millie to a local department store and buy a jacket and some warmer clothes for her Chicago arrival. She complained, saying she would be all right.

"No! I'm not sending you back to your father looking like a refugee."

Hutch stayed with the boat. He wanted to take on fuel and fill the water tank. It was agreed that Stu would take her shopping and deliver her to the airport in time for her plane. She thanked Hutch before they left, giving him a kiss on the cheek, saying he had saved her life.

The dock master had a taxi waiting for them. At the shopping mall, they both spotted a denim jacket with a wool liner.

Stu said, "That has to be yours."

It was a quick sale for the clerk. Next, they purchased some red leather, short boots. She said if he wouldn't mind, she would like to purchase some undergarments as well.

"No problem. You might say everything is complements of Les."

After purchasing her Delta ticket, he handed her two hundred dollars. She didn't want to take it, but he insisted.

They had lunch at the airport lunch counter and then proceed to the Delta gate. She again thanked him, saying how happy she was to be going home to her father.

Stu said he would like to ask her one question if she didn't mind.

She nodded with a questionable look, wondering what type of question he would ask.

Stu asked, "Millie, how old are you?"

She answered, "Fifteen."

When he returned to the boat, Hutch said, "You will never know what a change you have made in Millie's life."

Stu asked Hutch, "How old do you think she is?"

Hutch guessed eighteen or nineteen.

Stu said, "Would you believe fifteen?"

Hutch responded, "Oh, shit. Les must be crazy."

"Because you are a savior of young maidens," Hutch said, "I'm going to reward you with a steak dinner ashore."

The dock master made a recommendation. They were very pleased with his selection. During dinner, they talked about their day's adventures.

Stu said he couldn't do any more than bluff Les into paying. Anything else might have landed him back in Eddyville.

The steaks arrived at the table along with doggy bags. The meat was three inches thick and overhung their plates. They both agreed that they would still be eating this when they reached New Orleans.

The rest of the trip down the river was uneventful. Every day was like the day before and they never saw a sign of Les again.

Chapter 11

Three days later, as they moved in toward New Orleans, Henry pointed out that it was going to be a night arrival. The shoreline was nothing but large industrial complexes. There just wasn't a place to anchor or dock. He guessed it might be a two or three hour run in darkness.

As they motored, Hutch brought up Les's name, saying he must be pretty pissed, about now. He listed the events that had happened: beat him at backgammon, found his hiding place, and stole his girl.

Stu said, "Yeah, I guess you could say Les and I are not friends anymore."

The New Orleans river traffic was a little of everything. There were ferries moving back and forth, large seagoing vessels, and tows pushing barges. Hutch was looking for the entrance to a lock that would take them into the Industrial Canal. Hutch radioed for directions, saying they were the sailboat, *Henry's Dream*, running under power and had just cleared the two bridges. He needed help in finding the Industrial Lock.

He received an immediate response. "*Henry's Dream*, this is the *William Ruth*. Switch to channel six."

The *William Ruth* was directly behind them. The pilot of the William Ruth told them the lock was straight across the river. He said, "That red light is marking the entrance, but hold up going until that ship moving upstream has passed." The running lights on the ship were up so high, that neither Stu nor Hutch had noticed them.

They locked through into the Industrial Canal with two small towboats. The tows were pushing several small barges loaded with white rock. Hutch tried talking to one of the deck hands as they were locking, but he couldn't understand the Cajun language. The lockmaster had moved them up alongside of the tows so that they would be the first out of the lock.

Once in the canal, they found an old barge in one of the side-cuts off the canal, and tied up for the night. Hutch reported their New Orleans arrival to Patrish as Stu fixed a stew with some of the leftovers from Greenville.

The next morning they motored out of the canal into Lake Pontchartrain. They had now gone from fresh water to salt water. Their race with the Cumberland water was over. Hutch figured that they had won by more than a day.

Upon entering the Municipal Marina, their plans were to refuel and take on a few provisions. They were hoping to be able to rent a slip for a day.

The dock master said if they only stayed one night, they would be the first pleasure boat to stay only one night after making the hard trip down the Mississippi. He asked if they were in some kind of trouble, because they seemed to be in a hurry.

Hutch said, "No, we have no problems that we know of."

The dock master responded that once they signed the register, it was a matter of record and he would have to report that they were there.

Hutch spoke up, saying, "Report it, report it to who?"

They had no idea what the dock master was talking about.

At that, the dock master turned to Stu. "Your name Vogel?"

Stu was surprised and starting to feel guilty, but he didn't know why. "Yes, I'm Vogel, what's the problem?"

The dock master asked if either of them had ever heard of Tony Mandolino.

Shaking their heads they asked, "Who the hell is he?"

"I'll tell you who he is. He is one of the most powerful men in New Orleans. Tony is into everything and has a reputation for playing pretty rough. Two of Tony's men were in yesterday." They had evidently checked to see if Henry's Dream was registered. He went on to say that they were the type that wore pointed shoes. They had told him who they worked for and left a phone number for him to call when Henry's Dream arrived. The dock master told them he would have to make the call, but he would let them refuel before he called.

Hutch suggested it might be best if they left after they fueled.

Stu was just curious about what was going on. He wanted to make the call. Otherwise, he felt they might never find out.

The dock master was hoping they would leave because he didn't want to have to deal with any problems involving Mr. Mandolino. He assigned them a slip on the other side of the marina, commenting that they would be able to see anyone coming long before they made it to their boat.

After they had the boat secured in the slip, Stu suggested that Hutch go to the grocery store and take the hand-held marine radio with him. They could have both radios on the same channel and Stu could tape the mike open on his end.

As Hutch was getting off the boat, he saw two men walking toward them. They looked like a Hollywood version of gangsters. The dock was kind of a U shaped arrangement and they had not spotted *Henry's Dream*.

Stu told Hutch to hurry and go out to the end of the dock and get out of sight.

Hutch said, "Okay, but I feel like a shit leaving you here."

Stu was busy mopping the deck when the two men arrived. The smaller of the two said, "Good afternoon. Are you Mr. Vogel?"

Stu noticed that both men had a bulge inside of their jackets. No doubt about it, they were carrying. He acknowledged, "Yes, I'm Vogel. What can I do for you?"

The smaller of the two men said that their boss wanted to meet him and his friend and invite them to dinner.

"And who might your boss be?"

The smaller man responded, "Tony Mandolino."

Stu said that he didn't know Tony Mandolino and asked why he wanted to invite them to dinner.

"Mister, we know you don't know Tony, but we just work for him and when you work for Tony, you don't ask questions."

Stu started to get the feeling he wasn't on dangerous ground and asked about what time they would be picked up.

They said they would be back at six thirty.

Stu said, "That's fine, but would you boys mind leaving your hardware at home."

The little man responded that he was sorry, but the hardware went with the job.

Then Stu asked what type of job required them to carry.

The response was that they would be back at six thirty.

After Hutch reappeared, they reviewed Stu's conversation with Tony's men. They both felt that they were no longer in danger, agreeing that Tony's men would have never given them the chance to run.

With the visit from Tony's men out of the way, Stu said he would go to the grocery and help Hutch. They stopped by the dock master's office to have him call a taxi for them. As they were leaving in the taxi, they noticed a car parked outside of the marina gate. Tony's two men were in the car. Oddly enough, the car didn't follow the taxi. When they returned, the car was still in the same spot.

After finishing with washing the boat down and doing routine boat and engine chores, they cleaned and dressed for dinner.

As they waited to be picked up, Hutch suggested that he fix a small drink.

Stu said, "Why not? A drink might ease the pain of a bullet in the back of the head."

While they sat there enjoying their drinks, Stu remarked that he thought the whole thing somehow related to Les. He didn't think they ever would have mentioned Tony's name if the shit was going to hit the fan.

When the car pulled through the gate, they spotted it and started walking in that direction. The shorter of the two men got out and met them halfway on the dock. He was very pleasant. "Good evening gentlemen. Your car is ready."

Walking back to the car, Stu asked the short man his name. He said he was Earl, but everyone called him Oil. "Sammy is our driver. You might notice he doesn't talk much."

The car was a Chevy. Hutch had logged many a mile in the back seat of Chevy taxis and he could tell this wasn't the norm.

"Oil, tell me about this car. I know it's special."

Oil said he was right about that and it cost over three hundred thousand dollars to build. He went on to say that the engine was close to five hundred horsepower and that Tony had another one just like it in reserve.

Reaching the French Quarter, Sammy pulled the car around a sign that read, NO AUTOS PERMITTED BEYOND THIS POINT. There were two runners waiting that ran ahead of the car, warning tourists to clear the way. They stopped in front of a beautiful building with decorative wrought iron.

A large man dressed in a white uniform opened the car door. "Good evening, gentlemen. Welcome to Chez Orleans."

Oil led them inside and up some stairs. The stairs had been roped off. One of Tony's men removed the rope as they approached. Stu noticed that the rope handler also had a bulge in his jacket. Oil ushered them into a large private dining room, but did not enter, himself.

As they entered the room, a small gray-haired man rose from a chair. He must have been in his seventies and weighed no more than one hundred and ten pounds.

"Good evening, gentlemen. I am glad you were able to come on such short notice." He introduced himself, saying he was actually expecting them yesterday. Turning to a young, attractive lady, dressed in a long black skirt and wearing a white silk blouse with long sleeves, he said, "Mary will take your drink orders." Mary was indeed very French and spoke with an accent.

Hutch ordered a Rob Roy, but Stu thought he had best stick with beer.

After Stu had his drink in hand, he asked Tony why he had invited them as his guests.

"Gentlemen, let me explain. I'm an old man with many business interests. I have business friends all over. My friends mean more to me than anything I have. You two did a special favor for one of my good friends. Valmar wanted to fly down and thank you himself, but he knew he could trust me to thank you. He also wants me to repay you the money you spent helping his daughter."

Stu said that certainly wasn't necessary, but in the spirit of the evening he would accept it.

Then Tony reached in his pocket and pulled out the envelope with the money. He went on to explain that Valmar Kurshski had been a good friend and customer of his for at least twenty-five years. "Meeting you two is my pleasure. Valmar called me and told me about how you rescued his daughter."

Stu asked how Millie was doing.

"She's pregnant. Valmar and his wife are both Polish Catholic, so they will raise the child as their own."

As the evening wore on, Tony explained that he was mainly in the import business. He shipped fish to Chicago that was brokered through Valmar. Most of his suppliers were from Central and South America and he had to have those damned high-priced gas burners to protect his friends when they were in town. They wouldn't feel safe in a normal limo. He said that it's a hard world out there and most of them knew it.

Before they departed for the evening, Tony told them that if they ever needed a special favor, to call him. He gave Stu a private phone number, advising him not to lose it.

In the morning, a marina worker showed up, saying there was a package for them in the dock master's office. As they were ready to head out on the next leg of their trip, they motored in the boat over to his dock.

The dock master said he didn't know who they were, but it looked like they were on the good side of Tony. One of Tony's drivers from his liquor wholesale house had delivered a case of wine for them. He said, "This stuff is almost too good to drink."

Just as they were leaving, the dock master asked if they happened to know Les Reinhart. He was supposed to be on a sailboat, too.

Before Hutch could say anything, Stu answered very quickly, "No, we have never heard of him."

Once they were clear of the marina and motoring on Lake Pontchartrain, Hutch asked Stu why he denied knowing Les. He responded that their dog wasn't in that fight and they didn't want their names associated with Les.

Hutch said he was glad they had met up with Les. It really had made for an interesting visit to New Orleans.

Stu said, "Don't to be too happy until after we have tasted the wine."

Chapter 12

Sailing along the Gulf Coast was a big change from the river trip. They were able to sail for the first time and could run for up to five hours without changing course on the autopilot, with porpoise accompanying them from time to time. With the clear blue water instead of muddy river water, and no engine running, they were enjoying every minute of their day. There were absolutely no other boats in the area. Their last port was Apalachicola, before they were to make the hundred and fifty-four mile crossing.

They waited two days at Apalachicola for a good weather report. They started their crossing at two in the morning. Other than a beautiful sunrise and sunset, the trip was uneventful. Two days later, they arrived at Bradenton, their final destination. Hutch had the boat pulled out of the water and gave the boatyard a long list of maintenance and repair items.

Hutch booked their flights back into Evansville.

After arriving back in Evansville, Stu had dinner with Patrish and Hutch. Patrish was amazed at their stories. She was very interested in hearing about Les and the time in New Orleans.

Patrish asked, "Do you think you will ever hear anything about Les?"

Stu looked at Hutch and said, "Maybe."

The next morning, after calling Catherine, he was on the road to Bloomington. He was really enjoying his Volvo and wanted to call Bruce to report how great the car was.

The big surprise in Bloomington was that Fred had kicked Nel out of his condo. She was, apparently, pregnant and Fred knew he couldn't have children. Catherine was pretty distressed over it. She knew Fred through many of his romances, but Nel was the first one she had actually liked.

Stu took it upon himself to go visit Fred. Fred hadn't seen his car and was surprised to see him.

It was clear that Fred had been drinking and his place was a mess. After inviting him in, Fred offered Stu a drink.

"No, I just want to visit with you and I would appreciate it if you didn't have one."

At that remark, Fred sat up and gave Stu a very sober look.

Stu had something he wanted to say, but first he wanted Fred to understand that he wasn't the father of Nel's child.

"Hell, I know that. Shit, you were still in prison when she got knocked up. She's been carrying the little bastard for three months."

Well, Fred had caught Stu off guard when he mentioned his being in prison. It had to come out sooner or later, but it still surprised him.

"I'm glad that is not an issue because I want to suggest something to you. I admit that I really don't know Nel, but I do feel like I know you. Let's talk about Nel. It's my guess that she hasn't got much more than a fat belly and is not in any position to raise a child. It might be a hard nut for you to swallow, the thought of raising another man's child, but there have to be some plusses. Having a young child to enjoy could add meaning to your life. Nel, I am sure, would be the most grateful wife ever if you helped her through her pregnancy. As dumb as it may sound, I'm saying I think you should take her back and be the child's father."

Fred sat there, without saying a word. He just looked at Stu. His facial expression was almost blank. Finally, he said, "Don't go, but I think I need a drink."

After pouring his drink, he walked over to get some ice. He really wasn't happy with Nel being gone and maybe Stu's thoughts weren't all that bad. Actually he wanted to talk to her, but maybe when he hadn't been drinking.

Later, when visiting with Catherine, Stu relayed his experiences from his recent trip. He had mixed feelings about Les and was a little concerned. Somehow he needed to know, but was afraid to pursue it. He would just have to give it time.

They were interrupted by Fred barging in. "Catherine! This S-O-B thinks I should take Nel back and help raise her little bastard. So you better lay in a supply of diapers." With that remark, he turned and walked out just as abruptly as he had entered.

Catherine said, "Well Stu, maybe you should look for a position in sales. I don't know how you did it, but you just made a real person out of Fred."

Stu asked if she had any ideas about who the father was.

She replied, "Certainly. He worked at the marina and took off the minute Nel said she was pregnant. I had noticed him coming and going, but I was afraid to say anything to Fred. You just never know. Something really bad could have happened and then I would feel guilty."

Later, Catherine called Fred and invited him over for dinner. Fred had had time for a nap and shower. Re-entering Catherine's condo, Fred announced that he had invited Nel to come back, and that his lawyer had just lost out on a big fee.

Stu added, "I think this calls for a very special celebration."

Stu went out to his car and came back with two bottles of Tony's wine. He explained that a friend had given him a case in New Orleans.

Fred reached out and took one of the bottles. "This must be some kind of a friend. This stuff is over a hundred dollars a bottle. You sure you didn't win it in a backgammon game?"

Stu knew it was exceptional because he and Hutch had shared a couple of bottles on their trip. During dinner, he was relating some of the experiences he had had on his trip with Hutch, when Catherine's phone rang.

Catherine got up to answer the phone, saying the damned telemarketers all called during dinner. As it turned out, it was Susan, trying to find him.

She explained that she was calling from a pay phone because she couldn't be too sure her phone wasn't being tapped. She suggested that he meet her the next day for lunch at the country tavern where he had taken the girls for lunch. He agreed, but even with a wild imagination, he still had no idea what was going on. His only thought was it might have something to do with Les. Susan, calling from a pay phone, saying her phone might be tapped? What the hell was going on?

Back on the road the next morning, enjoying driving his Volvo, his thoughts turned to Bruce. He needed to thank him again and tell him how much he was enjoying the car.

Susan was waiting for him when he arrived at the tavern. She had taken a corner table in the family room, which was next to the barroom. After going through the brother and sister hugs and kisses, he asked what was going on.

She explained that she had had a visit from Bruce. "Bruce said something major is going on and he needs to visit with you as soon as possible," she relayed.

Stu said, "Well, I guess that would be today."

Bruce had given her a phone number for Stu to call when he arrived in Louisville. His instructions were like something out of a spy novel. Bruce wanted Stu to tell the person answering the phone that the fish were biting and then to proceed to the upstairs bar at the Galt House Hotel and just wait for him, even if it took all day.

After a short visit and lunch with Susan, he was back on the road again. He knew Bruce wasn't playing games and that it had to be something major. He certainly was taking every precaution.

After parking his car in the Galt House parking garage, Stu phoned the number that Bruce had given to Susan.

Thirty minutes later, he and Bruce were having a beer in the barroom of the hotel.

Stu asked, "Okay, why all of this spy stuff? What's going on?"

Bruce asked Stu, "Do you know who Senator John Wathen is?"

Stu said, "After twenty-five years in jail, I'm doing well to be able to tell you who the President is. No, I don't know the Senator."

Bruce said, "Well he remembers you and wants you put back into Eddyville for a parole violation."

"Parole violation? What did I do?"

Bruce explained that Stu hadn't made a violation, to his knowledge, but the Senator's office had left it up to him to get Stu back into prison.

Stu asked, "Why?"

Bruce said, "It looks like you have forgotten John Wathen, from your past. Senator Wathen was the prosecutor responsible for your conviction. You were the first major step in his political career." Bruce explained that they both had to be very careful. Wathen was an extremely powerful man and had the resources to get anything done. He said he was pretty certain as to why Wathen was after him. Bruce said, "I have read through all of the old newspaper accounts of this trial. There is one thing that really stood out. Why weren't you tried in Federal Court? I have a friend who is a retired Federal prosecutor and he remembers the case. He said, 'Maybe Wathen convicted an innocent man and he knows it. It is clear that Wathen needs him back in Eddy. If the truth ever came out, it would be the end of Wathen's career.'"

Bruce suggested, "Stu, we need to hide your car and then get you out of town. I have a friend who has a spare garage that you could use.

After they succeeded in ditching the Volvo, Bruce said he wanted Stu to meet his friend, the retired federal prosecutor. Bruce said, "He's living in a small apartment in the downtown area. His wife died a few years ago and he just enjoys spending his time in and around the court buildings."

As Bruce introduced Stu to his friend, Joe, he explained the pressure he was getting from the Senator's office.

Joe advised them that they couldn't be too careful. "Bruce you could end up floating down the river and you, Stu, could be held responsible. Wathen didn't get where he is today by accident. He climbed over many a good man to get there. I wouldn't trust the snake. Stu, you need to disappear, and Bruce, I don't want you to have any contact with Stu. It's very important that Wathen thinks you're playing on his team."

Joe went on to explain that they would need help and a plan to take Wathen down. Joe had friends in the FBI he could trust. Looking at Stu, he said that he needed to disappear. Joe said he could work on the case without calling any attention to himself. He handed Stu a business card, saying he should call him from time to time. Joe said, "Just say you're my cousin, Willy. We might be working around phone taps, so we need to take every precaution."

Joe suggested that Bruce ask Wathen's contact to get him a pistol that could not be traced, saying it would be his plan to arrest Stu with the gun in his possession. Joe was pretty sure where the gun would come from and he wanted to make sure the gun could be traced. Joe had no idea as to how long it would take for his plan to work. Joe said, "I'm really going to need help from the FBI."

Later in the day, Stu was on a Greyhound Bus headed for Cincinnati. He was running, but to where? Once in Cincinnati, he took a taxi back across the Ohio River to a motel overlooking the city.

The next morning, he was planning to ask where he could find a cheap used car. He actually found a used car lot three blocks from the motel, while out taking an early morning walk. He returned to the lot after nine in the morning and was able to purchase an old Ford for five hundred dollars. They gave him a cardboard temporary license that was good for twenty days. The fuel light was on when he drove off the lot. The car barely made it to a gas station.

Stu had no thoughts about where to head next, but with winter on its way, the South seemed sensible. The interstate highway, southeast out of Kentucky took him into a mountainous area. His old clunker of a car was being put to a real test. He made the decision to abandon traveling on the interstate highway and travel on the state and county roads. It was nearing the noon hour when his right rear tire blew out. He wasn't so sure that there was a spare tire in the trunk, or even the tools to change it.

His luck suddenly improved. He was in the process of changing the tire, when a North Carolina highway patrol car pulled up behind where he had pulled off the road. Just as the officer approached, the lights in the patrol car started flashing. The patrol officer just had time to tell Stu that there was a service station two miles ahead.

As it turned out, Jeff's Texaco was open. The area didn't look very prosperous, but Jeff's station was very well-kept. The gas station wasn't paved, but was covered with white rock. Apparently, Jeff's Texaco was a one-man operation and Jeff was the man.

Stu pulled his car up to the gas pumps and was in the process of filling his tank, when Jeff came out of the station. Stu explained that he had a flat tire in the trunk and wanted to know if Jeff could fix it.

Jeff said he should drive his car over to the garage door when he was finished with the gas pump.

Stu had guessed that Jeff was somewhere in his early seventies.

While Jeff worked on fixing the flat, he complained to Stu that he wasn't able to hire help. Jeff said, "All of the young bucks skip out of these hills the first chance they get. It's a great place to live, with good fishing and hunting. Lived here all my life and wouldn't trade it for anyplace. Try to explain that to these young men with hard-ons for city girls." He didn't want to close his station because everyone in the area depended upon him. They had supported him for years and now he was paying them back by staying in business.

Just as Jeff was finishing with the flat tire, a car pulled up to the gas pump.

Stu told Jeff to go ahead and take care of his customer.

Jeff went into the station and was waiting to get paid. Stu was watching as the customer opened the trunk of his car and took a pistol out. He then proceeded to snap the magazine clip into the pistol. The customer, a young man of about twenty, proceeded to walk into Jeff's station. He hadn't noticed Stu watching him.

Once he was in the station, Stu hurried out and took the keys out of the young man's car, realizing there was going to be a holdup. He then hurried through the same station door. Stu surprised the young man by yelling at him, "What the hell do you think you're doing?"

The young man pointed the gun at Stu and said, "If you weren't such a dumb mother-fucker, you might see that this is a stickup and you just might get a bullet hole in your dumb ass."

Stu said, "Ten years for armed robbery. They will be fighting over you to see whose bride you're going to be in the state prison. After your first week, you will never hear yourself fart again. Now, get the hell out of here and throw that pee shooter of a gun away before you shoot yourself in the foot."

Jeff was surprised when the young man turned and ran out the door. He told Stu he had never seen anything like the way Stu talked, with a gun pointed at him.

Stu said, "Just wait. It isn't over yet!"

Sure enough the young robber reappeared and pointed his gun at Stu, saying, "Okay, smart ass, give me my car keys."

Stu told him that he forgot to pay for the gas and that he needed to pay first.

"I haven't got any fucking money. Give me my fucking keys."

Stu told him that he would have to work for Jeff to pay his gas bill. "If you do a good job, Jeff might even give you a full-time job. Now take the clip out of that pistol and hand it to me."

Jeff was surprised when the young man did as Stu told him.

Stu proceeded to take all of the bullets out of the clip and then smashed it with a tire iron. "Now hand over the pee shooter."

Stu opened the firing chamber and saw there wasn't a bullet in the chamber. Stu's bravery was actually based on his belief that the robber didn't know enough to load his pistol. He then took the barrel loose from the pistol. Stu knew guns, even though it had been over twenty-five years since he had handled one. He threw the pistol in the trash and stuck the barrel in his pocket. Handing the keys back to the "would-be" holdup man, he told him to park his car next to the building, so paying customers could get to the gas pump.

While the kid was parking the car, Stu paid Jeff for his gas and the tire repair. "I wish you luck with that young man. He might see the advantage of working for a living."

Two days later he was in Beaufort, South Carolina. Stu had it in his thoughts that he could purchase an inexpensive boat and live on it. He certainly wasn't short of cash and living on a small boat could work perfectly. He was checking the boats for sale at the Beaufort Marina, when he noticed an old hotel across the street from the marina. He asked the dock master if that would be a good place to have lunch.

His reply was that it was the best place in the entire county. The place wasn't busy, partially because he was a little ahead of the lunch hour crowd. The hostess seated him and handed him the menu. He had barely opened it when she returned to the table.

The hostess said, "We have one of our most distinguished customers just coming in, and he always likes to be seated with someone."

Stu nodded that it would be okay. She returned with someone that looked to be in his seventies and introduced him as General Tom Lavery.

Stu jumped to his feet, saying it was indeed an honor and said that he had lunched with the General years ago.

General Lavery said, "Now, young man, I can't say that I recall. Where might that have been?"

Stu replied, "Chosin." Stu went on to tell the General that he had also pinned the Silver Star on his chest a few months later.

The General held out his hand, saying, "I, too, am honored." He proceeded to question Stu as to why he was in Beaufort.

Stu said, "I'm boat shopping."

After lunch, the General invited him to his home. "We need to swap war stories."

With nothing better to do, Stu took him up on the invitation. Before the afternoon was over, Stu had told the General the entire story of his life and about how Senator Wathen was trying to get rid of him.

After hearing Stu's stories, the General invited him to be his house guest for a few days. He also had a retired Marine Sergeant Major living with him. The Sergeant Major had looked after the General and his wife for years, and then after she died, he took over the running of the entire household.

Later in the day, the Sergeant Major returned. General Lavery introduced him as Sergeant Major, with no other name following.

During dinner Tom explained to Sergeant Major about what was going on with Senator Wathen.

Sergeant Major said, "We need to get Kenny moving on this quick."

Tom told Stu that Kenny is Kenny Dillman, the director of the FBI. "Kenny was on my staff in Korea. He was Major Dillman then."

Turning to the Sergeant Major, General Lavery commented, "I actually put a call in to him earlier. We should be hearing from him shortly."

Later, when the call came, Dillman was surprised to hear that Tom had Vogel as a house guest. He commented that they were getting some serious smoke out of Louisville from an ex-federal prosecutor, named Joe Ward. Dillman said, "This is starting to look like another Watergate. Let me send a jet down for you two in the morning and we can have a meeting with the Attorney General. Wathen is a big man up here and we have to be careful where we are going on this thing. I'll have Joe Ward flown in too. I think it best if we use the WFO for this. There are just too many people paying attention to the comings and goings here."

Tom asked, "What is the WFO?"

Dillman answered, "Washington Field Office. I'll have a jet pick you up at Paris Island. Bring the Sergeant Major, too. I would sure like to see him. Knowing him, he might even offer some helpful input. I always felt he should have been the General and you the Sergeant Major."

What a change. All of a sudden, Stu started feeling like he wasn't a fugitive. He had no idea how this was going to pan out, but it was great having someone like Tom Lavery on his side.

Chapter 13

They had an early breakfast the next morning, with Sergeant Major doing the cooking and Tom cleaning the kitchen when they were through.

Stu decided to dress casually because he really didn't have much of a choice. Both Tom and the Sergeant Major did the same. Stu had some worries, but he was very excited and did feel safe with General Lavery at his side.

As they entered the security gate at Paris Island, the Marine guards really snapped to attention, when they recognized the General's car. The jet was already waiting when they arrived at the airfield.

They were in the air in short order. There was a young FBI agent aboard who had flown down from Washington with the plane. Once they were in the air, he offered them coffee and donuts. He barely had the coffee served, when the captain announced that they would be landing shortly. It was a cloudy fall day and Stu really couldn't see much as they landed.

After the plane taxied to a stop, the agent escorted them to a black suburban. The agent said that they had another plane coming in from Louisville and it was on its final approach now.

Stu looked at Tom, saying he guessed that would be Joe Ward.

The agent nodded, hearing Stu's comment. Ten minutes later they were all in the suburban and crossing over the Potomac River into Washington.

Joe Ward appeared friendly, but also very serious. There was very little conversation during the ride. Ward did comment on the plane ride, but that was it.

They all entered the FBI office without attracting any attention. Kenny Dillman greeted them as they were led into a wood-paneled conference room. The room had a long table with twenty red leather chairs. There was a small coffee bar to one side.

After the introductions were made all around and they were seated, they were offered coffee, tea, or juice by the agent who had flown in with them. There was already a plastic bottle of water at every seat, plus a note pad of paper and a pen.

Kenny called the meeting to order and announced that it was being recorded. He said, "I feel that Joe Ward is up to date on this case, and I would like to start with him giving us a total breakdown on what he knows and thinks is going on." Turning toward Joe, Kenny said, "Let's hear it."

Joe pushed his chair back and stood up, saying, "If you don't mind, I'll stand." He went on to say that they needed to understand how this developed from the start. "The crime that took place in Louisville, by all rights, should have been in Federal Court. The reason it wasn't, was because I was the leading Federal Prosecutor in Kentucky. When Mr. Vogel was first arrested, I sat with FBI agent William Green when he interviewed Mr. Vogel. The reason Vogel was brought in was because he was identified by Margaret Dunn as a possible suspect. Miss Dunn was one of the tellers on duty during the holdup. During the interview, Mr. Vogel told us that he was an over-the-road driver for a moving company. The morning of the robbery, he was actually driving a truck to Cincinnati. One hour before the robbery, he had stopped at a Kentucky State Highway weigh station. With this proof, I was no longer interested in him as a suspect. During the trial, Wathen had a truck driver appear as an expert witness. This driver testified that he was able to drive his truck from the mile marker of the weigh station, park his truck, and drive a car to the bank. Afterward, he departed Louisville by crossing the Ohio River into Indiana, and driving on to Cincinnati, without passing another weigh station. Now, what the expert witness said was correct, except that he was driving west when he passed the weigh station. Had he been driving east, he would have actually had to drive another fourteen miles before he could get off the highway and turn his truck back toward Louisville. So, add another twenty-eight miles to the time and there is no way it could have been Mr. Vogel. Mr. Vogel's court-appointed attorney, Sammy Johnson, wasn't ever interested in anything other than Kentucky whiskey. Everything flew by him like a bunch of geese headed south for the winter."

Stopping to take a drink of water, while still standing, he said, "Like Paul Harvey, I want to tell the rest of the story.

"Senator Wathen used his conviction of Mister Vogel as the stepping stone into being Governor. 'Tough on crime, with criminals going to jail' was the main point of his platform. He served two terms as Governor before moving on to the U. S. Senate. Now, in his path to glory, there was always one person riding on his coattails: Margaret Dunn. Shortly after the trial, she was given a job in his office. She has followed him through his political career and no one ever saw the connection. It was thought for years, that she was just his mistress. I have no way of knowing if that is true or not." Looking toward Kenny, he commented that he was sure the FBI never snooped on a U.S. Senator.

Ward went on, saying, "Now, the next step of the puzzle happened five years later, when John Wathen was sitting in the Governor's seat. A man named Shirley Austin, after being convicted of a capital crime in Texas, confessed to several other crimes he had committed. The bank robbery and killing in Louisville was on that list. Somehow it escaped the Kentucky news media. The recent interest in Mr. Vogel, and my asking questions in the Louisville FBI office, uncovered this. It was also a matter of record that Governor Wathen was informed at that time. Having centered his entire career around Vogel's conviction, it certainly would be harmful if it came out that he had convicted an innocent man, a veteran of the Korean War."

Stopping to take another drink of water, he said he was just about through. Ward continued, "The reason we are here today is because Senator Wathen wants this man back in prison. Wathen's office, by way of Margaret Dunn, told Stu's parole officer, Bruce Roach, to get him back in prison. His reason, I think, explains itself."

After Joe sat down, Kenny spoke up, asking if anyone wanted to make a comment on what they just heard.

The Attorney General stood up, saying, "I have to make a phone call so you can take a break. I'll be back shortly."

Tom Lavery turned to Sergeant Major. "Okay, tell us who you think he's calling."

Sergeant Major answered, "There isn't any doubt in my mind. He's calling the President. This thing is far too political."

Kenny spoke up. "Now you know, Tom, why I wanted you to bring Sergeant Major. He has always had this knack of seeing the next move."

When the Attorney General returned, he announced that he wanted to take everyone that had flown in that morning to lunch. "Kenny, I need to have a little private time with these gentlemen before we proceed."

Kenny nodded his approval, asking if he wanted one of his men to take them to the White House.

The Attorney General laughed, saying, "I can see why you are so good at this job."

Kenny looked at Sergeant Major and winked. Before they left, the Attorney General told Kenny that he wanted the tapes of this morning's meeting. "I don't want to hear about any copies either."

In no time, they were back in the black suburban and driving though the gates of the White House. Stu could tell that everyone seemed a little tense, with the exception of Sergeant Major.

Entering the White House, they were taken directly to the Oval Office. Only the President and Vice President were in the office. As the Attorney General entered the office, he held his finger to his lips and then pointed to the recording microphones, while making a twisting sign with his fingers.

The President reached under his desk and flipped a switch. "Okay, they're off."

Just as they were completing the introductions, the President received a call. "I thought I said we're not to be interrupted."

The President was told that there was an extremely urgent call for the Attorney General, from Kenny Dillman.

The President looked at the Attorney General, saying, "I hope you don't make a habit out of taking your calls in my office."

Once Kenny had the Attorney General on the phone, he asked him to have the President put the call on his speaker so they could all hear.

Kenny reported, "There has been a major development in this case. Bruce Roach was shot three times this morning while we were having our meeting at the WFO. He is in critical condition, but there is a good chance he will survive. The gunman wore a ski mask and drove a Volvo, registered to Mr. Vogel. The Volvo has been found, along with a recently fired gun and the ski mask. The Kentucky State police have road blocks all over the state. Senator Wathen is in Louisville and will be making a statement, shortly. He is in town for a major fundraiser that is being held at Freedom Hall tonight. Hold on. I just got the word that ABC news is starting an interview with him on national TV."

The President wasted no time in telling the VP to turn on the TV to the ABC channel. When the picture came on, the set was on the NBC channel. They were covering the same interview.

The Senator was talking. "Twenty-five years ago, I was the local prosecutor, responsible for putting Stewart Vogel in jail for life. Our current Governor, with his 'soft-on-crime' approach, allowed Vogel to be paroled. Now, we have strong proof that he shot Bruce Roach, his parole officer, three times this morning. Well, Mr. Vogel, if you are by any chance watching this interview, I want you to know that Kentucky's 'hard-on-crime' Senator is out to get you."

Next, the news program showed pictures of Stu's Volvo and the house where Bruce Roach was shot.

The Attorney General turned to the General and his group and said, "It looks like Senator Wathen has just changed our game plan. We were planning to stall this situation for two months. You have to understand that Wathen's Senate seat is vital to our party. He is a big favorite in all of the polls. The current Kentucky Governor, who is not a member of our party, is up for reelection. He is way behind in the polls. Now, on top of everything else, the damnable election is in three days. We had hopes of seeing him elected and then taking him out when a new Governor could appoint his replacement. I guess that plan could still work, but with Mr. Roach being shot this morning, things have to change. We just cannot sit here with our heads in the sand for two months. There has to be an answer, but I'm not even close to an idea. The main thing is, whatever plan we can come up with, it has to stay in this room."

Both the President and the VP were quick to agree. The President asked Tom if he had any suggestions.

Tom responded, "Mr. President, this is a different battle than what I have been trained for. However, whenever I was in a tough spot, I always turned to one man. If you don't mind, I'm going to ask that man what he would do."

The President said, "General, I appreciate your offer to help, but none of this can leave this room."

Tom said, "It doesn't have to. That one man is in this room."

Tom then turned to Sergeant Major and said, "Okay you have all of five minutes to think about it. Let's hear it."

Sergeant Major smiled at the General, saying, "You old son of a bitch, I just knew you were going to do this. Sure, I have a plan and I think it just might work."

The President was excited and said, "Let's hear it."

Turning to the President, Sergeant Major, said, "Sir, I never dreamed I would be part of a meeting in this office, but now that I'm here I would sure like to add to my dreams by sitting in your chair."

The President stood and stepped aside.

Sitting behind the President's desk in the Oval Office, Sergeant Major began with his plan. "First, there will be no delay or cover-up. Second, Wathen's office will be informed that the VP will attend his rally tonight in Louisville and would like to speak, too. I want all of the national networks to carry both Wathen's and the VP's speeches. Wathen needs to speak first. Let him get into his hard-on-crime story and the Stewart Vogel connection. At that point, I want two FBI agents to step forward and arrest him. The Attorney General can list the charges. Then the VP needs to take over. As he steps up to the podium, holding up his right hand to quiet the crowd, he should say, 'This morning, we received information that connects Senator Wathen to several crimes. The President has instructed me to be here to talk to all of the voters in Kentucky. Three days from now, you will be voting for both a Senator and a Governor. Our party's candidate will be behind bars. The President has asked me to ask the voters of Kentucky to vote for Wathen for Senator. In turn, he promises you that Wathen will never see the inside of the Capitol Building. Elect Jimmy Curtis as Governor and the Governor will promise you that retired basketball coach Warren, from the University of Kentucky, will represent you for the next six years as Senator.'"

Sergeant Major stood and gave the President back his seat.

As the President was regaining his chair, he asked for comments.

Both the VP and the Attorney General said the plan was brilliant. The President agreed. The Attorney General said he needed to get all of the criminal charges to Kenny Dillman. He wanted some of his agents from here to make the arrest. They could fly out with the VP as Secret Service.

Turning to the VP, the President said, "Paul, you had best get your ass in gear and have a nice flight. I'll be watching, while enjoying some thirty year old scotch." The President then invited everyone that had flown in that day to join him for lunch.

During lunch, the President praised Sergeant Major, saying that after this was over, he would receive a Presidential Citation. The President said, "I guess you are the first black person to ever sit behind The White House desk, but most likely not the last." The President was very impressed by Sergeant Major's fast availability to come up with a workable plan. The President also wanted Sergeant Major to be available from time to time as a special consultant.

After lunch, they were driven back to Dillman's field office. Dillman informed them that Margaret Dunn was also being arrested and that they expected to scare the hell out of her. Dillman said, "We'll be making her arrest prior to the rally. She will be picked up leaving her hotel. Our plan is to have a TV blasting away in the outer office. The FBI will be walking through that office just as Wathen is starting his speech. Once she enters the next room, she will not be able to know what is taking place at Freedom Hall. I'm going to tell her that Wathen is just too big in Washington and we will agree to back off if she will help us put him behind bars. By the time we get Wathen in, she will already have spilled the beans."

Dillman thanked them for flying in. "I did hear the plan from the Attorney General. Tom, I have a question. Was this all Sergeant Major's idea?"

Tom responded, "Who else?"

Kenny told Stu that the Attorney General's Office was preparing a news release that would be handed to all media after Wathen's arrest.

Kenny asked Joe if he was still a member of the Kentucky Bar?

Joe said, "Yes, I'm really not active and I haven't even got an office. However, I do manage to take one or two pro bono cases every year."

Kenny said, "Well, I was just thinking, after the shit hits the fan tonight, every ambulance chaser in Kentucky will be trying to represent Stu, here. Why don't you agree to represent him? You know the ropes and you need to freeze Wathen's assets as soon as possible."

Stu agreed and asked Joe to represent him.

Tom told Kenny that they needed to get back home because there was a program on TV tonight that he didn't want to miss.

Kenny told Joe that they would be sending him home on the VP's plane.

Just as they were leaving Kenny's office, an agent met him at his office door.

The agent said, "Mr. Dillman, one of our agents in Louisville needs to talk to you. He said it's important."

Kenny signaled the group with his finger to turn around and return to his office, then told the agent to put the call through to his office. Picking up the phone after it rang, Kenny said, "Dillman here."

After Dillman had listened, he responded, "I'm not surprised. Wathen needed to limit the players and he wanted someone he could trust. Let's stick with the arrest plan. I wouldn't want to tip Wathen off."

After he had replaced the phone, he informed the group that the local police had found several blond hairs inside of the ski mask. The locals had not a clue as to whom the hairs belonged, and they were not releasing any information at this time.

Flying back on the plane, Tom joked with Sergeant Major, "Taking the President of the United States' chair away from him needs to be in the history books someday."

Stu asked the agent if he could use the phone to make a few calls.

The agent explained that it was a safe phone and the number could not be traced back. "You're more than welcome to use it."

Stu called his friend, Bob Henderson, first. Bob raised a little hell about him not keeping in touch.

Stu said, "I'm kind of up in the air right now. We can visit later. I just called to tell you to watch Senator Wathen's speech tonight. I'll get back to you tomorrow."

Next, he phoned the beer distributorship in Jasper, where Al worked. Al answered the phone.

"Al, this is Stu. I'm short of time, but..."

Before Stu could say another word, Al said, "The police came by our home, looking for you. Please stay away from Susan and turn yourself in."

With that remark, Stu had second thoughts on mentioning anything about Wathen.

Next, he called Catherine at the bank, giving her the same short message.

Just as Stu had finished with the phone, a call came in. The agent flying with them handed the phone to Tom. "General, it's for you."

It was Kenny, saying he was in the plane with the VP and Joe. He had been thinking about the hair in the ski mask. The Louisville police had no idea whose hair was on the ski mask. Kenny wanted to be there when Margaret Dunn was taken into custody.

Kenny said, "I think we can get a statement out of her that will help wrap up the whole case. She has no idea as to who I am, so I will be just another local. It's my plan to tell her we found her through the Senator. I'm going to tell her that the Senator told us he was very suspicious of her and feels she lied to him from the very start. I'll have her thinking she is going into a black hole and if she has anything to say, she had best speak up fast as the Feds are already on their way to pick her up. I'm going to tell her if she is ever going to make a statement, this might be her only chance. I will be making a video recording and I plan to say that we'll keep it away from the Feds. If she goes into the black hole, she will never see the inside of a court room. The most we can charge her with is attempted murder. I will tell her she could be out of jail in seven years. Then, she's got to give us something to help us keep her here."

Tom said, "Kenny, you sound like a man with a plan."

Once they had landed and were back in the General's home, Tom suggested that they have a drink before dinner. It had been a day like no other and they all needed to just relax. Sergeant Major said he would fix some steaks on the grill.

Tom spoke up and said, "Not until after you have joined us for a scotch."

Sergeant Major said, "There's a good football game on TV tonight. We might want to watch that instead of the Senator's speech."

The phone rang and Sergeant Major handed it to Tom. "It's Kenny again."

Kenny said, "Tom, I have some updates for you. First, the parole officer that was shot this morning is going to make it. He took two shots in the upper chest and a flesh wound to his right arm. Second, Paul has just talked to Coach Warren, and he will agree, but only if he can serve as an independent. He said if he was going to serve the people of Kentucky, he would want to serve all of the people. Paul is going to tie the coach's comments into his speech tonight. Thanks to Sergeant Major, this will be the greatest speech he will ever make. There has always been some question as to who would be the next President. Tonight, the Vice-President feels he will be making a major step in that direction."

Stu said, "General, I have been sitting here thinking. Tomorrow, why not take that piece-of-junk car that I purchased to Louisville and pick up my Volvo? I have some friends that I would like for you to meet, and we can call on Bruce in the hospital, too."

The General said, "I don't know if I can stand any more excitement, but so far it's been fun. I never thought I would see Sergeant Major, here, sitting in the Commander in Chief's chair. We have been together forever and he has pulled a lot of things, but I have to admit, he hit a new high today."

The phone rang and Sergeant Major answered it, "Yes."

Then, a long silence while Sergeant Major was listening.

"Yes sir, Mister President, but I have promised to drive the General and Mr. Walker to Louisville tomorrow. If you wouldn't mind having the jet drop them off in Louisville, it would get me out of a pinch... Yes Sir, I will pack an overnight bag and we will meet the jet at 0830."

The General looked at the Sergeant Major and said, "Don't tell me you just conned the President into flying the two of us to Louisville."

Sergeant Major just nodded with a smile. Sergeant Major said, "The President has a couple of situations that have been bothering him and he would like for someone outside of his staff to take a fresh look. The President said he would be very interested in hearing any suggestion I might make."

Sergeant Major said that he would pack the General's bag for his trip and wondered how many days they would be gone.

Stu suggested that they pack for at least a week.

As the three of them were finishing dinner, the phone rang again. It was Kenny Dillman.

Sergeant Major said he would put the phone on speaker so everyone could hear.

Dillman said, "Margaret is in jail. We read her her rights, and then told her that Wathen had squealed. We explained that we were short on time because we were going to have to turn her over to the Feds. We told her that we have been told not to enter her name into any of our records. If she wants to make a statement, we will record it. I told her about the 'black hole' and she fell for it. After I explained that Bruce was still alive and was expected to recover, she loosened up. She talked for over an hour, nonstop. After she finished, I promised her that we would do all we could to help. With her help, she could be out in seven or eight years. Wathen, on the other hand, will be looking at life. She was still worried about the black hole. I told her we would hide her from the Feds until we could get her story out."

Kenny needed to get to Wathen's rally. Kenny said, "You can watch the rest on TV."

They were still eating dinner when Wathen started his speech on national TV. He began, just as predicted. He mentioned a parole officer being shot by someone he had convicted twenty-five years ago of murder. "This man, Stewart Vogel, is now being sought by the police. His car was seen at the scene of the crime and was later found with a revolver, which had been recently fired...Wait a minute...What's going on here?"

Kenny stepped forward, saying, "Senator, you are under arrest."

Just as quickly, Paul stepped behind the podium that Wathen was removed from. His speech was, indeed, the best he had ever made. He explained that Stewart Vogel was actually in Washington this morning, meeting with our Attorney General at the time the parole office was shot. "Stewart Vogel is an ex-Marine who served in combat, in Korea. He was awarded the Silver Star, which is two steps down from the Medal of Honor. This man, this war hero, was fraudulently convicted by Senator Wathen. And today, Wathen tried framing him again by having the parole officer shot and planting a smoking gun in his car."

The network news people were going wild. This had to be one of the most spectacular events they had ever covered. They hadn't even come up with a picture of this man, Steward Vogel. No one knew of his whereabouts. However, they did manage to come up with a picture of his Volvo. One news lady did manage to get the warden at Eddyville on the phone. He, like everyone else, was stunned.

The warden said, "Yes, I knew Vogel. No, he was never any trouble."

That was all she was able to get out of the warden.

Stu called Susan to make sure she had seen the show.

"How could I miss it? It was on every major news channel. I'm surprised you were able to get through. Our phone has been ringing off the hook. My lawyer, Goehausen, even called, saying he wanted to represent you."

Stu reported that he would be in Jasper soon.

Chapter 14

In the morning, once they were in the air, Tom called Kenny. He told Kenny that they would be landing in Louisville in about one hour. He requested that the local FBI get Stu's car out to the airport.

Sergeant Major spoke up. "Tell them to fill the gas tank."

Kenny laughed, "Will that man ever quit?"

Lavery said, "You haven't heard the best of it. He's flying on to Washington for a couple of days to be with number one."

The Volvo was waiting when they landed. Kenny was there, also. He suggested that they have one of his agents take the Volvo downtown. He could escort them to the hospital to see Bruce. He also mentioned that the Attorney General was flying in, too.

Kenny said, "The arraignment for Wathen is to be at eleven this morning. There could be a problem because the Federal Judge is a Wathen appointment. Margaret told us that Wathen has two million in a Swiss account. If he would be allowed to make bail, he would be a high risk to flee the country. That is why the Attorney General is coming in. The courtroom is going to be packed, but I can slip you in as members of the press. We just don't want you down front. Joe will be there, too."

Bruce was in better shape than they expected. He had several tubes attached, but seemed to be in good spirits. He was glad to see Stu and had seen the TV news, so he was pretty much up to date.

Wathen was confident that he would be able to make bail in Judge Reese's court.

Judge Reese had received his appointment with Wathen's backing and never would have been appointed, otherwise. It was payback time and Wathen felt sure Reese would come through for him. When he spotted the Attorney General sitting at the table with the Federal Prosecutor, all of a sudden he wasn't too sure.

As the proceedings started, the Prosecutor introduced the Attorney General to the court. Judge Reese had never met the Attorney General, but he commented that it was an honor to have him in his courtroom. Reese asked if the Attorney General wanted to make any comments prior to the proceedings.

The Attorney General stood and thanked the judge. "I am here today, because criminal charges are being filed against a U.S. Senator. This is, indeed, a very serious and unhappy event."

After the charges were filed, Wathen's attorney made a request for bail, stating that these charges will all be proven wrong. His client would be proven innocent of all charges. The Prosecutor said that Wathen was a flight risk and they knew of a two million dollar Swiss bank account the Senator had.

Wathen was stunned. No one knew about this account, that is, except for Margaret. Wathen wondered, *Where the hell is she? They had to have gotten her to talk. She could be ruining us both.*

Reese denied the bail request.

Joe came up to Stu in court, as Wathen was being led away, and suggested that they go to lunch. The VP had not attended Wathen's arraignment.

Kenny spoke up and said Paul was still in town and had booked a private dining room so all of them could meet for lunch.

As the court room was clearing, a few of the news people spotted Kenny talking to Stu and Joe. They knew who Joe was and thought Stu might have been another government agent. Two of them followed the group downtown to the hotel where they were having lunch with the VP.

After seeing the entrance to the dining room blocked by Secret Service agents, one of the reporters headed for the kitchen. He offered one of the waiters a hundred dollars to let him borrow his white jacket. The reporter was pouring water into the glasses. The men were all still standing and greeting each other. The reporter heard Paul greet Stu, so he turned to get a better look at him.

Stu noticed the reporter looking at him, so he, in turn, looked at the reporter. He noticed that the reporter was wearing what looked like expensive shoes. He moved closer to the VP and put his hand up to his ear. "Sir, I think we have a mole."

The VP pushed a button on a device that he carried at all times in his pocket. Two Secret Service men enter the room immediately. The reporter was taken out through the kitchen and turned over to two other agents.

During lunch, Joe told Stu that he had filed papers with the court to freeze all of Wathen's assets. He was also filing charges against the State of Kentucky. He suggested that they go easy on the state and make a settlement out of court. The big settlement would come from Wathen.

The VP said he thought Sergeant Major would have come, too.

Tom said he thought he had some other business he wanted to take care of.

After the luncheon, all of the Washington people headed to the airport to fly back.

Stu suggested to Joe that they have a meeting with the media and answer a few questions for them.

Joe agreed. "I'll book this same room and set up the meeting for four this afternoon."

The General booked a suite for himself and another for Stu. Their luggage was moved by the agents into the rooms.

At four in the afternoon, they entered the reserved room, which was full of TV news reporters and cameramen. Joe had arranged to have a small podium set up with a mike. As Stu walked to the podium, the reporters started yelling questions. Stu raised his hand to quiet them as he reached the podium.

"Gentlemen of the media, this is my meeting and you are here at my invitation. I want to make a statement and allow you to take your pictures. I will answer questions after my statement. There is to be no yelling or shouting of questions. If you have a question, raise your hand after my statement. If anyone asks what I would consider a stupid question, I will answer it by saying, 'stupid,' and move on to the next question."

Stu introduced his attorney and the General. He gave a short history of his life. He mentioned his service in the Marines. He listed the metals he received while in service. Eddyville, his home for the last twenty-five years, by all means, was a place to stay clear of. He went on to say that he had no plans, as of this time.

Stu asked, "Any questions?"

Every hand in the room flew up. Stu pointed to an attractive lady reporter.

"Mr. Vogel, do you have a girl friend?"

Stu laughed, "I guess I pointed to you first because I knew you were going to ask that question. I figure the sooner I answer that question, the better my chances are of getting one."

Stu pointed to one of the older men in the room next.

"Mr. Vogel, you have been out of prison for well over a month. What have you been doing?"

Stu said, "Visiting friends and boating. I helped a friend move a large sailboat down to Florida from Kentucky Lake."

Next, he pointed to a young black reporter.

"Sir, I interviewed the warden from Eddyville. He said you were a champion backgammon player. Is that correct?"

Stu smiled. "Let's put it this way. Could you be a golf champion if you had never played in a golf tournament? They don't have backgammon tournaments at Eddy. Yes, I know how to play backgammon, but I have never entered a tournament."

Stu said, "One last question."

He pointed to a tall reporter standing in the back of the room.

"Sir, one of our reporters was taken from this room today. Can you tell us where he has been taken and who those men were?"

Stu said, "I will answer as much of that question as I can. The men that escorted the reporter out of this room were Secret Service. I have no idea where the reporter is or when he will be released. I can't tell you if any charges are being filed. This has nothing to do with me. However, I will suggest to all who are here that you never try to breach an area that has been secured by the Secret Service. These men serve with a very intense dedication. They are ready to step into harm's way, when needed. Don't screw around with them. Thank you all for coming. My lawyer will make any news releases in the future. Truthfully, I don't expect to be making any news that is worth reporting in the future."

That evening, they stayed in the hotel suite and watched TV. Tom called Sergeant Major, who reported that he would be staying in Washington for a few days. Tom knew better than to ask him what was going on.

Stu called Susan. She was excited to hear from him and wished everything had come out like this when their parents were still living.

Stu said, "I'll be traveling with a friend. We will be in Jasper tomorrow and would like to take your family out to dinner."

Susan had seen the coverage from his meeting with the media. She said, "I think it would be nicer if I fixed dinner here for you and the General."

They had breakfast sent up to their room in the morning. Stu received a call from one of the FBI agents, advising him that his Volvo was in the hotel parking garage. The agent also mentioned that if Stu was interested in selling the Volvo, he would be interested in purchasing it.

After checking out of the hotel, Tom and Stu crossed over the Ohio River into Indiana. The Volvo was running well and they had a beautiful day for a drive. Tom wanted to know more about Stu's time in Korea.

Stu said, "Well, if you promise not to have me arrested, I'll tell you how we managed to steal a generator from the Army. Our outfit didn't have a generator. I borrowed a typewriter from the company clerk and typed up a phony requisition for a generator. Would you believe those Army guys even helped load it on our truck?"

The General said, "That's interesting. Whose name did you use on the phony requisition?"

Stu answered, "Do you really want to know?"

Tom said, "I think I already know."

Stu said, "I guess there is very little I can say about Korea that you don't already know. I know in WW2 you fought your way through the South Pacific. Tell me about it."

"Most of it was very bad," said the General. "There were Japs behind every rock and tree on the islands. We fought for six months on Guadalcanal. It wasn't until we invaded Guam that we had a battle without a jungle. Guam was different. We had pushed the Japs to the end of the island until they only had the sea at their backs. Sergeant Major and I were in a foxhole, close to the front line, when they started a bonsai attack at two in the morning. There were close to three hundred charging toward us, with their sabers reflecting in the moonlight. They were screaming as they charged into our line of fire. They wanted to die for the emperor. We made sure they did."

Tom wanted to know what their plans were for the rest of the day.

Stu said, "I might get us a free lunch, first thing. Then I have two rooms reserved for us at the local Jasper Hampton Inn. Later, we will get a home-cooked meal at my sister's house."

Tom said, "You sound like a man with a plan."

When they entered Gus's tavern, someone other than Gus spotted them and started clapping. Before long, everyone in the tavern was clapping. Most had seen the TV news and everyone in Jasper was bragging that they knew Stu.

Stu held up his hands, signaling them to stop.

"Thank you for the warm welcome. I want to introduce to you another Marine who led Gus and me through that frozen hell in Korea, General Tom Lavery."

The General waved a "thank you" and they proceeded to the bar, where they found two empty stools.

Gus said he had a table in a back room and then he proceeded to lead them there. He remembered the General. The General had come through the hospital and pinned the Purple Heart on him. Gus told how Stu had saved his life, and he then proceeded to show him the web belt and rosary.

After lunch, they checked into the motel. Stu called Susan and told her they were in town. This wasn't news to her, because she had received several calls from people who were at Gus's for lunch.

"I'm glad I planned on having you here for dinner. Anywhere we would go, you would run into news people with their TV cameras. I'm going to leave the garage door open. Park that well-known Volvo in it and close the door."

Tom was out of touch with Sergeant Major. He really wanted to hear about how he was getting along. He called Kenny and caught him in his office.

Kenny gave Tom a number to call. Kenny said, "I think the operator who will be taking the call will connect you."

A White House operator answered the phone, saying all messages would be recorded.

When Tom asked for the Sergeant Major, the call was put right through to him. Tom reported that they were in Jasper, Indiana, and according to Stu's plan, Bloomington was the next stop. Neither he, nor Sergeant Major, knew when they would get back to Beaufort. They didn't say much, knowing everything was being recorded.

During dinner, Tom suggested that Stu should give Joe's phone number to Susan. "He might want to represent her against Kentucky's spurious Senator."

Stu agreed. Later in the evening, he called Catherine. He said that he was traveling with a friend and would like to visit her tomorrow.

Catherine said, "Hell, yes! Fred and Nel have been driving me nuts with questions. Who is your friend?"

Stu answered, "Tom Lavery."

Catherine was relieved to hear a man's name.

Stu said they would be there in time for dinner. He said, "I'll pick up some steaks if you can get Fred to fix them on the grill."

Catherine was excited to hear from him and wondered if Tom Lavery was another ex-con.

The drive from Jasper to Bloomington is through a beautiful area of Indiana. During the trip, Tom asked Stu if anything funny ever happened in prison.

Stu explained that the Eddyville prison needs to stay in lockdown a good deal of the time. He said, "Prison just isn't a happy place. Actually, it is a miserable place to be. All the years I was at Eddyville I cannot recall anything happing that I could say was funny. Before I was sent to Eddyville, while I was in jail in Louisville, something happened that I thought was funny. You need to understand that there is a major difference between a jail and a prison. The inmates are of an entirely different class. You would have people in jail who were just picked up because they were drunk. They had a daily turnover of inmates.

"While I was in jail in Louisville, one night after the evening meal, several of the inmates refused to enter their cells. They stood on the walkways in front of their cell doors and refused to enter their cells. I really didn't understand why they were doing this, other than the fact that they were just plain stupid. The head jailer called the local sheriff to see how he wanted to handle the problem. The sheriff told the jailer to go ahead and close and secure all of the cell doors. He said he would be there at nine the next morning. Ten minutes later, the jailer again called the sheriff, saying the inmates were now willing to enter their cells. He asked the sheriff what he wanted him to do. The sheriff's answer was to keep the doors locked and tell them he'd be in at nine in the morning. Well, these young punks could only piss and shit on the walkways as that was all the area they had. Sleeping on the cold cement floors didn't work too well for them, either. Since I had a good night's sleep in my bunk, I do look back and think it was funny. I am sure it never happened again."

They had a wonderful evening and watched the election news from Kentucky. Everything had gone just as Sergeant Major had planned.

Coach Warren was interviewed in his home. He said that after his appointment he would be working both sides of the aisle. He said, "You might say I'm going to play offense and defense."

After they arrived in Bloomington, as always, Fred wanted to play some backgammon.

Catherine said, "Okay, children, play your little game, but Tom and I are going for a walk."

After they had departed, Nel commented that she thought Catherine and the General were a little sweet on each other.

They didn't return for over two hours. When they did return, Catherine said they had stopped by the Lodge and had a drink. Nel had already gone back to their condo.

Catherine said, "Fred, I hope you didn't lose too much."

Lucky Fred managed to lose over a thousand dollars to Stu again.

When Stu and Tom were upstairs getting ready for bed, Tom asked Stu if there was anything special between Catherine and him.

Stu said, "If you mean romance, the answer's 'no'."

Tom responded, "Good."

Chapter 15

During breakfast, Catherine announced that she was taking the day off so she could show Tom around Bloomington.

Just as Stu asked if he would get to come along, the phone rang.

Catherine answered with a cheerful, "Good morning!" Then after a few seconds she said, "Well, you're in luck, because he is here."

Handing the phone to Stu she said, "It's for you."

It was Henry's wife, Patrish. She reported that Henry had had a light stroke and was now home from the hospital and wanted to see him as soon as possible.

Stu asked Patrish, "Would today be too soon?"

After Stu hung up the phone, he said, "Catherine, I need to make a quick run to Evansville. Tom, will you be okay with staying here while I'm gone? I should be back for dinner." There just wasn't any question about it. Three was a crowd.

Stu took his bike off the rear of the Volvo before making the drive. He had become attached to the Volvo. He was kind of like a high school kid when it came to his car.

Once in Evansville, Stu drove directly to the Hutchinson home.

Henry seemed to be in pretty good shape, but he needed a cane to walk.

Henry suggested that they have their little meeting and then go to the country club for lunch. He hadn't been out since he had had his stroke.

They sat in Henry's study. Henry began by telling Stu that their river trip had been an adventure of a lifetime. "If you hadn't come along when you did, I never would have been able to make it. The experiences were even greater than I expected. Now, it is clear to me that my boating days have come to an end. Both Patrish and I feel indebted to you and we would like to sell you my boat for a dollar. We have already filled out the documentation transfer papers. We didn't know what you were using as a mailing address, so you will have to fill that part in yourself."

Stu loved Henry's sailboat and just couldn't believe that it was going to be his. "I cannot thank you both enough. I hope you will think of me as more of a caretaker than an owner."

Before they left for the club, Stu borrowed their phone and called Catherine. He told her that he was driving through Louisville on the way back to check on Bruce.

She reported that his attorney needed to talk to him and wants him to call.

He made the call to Joe.

Joe said, "Vogel, I need for you to come to Louisville. How soon can you make it?"

Stu answered, "Actually, I'm in Evansville and was planning on driving up to check on Bruce later this afternoon."

Joe replied, "Good. I'll book you a room at the Galt House. Call after you have checked on Bruce and then we can meet for dinner. The room is going to be in my name. We don't need any reporters spying on us."

Stu drove in his Volvo to the country club because he wanted to leave directly from there for his drive to Louisville.

During lunch, Henry asked Stu if he had any ideas about what he would do with the boat.

Stu said, "I hadn't thought about it. If everything works out, I might like to take it to the Bahamas for the rest of the winter."

Hutch said, "Not a bad idea."

An Indiana Senator was also having lunch at the club and stopped by the table to say hello to Henry. Henry introduced him to Stu. Hearing Stu's name, the Congressman commented that he wasn't happy with what Stu was doing to his good friend, Senator Wathen.

Stu looked up at him. "Senator, that's an interesting statement. I think I'll need to comment on it when I next meet with the media."

The Congressman said, "Wait a minute, you misunderstood me."

Looking him straight in the eye, Stu said, "I spent twenty-five years in prison so your friend, Senator Wathen, could advance his career. Make your stupid statement to the press and see where that gets you."

The Congressman said, "Mr. Vogel you have no idea of the power of the people on the Hill, so you had best be careful."

Stu said, "Senator, that almost sounds like a threat."

He replied, "Let's just say it was a word to the wise."

Picking up the menu, Stu said, "I'll consider the source."

After the Senator had left the table, Henry apologized. "I'm sorry. That was unpleasant."

Stu answered, "No, it was stupid of the Senator."

Patrish said, "Aren't you a little concerned?"

Stu said, "No, I have friends, too."

Henry thought he was talking about Tony in New Orleans.

Later, as the conversation came back to talking about the boat, Stu couldn't thank them both enough. He said, "I really don't feel right accepting it, but I'm going to do it anyway. I think I will be coming into some money. When that comes through, I would be more comfortable paying you."

Leaving the Club, Stu passed the table where the Senator was dining. The Senator held his head down and acted as if he hadn't seen Stu. Stu said, "Nice meeting you, Senator," as he walked past.

Once he was back on the highway, he found a truck stop and called Joe, to let him know when he expected to arrive at the Galt House.

When he arrived, Joe was waiting in the lobby. Joe handed him his room key, saying, "Let's have our talk upstairs."

Joe had booked a larger room with a sitting area. Once they were seated, Joe began to explain what was going on. Joe said, "I filed the papers yesterday in your suit against Wathen. Wathen's attorney is an old friend and we go way back, so we have no problem with getting along. I need to explain to you the difference between a civil suit and a criminal case. In a criminal case, the defendant never needs to make a statement. In the civil case, both sides will have to go through a deposition with a court recorder making a complete record of everything that is said. Roger, Wathen's attorney, wants to meet with you as soon as possible. He wants to make you an offer. They want to have the civil suit dismissed before the prosecutor for the criminal case gets word of it."

Stu said, "Well, I guess there isn't anything wrong with my hearing their offer."

Joe said, "I was hoping you would agree. We have them over a barrel and they know it."

Stu asked, "What about my sister, Susan?"

Joe replied, "We can direct part of the settlement to be in her name."

Stu asked, "How about Bruce?"

"Roger said Wathen had nothing to do with Bruce getting shot and it was all Margaret's doing. No one is going to walk on the criminal charges, but I doubt either one of them will spend more than ten years behind bars. However, if it comes out in the criminal trial that there was a conspiracy, it might add another ten years to Wathen's time."

Jo then said, "If everything is a go, I'll tell Roger we will meet him in his office tomorrow at ten in the morning."

Stu checked in with Catherine. She didn't seem disappointed to hear that he would be staying overnight in Louisville.

Joe set up the Sunday morning meeting with Roger and then went with Stu to visit Bruce. It was remarkable how fast his recovery was going. He was out of the bed and sitting in a chair when they showed up.

"They are sending me home tomorrow!" exclaimed Bruce.

Joe and Stu reported to Bruce about all that they knew concerning the criminal case.

Bruce was interested in knowing what Stu planned on doing, now that he was really a free man.

Stu told them both, "Actually, my plans change almost every hour. At the present time, it looks like I will be spending the rest of the winter on a sailboat in the Bahamas."

Joe spoke up, saying, "If that's what you are planning, maybe you should let me get started on a passport."

Stu thanked him, saying, "I appreciate it, but I think the Sergeant Major can get that job done in a day."

Bruce wanted to know who this Sergeant Major was.

Stu said, "Just a smart guy who seems to be spending a little time in the Washington area."

Driving back to the hotel, they decided to have dinner there.

Joe said, "I don't know if you're a bourbon drinker, but the bar at Galt House has over 100 different Kentucky whiskeys."

Stu said, "It's kind of late in life for me to develop any new bad habits, so let's go with your first choice. I'm sure you just happen to have one favorite out of the hundred."

Joe said he was right about that.

They sat at the bar to have their drinks. Joe felt whiskey was more enjoyable when you were seated at a bar. It was still a little early, so there was just one bartender on duty. Stu wasn't surprised when the bartender called Joe by name. He filled a cocktail glass with ice and poured from a whiskey bottle and set it in front of Joe.

"What will your friend have?"

Joe said Stu was having the same.

The bartender asked who was doing the buying.

Joe said, "Well, seeing that he is my only client, I guess I am."

They sat for almost an hour at the bar. The view of the river was the best in Louisville.

They moved into the dining room just as a piano started playing. Later, when the check came, Stu said he would get it. He said, "I'm afraid it might cost me more if you pay it."

Joe said, "The coffee shop is down off the main lobby. Let's meet there at 8:30 for breakfast. Roger's office is just three blocks from the hotel, so if the weather is nice, we can walk."

Chapter 16

I t was indeed nice outside as they walked to Roger's office. Roger had one of his secretaries greet them at the door. Since the office wasn't really open on Sundays, she locked the door, once they entered, and then led them to a small conference room. Roger was waiting and stood to greet them as they walked in.

The old lawyer said, "I'm sure Joe has explained to you why we are interested in getting this civil case off the books. My client, Senator Wathen, is offering two million dollars to make an out-of-court settlement."

Stu said, "Actually, Joe and I hadn't talked about a number. Years ago, if someone said they would pay me eighty thousand dollars a year to stay in prison for twenty-five years, I would have walked away. Today, I've already spent the twenty-five years, so it's kind of an after-the-fact deal. Somehow, I think you would pay four million, but I will settle for three."

Roger sat there for two or three minutes. His elbows were on the table and he was leaning forward, with his hands covering his face. Next, he leaned back in his chair and said, "Agreed."

Once the agreement was made, Stu announced that he wanted his sister to receive five hundred thousand out of the settlement. Roger said they could wire the money on Monday morning. They would need the bank's numbers as well as their account numbers. Stu had his checkbook, which supplied him with his account numbers, but he would have to call Susan to ask for hers.

Roger asked Joe if he had Susan's power of attorney.

When Joe answered no, Roger said, "What we need to do is have your sister drive down here today to sign the release."

Stu was lucky to get through to her. Susan had just returned from Mass. Stu explained, the best he could, where he was and what was going on. "We need you to drive to Louisville now. I have just reached a settlement agreement with Senator Wathen's attorney. I have included you in the agreement for a very generous amount. They have their reasons for getting this done today. My lawyer and I are in full agreement, and trust me, this is as good as it gets. Bring a deposit slip or a blank check for them to get the bank and account numbers. Once they have the agreement signed, they will make arrangements to have the money wired in the morning."

Stu continued, saying, "This whole event is not public information, and the less said, the better. I'm thinking while I'm talking. Maybe it would be best to have Catherine open an account for you at her bank in Bloomington. I'm sure a half million showing up in the Hartig's checking account would get around Jasper pretty quickly."

Susan said, "Did you say a half a million?"

Stu replied, "Yes, and I am still thinking. I think this account should be in your name only. You can tell Al that I have set up an account from which you can draw funds from time to time."

Susan agreed, saying, "I hear what you are saying, and yes, I think it would be smart."

She said she was home alone because Al and Anna had gone up to Bloomington in the pickup truck to take some furniture to Sally.

It was agreed that they would meet her at the Galt House in about two hours.

Joe turned to Roger and asked, "Can I use one of your word processors? I need to file a lawsuit, on Susan's behalf, first thing in the morning. This needs to be a settlement, not a gift that can be taxed later."

Roger turned to Stu and said, "That's why you have a lawyer. However, I think this will be the first and last time I let someone use my office and equipment to file a suit against my client."

Susan made it to the Galt House in a little less than three hours. She hadn't met Joe. Stu explained to Susan how Joe had been responsible for a good part of clearing his name.

Roger was waiting in his office when they returned. He had brought in a notary to witness the signatures on the agreements. Stu told Roger that he would stop by in the morning with the transfer number for both accounts.

Walking back to the Galt House, Susan said she wanted to get on the road. She wanted to be home when Albert returned from Bloomington.

Stu said, "Understood."

After Susan and Joe had left, he called Catherine to report that he wasn't through with his business in Louisville. "I am in the process of making a settlement with Wathen's attorney. They will be wiring money into my account in the morning. I need you to open an account for Susan, as soon as the bank opens. She has been part of this settlement, and they will be wiring money into her new account, too."

Catherine said, "Okay, but after tomorrow don't be asking me to be your personal banker."

Stu asked, "And, why, may I ask?"

She was quick to say, "I'm going to retire from banking."

He asked, "And, do what?"

Catherine said, "We will tell you at lunch tomorrow."

Stu answered, "Enough said."

Back at the Galt House Hotel, Joe and Stu returned to the barroom. This time, they sat in a corner lounge area and ordered two glasses of beer. Stu said, "I have to admit I didn't drink much as a young man. I remember there were three breweries here in Louisville. I think I can remember the names were Oertel's, Falls City, and Fehr's."

Joe said he had forgotten about Fehr's. Fehr's had gone out of business way ahead of the others.

Joe was very curious about Stu's life at Eddyville. He had dozens of questions. It made for an interesting topic, but not something Stu would normally be comfortable talking about. They also talked about the State of Kentucky and wondered how much they would offer to settle with Stu.

Joe said, "One thing is for sure; it won't come as fast as the last deal."

Joe suggested that they get Stu's Volvo and drive across the river to New Albany. "There is a nice little Italian restaurant that's open on Sundays."

Every time Stu got behind the wheel of the Volvo, he appreciated it more.

The restaurant was fairly busy. The owner was actually a friend of Joe's, so he had them seated, without delay.

Stu asked Joe what he should do for Bruce.

Joe answered, "Nothing, for the present moment. I'm going to represent him in lawsuits against both Margaret and Wathen. Margaret has filled her pockets riding on Wathen's shirttails. This isn't going to be as easy as your case, but at least I know I'm on the right side of the table. Believe me, Wathen isn't short of money. He had his hand in other people's pockets for all the years you were in prison."

Stu asked, "Okay now, when do I get the bill for your services?"

Joe said, "Actually, I hadn't planned on charging you anything. How about if I pick a local charity, here in Louisville, and have you make a contribution to them? Let's finish with the State of Kentucky and then we can talk about it."

Stu wondered if there was some way, in Joe's dealing with the State, that they could incorporate a parole for his old cellmate, Nick.

Joe answered, "That's interesting. Let me think about that idea."

Chapter 17

In no time, the morning business at Roger's office was over. Stu called Catherine before he checked out of the hotel. She confirmed that the transfers had come through for both accounts.

He told Catherine, "Okay, then I guess I can afford to buy lunch. I think I can make it in time."

She asked, "Any place special?"

Stu answered, "Yes, I think we should take Tom out with us and visit Sonny's father. Somehow, I have the feeling that neither of us will be seeing much of Bloomington in the future."

The drive out to Nashville was beautiful. The trees were giving their last performance of color before blanketing the ground.

It was a little after two o'clock when they entered the restaurant, where they had dined, previously. During lunch, Tom asked Stu, "Now that you're rich, what kind of car do you want to purchase?"

Stu said, "Actually, I wouldn't trade my Volvo, even on a new Rolls Royce. Better yet, let's hear your plans."

Tom said it was very simple. He and Catherine had fallen in love and were planning on getting married.

Stu asked, "Have you told Sergeant Major about your plans?"

Tom said, "Yes, and I'm sure it won't surprise you to hear that he is renting an apartment in Washington. He even suggested that we fly up to Washington. He said he could arrange for us to get married in the White House. I told him thanks, but we don't need that. He is going to fly in early next Saturday for the wedding. I want him to stand up with me. Stu, you can give the bride away."

Stu said, "And I thought my life was on a fast track. WOW!"

The visit with Sonny's father went well. He had read the papers and was glad to know that Stu was finally cleared of all charges. Before they left, Tom asked to have a few minutes alone with Sonny's father. Catherine and Stu had no idea what Tom said, but Sonny's father thanked Tom several times before they left.

It was very emotional for Tom, visiting with the father of one of his fallen Marines. Tom was very quiet during the drive back to Bloomington. He was crying, when he finally said, "War is hell and that was the coldest goddamned hell ever. It may sound stupid, but Sonny was lucky to have been killed in combat. There were thousands of our men taken prisoner. How they were killed, we will never know, and truthfully, we might be better off not knowing."

Fred and Nel came over when they returned. Fred said, "I knew it was going to happen sooner or later. Catherine was just too good of a package to not be snatched up by someone. Congratulations, General."

Tom had made arrangements for the chaplain of the local Marine Reserves to marry them. Both he and Sergeant Major were going to wear their dress uniforms. Sergeant Major would be bringing the uniforms when he came.

Stu said, "With your permission, Tom, I would like to wear a Marine uniform, too. See if Sergeant Major can borrow one in Washington that would fit me."

The next morning, Stu went by the bank to visit with Richard Elliot. He also wanted to take some of the cash out of the safe-deposit box.

Richard was very happy for Catherine, but he said the bank was losing its most valuable employee. Richard said, "Talk about a surprise."

Stu said he wasn't so surprised. He could tell there was something from when they first met. "They will be so darned good for each other."

Stu asked, "Richard, what do you know about getting a passport?"

"Well there isn't too much to it. You start by going to the county courthouse and get a copy of your birth certificate. While you're there, get three or four copies. I'm sure something will come up in the future, so save yourself another trip. Next, you need to go to the central post office. The U.S. Passport Office is on the first floor. They will provide you with the application. It normally takes six to eight weeks before you receive a passport."

Richard offered to help him invest some of his money.

"Yes, I guess I need to do something. What are your suggestions?"

"Well, it looks like you have more money than you are going to need anytime soon. I'm going to suggest we keep it in short term government paper. I'm sure you have things you will be doing, so let's put fifty thousand in your checking account. Any time it falls below ten thousand, I'll bring it back to fifty."

Catherine was busy with a real estate agent when he returned.

Stu announced that he was going back to Jasper for a few days and would return on Friday afternoon.

From Susan's house, he called Bob and told him about the boat he had bought. "I'll be in Bradenton in the early part of next week. I would like for Lu Sue to make up a shopping list for me. When the boat's ready to go, I want to head to the Bahamas."

The rest of the week flew by, and Saturday morning Stu was dressing in the Marine uniform Sergeant Major had brought for him to use. All of the time Stu was a Marine, he never had a Marine dress uniform. Both Tom and Sergeant Major had metals and ribbons galore on their uniforms. Tom spotted one ribbon on Sergeant Major's uniform and asked if that was what he thought it was. Sergeant Major didn't answer. Instead, he opened a case and pulled out the Medal of Honor and hung it from the blue ribbon around his neck.

Stu asked Sergeant Major to take care of some business for him when he returned to Washington. He gave him an envelope with the passport application and the document transfer papers for the boat.

When the wedding party arrived at the Pointe, there were TV crews for all of the major networks from Indianapolis. They had gotten the word through the Marine chaplain. They were filming the wedding party as they walked in. One of the newsmen asked if it would be okay if they got some of the footage from the actual wedding, too.

Tom turned to Catherine and asked if that would be okay with her.

Everything ran very smoothly and was over in no time. One of the cameramen had noticed Sergeant Major's Medal of Honor. After the service, Sergeant Major became the center of attention. He answered a few questions and then held up his hand, saying the interview was over.

Stu attracted about as much attention as wallpaper. None of the media even bothered to ask his name.

Someone in the White House had seen Sergeant Major on one of the networks' evening news shows. There was a call put through right away to the President. "Sir, we just picked up something on our news watch concerning the man you keep referring to as Sergeant Major."

The President thought, *Oh, shit. What's gone wrong?*

"Sir, maybe you already knew this, but it was news to us down here in the media watch room."

The President said, "Okay, damn it, let's hear it."

"Sergeant Major holds the Medal of Honor."

In a low voice, the President said, "I didn't know. Thanks for the information."

Chapter 18

S unday morning, Stu bid farewell to the newlyweds and then drove south. He guessed that he was now everyone's best friend and decided to try and visit Nick again.

He arrived at the Eddyville prison shortly after lunch. He parked in the same parking area, right in front of the main entrance. Stu had to walk up a good fifty steps to the front gate. The gate guard didn't know Stu, but told him there weren't any visiting hours today.

Stu said, "Would you please call the warden and tell him you have Stewart Vogel standing at the front gate?"

The guard knew who Stewart Vogel was. The television reporters had been to the prison and the papers were full of stories about him.

The gate guard said, "I'll put in a call to him, sir."

Stu laughed. In twenty-five years at Eddy, he had never had anyone call him sir.

The warden was in his home, a large white frame house, not very far from the parking area. He told the guard to just send him down there. He was extremely friendly when he greeted Stu.

It was a warm day and they sat on the porch, which was also in clear view of a guard tower. Stu was very aware that the guard in the tower was watching very closely. To start with, Warden, I want you to understand that I have no complaints concerning my treatment here at Eddy. I am on my way to Florida and I would like to have a short visit with Nick before I leave the state."

The warden said, "Well, this is highly unusual, but I don't see why I can't make an exception." He told Stu that he had been fairly sure about what Stu wanted and he'd already told the captain of the guards to have Nick moved to the visitors' room.

Walking back toward the prison, the warden said he hoped he didn't upset Stu's girlfriend on his last visit.

Stu laughed, saying, "Let's just say, you scared the shit out of her. You most likely did me a favor, because that romance was over before it even got a good start."

Nick was waiting when they arrived. The warden left them alone, while they visited. Nick looked like he had aged ten years since Stu's release. He said he had been sick with the flu. Nick had heard a little of the story about Senator Wathen. Stu gave him a pretty complete rundown of his adventures since he had left Eddy. Nick got a kick out of hearing about the backgammon winnings.

Stu said, "The state owes me big time. Joe, my lawyer is going to try to get you paroled as part of the settlement."

Nick said, "That would be great, but from the way I have been feeling, I think my chances of being carried out feet first is more likely."

Stu thanked the warden as he left. He commented to him that he hoped to have Nick paroled, before he died.

After leaving Eddy, Stu was back on the interstate, headed south. He hadn't had lunch, so he stopped at the first fast food sign he saw. He thought, *God, it felt good to be free.*

The drive to Bradenton took him another two days. Bob and Lu Sue had moved their boat to the Bradenton Yacht Club, so they would be close to where Stu's boat was.

Stu arrived in time for cocktails. It was great to be back with Lu Sue and Bob. Even more special was to be able to meet Bob's son, Eddy. They were full of questions, regarding all the things that had taken place over the last few weeks.

Stu didn't go into great detail. He kept the meeting in the Oval Office completely out of his account. He mentioned General Lavery and how the head of the FBI had been on his staff in Korea. Even though Bob only sold newspaper advertisements, he was still a newspaper man. Stu did say he had made a healthy settlement with Senator Wathen, but it wasn't for public information. Eddy was truly interested in hearing the details.

Stu asked, "Where is your friend, Art?"

Just as soon as he had asked, Art came walking down from the club. He came aboard and joined them for cocktails. Eddy said he wanted to swim a few laps before dinner. After Eddy had gone, they told Art that Stu was now the owner of a sailboat and was planning on spending the rest of the winter in the Bahamas. Bob asked Art if he had any advice he wanted to pass on to Stu.

Art made several suggestions. "First, you need to let me sponsor you for membership in our yacht club. For anyone planning on spending some serious time on a boat, a Florida yacht club membership is a must. Second, you need to have charts for everywhere you might be going. Third, you need to understand the dangers of the Gulf Stream. Fourth, take plenty of beer."

Stu said that the boat was at Sneade Island and that Lu Sue was going to check it out in the morning.

Art commented that Stu couldn't find a better surveyor.

Stu agreed to have Art sponsor him for club membership. They decided to have dinner at the club and asked Art to join them.

Art said that his wife had returned and was already in the middle of fixing dinner. Art said, "There is no way that I'm going back and announcing that we are eating at the club."

During dinner, Stu wondered if Bob had any suggestions about what he should do with his Volvo while he was off cruising.

Bob said, "That's simple. Just rent a storage unit. There is a place less than a quarter of a mile from here. Disconnect the battery and add a little bit of fuel stabilizer. Nothing to it."

Looking over at Bob, Stu commented that it was amazing how much someone could learn, just by asking a question.

Art walked up to the club with them so he could pick up a membership application for Stu. Art was an officer of the club, so all it took was his sponsorship and he was in.

Art said, "Turn it in at the office in the morning, along with your check, and you will get a membership card."

During dinner, Stu said he still needed to get his documentation certificate returned and he also needed a passport.

Bob said Stu might be in for a three or four month wait. "You never know."

No sooner than Bob had gotten the words out of his mouth, when two men in dark suits approached the table.

"Mr. Vogel, we have a package for you."

The men handed Stu a large envelope and then they left, just as quickly as they had appeared. When Stu opened the envelope, he found his new passport and the documentation certificate.

Bob reached over and took the certificate. "Okay, what's going on here? You damn near got your papers overnight and they were delivered by two guys who were packing. The envelope has a return address that just happens to be the same address as the White House."

Stu said, "General Lavery has a good friend in the White House. He's not anyone you would have ever heard of."

Bob said, "Well, he certainly must know what strings to pull."

Eddy was very impressed, too.

Before it got too late, Stu phoned Catherine to see how she and the General were getting along.

Tom answered the phone. He reported that he was packing boxes because Catherine was selling her place, furnished. Tom said, "We should be back in Beaufort by the end of the week. Fred is the only one who's not happy. He's talking about selling his place, too, and moving to Hilton Head Island."

Chapter 19

The next morning, Bob and Eddy were up early and headed back to St. Pete. Bob had rented a furnished condo, feeling that full-time life on a boat wouldn't work for Eddy. Lu Sue and Stu were at the boatyard, going through the boat, before the yard workers showed up for work.

After seeing the boat, Lu Sue made up a long list of things she thought he should have done to the boat. They sat in the cockpit of the boat as she explained each item. He agreed to every change. Somehow, Stu had the good fortune of not having to worry about the cost. The wind generator was the most expensive item, but, as she explained, it was very essential.

They took the list up to the office and talked with the boatyard owner about the things that Stu wanted to have done to the boat. The owner guessed that they could probably do all of the work in seven to ten days. He estimated that the total job would run over twenty thousand dollars. "We will need to be paid in full with a certified check before the boat is put back into the water."

Stu said, "I'll give you a twenty thousand dollar check now, so it will have plenty of time to clear. If there is any balance, I can pay in cash."

That was agreeable with the owner.

Lu Sue suggested that they should rent the storage area for the Volvo next. "We need a warehouse to store items we are going to be buying."

They returned to the Yacht Club next and Stu turned in his application for membership. The girl in the office told him she needed a three thousand dollar check, too.

"Okay, but I'm going to make it six thousand, because I'm going to be out of touch for a few months and I don't want to start off behind in my dues," Stu said.

She agreed that that would work.

He didn't have a mailing address, so he directed everything to Richard Elliot.

Stu and Lu Sue had lunch at the club and he was able to sign the check, as a dues-paying member.

Their next stop was at a marine supply store in Bradenton. They were able to find everything with just one stop. Lu Sue had him buy some warm clothing, too.

Lu Sue said, "It's likely you will still encounter some winter weather, even in the Bahamas."

They purchased chart books for every possible spot Stu might visit. Again, the bill was steep and ran over a thousand dollars. Stu used the bank card that Elliot had given him to pay the bill.

Next, they returned to the storage area and unloaded the Volvo. As Lu Sue placed all of his purchases in large garbage bags, she said, "These places have bugs and you don't want to be taking them to the Bahamas with you."

When they returned to the boat at the Yacht Club, Lu Sue said she would help him provision the boat, but they would need to wait until later to do it. "Bob is busy working on the upcoming boat show and I need to get back to my job. You're welcome to stay with us on the boat in St. Petersburg, but we just cannot spare the time to drive back and forth every day. And somebody has to be there for Eddy."

Stu said it wasn't a problem for him just to stay in the Bradenton area.

Since Lu Sue still had plenty of daylight, she said she was going to run their boat back to St. Pete.

He thanked her for all she had done. After helping her to get the boat away from the dock, he drove to Bradenton.

The Bradenton Yacht Club isn't in Bradenton, but across the river in Palmetto, Florida. It is a good five mile drive from Bradenton. Downtown Bradenton seemed to be nothing but commercial buildings. He continued to drive further south and found a nice Holiday Inn on the north side of Sarasota.

After checking in to the hotel, he used the phone in his room to check in with Joe.

Joe reported that the Governor, who was soon to be leaving office, was willing to grant a full pardon to Nick as part of the state's settlement with Stu. Joe said, "We settled for two million dollars on our wrongful imprisonment claim. I need you to sign the release. As soon as you can do that, they will cut a check and Nick will be pardoned."

Stu said, "I'm in Sarasota at the present moment, but we need to get Nick out of Eddy as soon as we can. I will get on the first flight that I can get out of here. Then I'll let you know what time I'm going to be in Louisville. I'll rent a car at the airport and pick you up."

Joe replied, "We can drive to Frankfort to sign the papers and pick up your check and Nick's pardon."

Stu called the same airline he had flown on before and found that they had a flight leaving at seven in the morning. He purchased a round trip ticket, planning on returning in three of four days. He then called Joe back to report that he could pick him up sometime after ten in the morning.

Joe said he would notify Frankfort first thing in the morning. "We should be able to have Nick out of Eddy before five."

After getting off the phone, Stu walked down to the barroom. He had enjoyed having the whiskey on the rocks with Joe at the Galt House, and right now, that sounded good to him. Sure enough, he heard the sound of dice, and there, at the end of the bar, were two young men playing backgammon. He sat there, enjoying his whiskey, and watching them play.

They asked Stu if he knew how to play.

He nodded yes.

They invited him to play with them, but he refused.

Stu said, "I've had a really hard day and I'm going to have an even harder day tomorrow. I expect to be back this way in a few days, so maybe if you are still here, I could play then."

He had a light supper sent to his room. He just didn't like sitting in a dining room alone if he didn't have to.

His wake-up call came at four thirty.

Checking in for his flight, he asked if breakfast was served on the flight.

The airline clerk said, "Only in first class."

Stu said, "Okay, move me up to first class."

She answered, "That will be an additional two hundred and twenty dollars."

Once on the plane, the first class section was empty, except for one other passenger. The other passenger asked Stu if he would mind if he sat with him.

Stu said, "That won't be a problem, as long as I get my breakfast."

The other passenger turned out to be a U.S. Congressman from Kentucky. He was very proud of his position and he didn't even bother to ask Stu his name. He mentioned that he always flew first class because the airlines complimented his tickets. The Congressman was on the House of Representatives' committee that regulated the airlines. He went on to say that he had a sweet little package in Sarasota that he checked on weekly. Then, after saying that, he turned to Stu and asked what business he was in.

Stu said, "Actually I'm a newspaper reporter. I'm working on Senator Wathen's case at the present time."

The Congressman was quick to say, "Hey, forget what I said. I don't need any problems."

Stu replied, "Congressman, it sounds to me like you are living on the edge. How would you enjoy seeing your name in thick black print on the first page of the Courier Journal and the Washington Post?"

The Congressman returned to his seat and didn't say another word for the rest of the flight.

As they were leaving the plane, the Congressman said, "I owe you a favor. Call me anytime I can be of service to you."

Stu said, "Congressman, do yourself a favor and get your head out of your ass before you break your neck."

The rental car company had an unlimited mileage special on rentals for less than a week. They offered a great selection, from top of the line European sports cars, to typical domestic cars. After looking over the selection, Stu chose an Oldsmobile.

Stu phoned Joe from the rental agency to tell him that he was on his way.

Joe was waiting at the curbside when he arrived at his building. They were on the interstate to Frankfort in no time.

Joe reported that Bruce was now back home and doing very well.

Stu talked about Nick and the time they had spent as cellmates. He was actually more excited about getting him pardoned than about the cash settlement with the State.

When they entered the state capitol, they were taken directly to the Governor's office. Meeting the Governor of Kentucky was nothing, compared to their White House visit, but it was still exciting. For someone who had just been defeated in the recent election, the Governor was very pleasant. They visited for quite awhile. The Governor was very interested in hearing about Stu's plans to live on a sailboat in the Bahamas for the rest of the winter.

The Governor said, "I'm leaving here in January. I have no intention of staying in politics. It's a hard life and I have had enough of it."

The Governor's office had faxed a copy of the pardon to the warden at Eddyville. They also attached a note stating that Stewart Vogel would be picking up Nick later in the afternoon.

On the drive to Eddy, Stu said he wanted to spend Nick's first night out in a really nice place.

Joe said, "I hope you've noticed that we haven't passed very much along this highway." Joe then suggested a state park lodge that was located on Barkley Lake.

As they turned off of the interstate at the Eddyville exit, they were stopped at a roadblock that had been set up by the state police. There weren't any cars ahead of them, so Stu stopped his car where the trooper directed him.

The officer said, "May I see your driver's license, please?"

After he had handed his license to the officer, he was asked to pull his car over to the side of the road.

Stu said, "Well, I don't know what this is all about, but at least I've got my lawyer here with me."

Once they had pulled the car off the road, the officer walked over, still holding Stu's license. As he was handing back Stu's license, he said, "The Governor asked us to find you before you made it to Eddyville. I am sorry to report that your friend, Nick, passed away this afternoon."

Joe reached over and touched Stu's arm. "Other than my wife, I've never had a really close friend. I can feel your loss."

The officer asked if he was okay before he left.

Joe offered to drive them back to Louisville. What Stu didn't know was that Joe didn't have a driver's license and hadn't driven a car in eight or ten years. As it turned out, it wasn't a problem.

Joe said, "I think we need to go to the Galt House and drink Kentucky's finest."

Stu agreed.

When they first entered the Galt House, Stu rented a room for each of them for the night. He said, "No one needs to leave here tonight."

Stu phoned Nick's son from the barroom. He told him that he was at the Galt House, in the barroom on the top floor. "My friend and I are holding a wake for your father."

Nick Jr. said he would be there in thirty minutes.

Stu had never met Nick Jr., but he knew who he was the minute he walked into the bar area. After handshakes all around, they sat down.

Nick Jr. asked how they were able to get the word so quickly about his father's passing. "It must have been after two this afternoon when I received the call from Eddyville."

Joe suggested that Nick Jr. should have a whiskey.

After the drinks arrived, Stu pulled a copy of Nick's pardon from an envelope.

Nick Jr. said, "What the hell is this all about? My dad dies and the State of Kentucky gives him a pardon?"

Joe took over and explained, the best he could, that Stu's settlement with the Governor included Nick getting a pardon, as part of the deal.

Joe said, "We were on our way to Eddyville, when we were stopped by a state trooper and told of your father's passing."

Stu was crying, "I'm sorry it happened this way. I loved your father."

Nick Jr. said he hadn't had time to think about any arrangements. He wasn't planning on putting a notice in the paper or having a viewing.

Joe handed him his business card and asked him to call him later. Joe also suggested that Nick Jr. should not drive, but take a taxi home.

Nick Jr. said he would.

As they left the barroom, they were a long way from being sober.

Chapter 20

It was after nine in the morning when Joe and Stu finally met in the coffee shop for breakfast. They both were still a little hung over. Stu checked them both out of the hotel and paid the bill. He offered to drive Joe back to his apartment, but Joe said he needed to walk.

Stu was back on the road again, driving to Bloomington. The Oldsmobile was a nice car, but there was just something special about his Volvo.

Richard Elliott was surprised to see Stu back in the bank so soon. Stu handed him the two million dollar check from the State of Kentucky.

Elliott said, "Let's see. A little over two months ago, you walked in here bare ass and elbows, and now you are worth close to five million dollars.

Stu said, "I guess I won't be needing a job anytime soon."

Stu told Richard about his boat and his plans to spend the winter in the Bahamas. He also mentioned that Henry had sold it to him for a dollar. Stu said, "I took the offer then, but I need to pay up, now that I can afford it."

Richard reported that Catherine and the General had left town that morning. "I'm going to handle the sale of her condo. I don't expect to see her anytime soon."

Stu asked Richard to increase the cash in his checking account to one hundred thousand dollars. "In two months you can back it down to fifty again."

He called the Hutchinsons from the bank and said he would like to take them to dinner.

They suggested that they should eat at their home. Hutch said, "We can talk without anyone bothering us. There have been several calls from the news people, wanting to interview us. They can't quite piece together your ties with us."

During the dinner at the Hutchinsons', Stu explained that he had received a very tidy sum from the State of Kentucky. "As a result of my recent good fortune, I would like to pay you for the boat."

Patrish said, "No, we are very happy with you having the boat."

Stu replied, "Okay, then, name a charity I can make a gift to."

Without any hesitation, Henry said, "The Little Sisters of the Poor. Each dollar they receive is never wasted."

Stu pulled out his checkbook and wrote a fifty thousand dollar check, payable to the Little Sisters of The Poor. He handed it to Henry, saying, "I'm sure you will make sure that this gets delivered."

Hutch said, "No. In the morning, why don't you take it there yourself? It will do your heart good to see the joy on their faces when you present this check to them."

Stu then went on to tell them about Nick and the pardon. Then he went into great detail, telling what was being done to the boat.

Henry commented that either he had received some very good advice, or he had studied up on cruising.

Stu said, "Actually, my best friend is married to someone who grew up working on boats in Hong Kong. She is having them replace everything from the cutlass bearing to the anchor chains."

The next morning, Stu drove to the Little Sisters of the Poor to deliver the check. As he entered the reception area, a young novice asked if she could help him.

Stu said, "No, but maybe I can help you."

He handed her the check.

She took one look at it and said, "Wait here, please. I'll be in trouble if Mother Superior doesn't get to thank you."

When Mother Superior appeared, she invited Stu to sit down with her for a few minutes. She read his name on the check. "Mr.Vogel, I can't begin to thank you enough for this very generous gift. It's almost as if God sent you. Just this morning, I was praying for help. I hate to pray for money when there are so many more important things to pray for. However, I did it this morning, and in walks God's messenger, or should I say, delivery boy."

Back in the Volvo, Stu felt really good about helping the Little

Sisters. Henry knew what he was doing when he suggested that Stu should deliver the check himself.

The Galt House was starting to look like home to him, as he pulled into the parking garage. He was lucky to catch Joe at home. The first thing Stu wanted to know was what arrangements were being made for Nick's funeral.

Joe said, "Let's talk about that at lunch. I can be there in fifteen minutes."

Stu waited in the hotel lobby for Joe, who suggested that they go up to the main dining room because it wouldn't be very crowded.

Joe said, "I hate to tell you this, but we attended the only memorial service for Nick two nights ago. Nick Jr. is having him cremated. His name isn't even going to be in the paper. No Greek funeral Mass. Nothing!"

Stu was very quiet. He sat there for a long time, without saying a word. Finally he said, "Okay, Nick is gone and we got three sheets to the wind. I would say there is nothing more we can do."

He told Joe about how he tried to pay Henry for the boat and ended up writing a check to the Little Sisters of The Poor. "I've been thinking about money. Not just my money, but all money. I'm guessing that if I managed to get lost at sea, all of what I have would end up in my sister's lap. That might not be a good thing. We need to work on my will. I would like to leave the bulk of my money to charities."

"I'm the lawyer. I should have suggested that you draw up a will. We can go to the office of a friend of mine this afternoon and borrow his word processor. I can write something up for now, and we can make changes, from time to time. Who knows? You're not too old. You might even get married. A guy with five million dollars wouldn't be too bad of a catch for someone."

While Joe was typing up the will, Stu confirmed his return trip to Sarasota for the next afternoon. He also phoned Nick Jr.

"Nick, Stu Vogel here. I'm wondering if you have any thoughts of what you are going to do with your father's ashes."

Jr. said, "Actually, I hadn't thought about it. Why? Do you have any suggestions?"

Stu said, "Yes. I'm going to be sailing to the Bahamas in a little over a week. If you don't mind, I would like to take Nick's ashes with me and spread them in the Gulf Stream."

Nick Jr. didn't know what the Gulf Stream was or where it was, but he agreed. He asked, "When are you leaving town?"

Stu said, "I have a flight out at noon tomorrow."

Nick Jr. gave Stu the address of the funeral home where he could pick up Nick's ashes in the morning.

Joe and Stu had an early dinner at the Galt House and then called it a day.

In the morning, Stu found the funeral home and picked up Nick's ashes. Stu asked if there were charges.

"No. We require payment in advance on cremations. We have close to a hundred boxes like this that have never been picked up, so we always get the money up front."

After returning the rental car, he checked in at the airport. The clerk who checked him in commented that it was quite common for people to be taking the ashes of their loved one to Florida. "We have even more coming back from Florida."

The return flight was uneventful. Stu hadn't bothered to upgrade for the return trip to Sarasota. His Volvo was waiting, just like an old friend.

After checking into the same Holiday Inn he had stayed at before, Stu called Bob. It was difficult for him to talk about Nick's pardon and death, but he managed to get it out. Stu said, "Truthfully, I thought the only way I would ever leave Eddy would be feet first."

Bob commented, "You weren't the only one!"

Stu said he was going to check to see how the boatyard was progressing with his boat. "I think Lu Sue did a great job making up her list, but there might have been something else the yard wants to add to it. If you have a number for Larry, I thought I might have lunch with him and play a little backgammon later, to pass the time."

He called Larry as soon as he finished his call with Bob.

Larry was excited to hear from him and said he looked forward to having lunch with him. "I do have a question. Are you the same Stewart Vogel whose name has been in the news?"

Stu answered, "Yes. Maybe tomorrow we can talk about it a little."

His next call was to the General's home in Beaufort.

Sergeant Major answered the phone.

Stu said, "Well, I'm surprised that you're home. I thought you had become a Washington bureaucrat."

Sergeant Major responded, "Hey, I had to check out how the General and his lady were doing. They both are doing great. I cannot begin to tell you what a wonderful change this has been for the General."

Sergeant Major asked, "What are we supposed to do with that old clunker of a car you left here?"

"Find someone and give it to them," said Stu. "The title is in the glove compartment."

Sergeant Major said, "Hell, I might take it back to Washington."

Stu thanked him for helping him with his passport and boat papers.

As it turned out, Catherine and the General were spending the day in Charleston. Sergant Major said he would leave a note that Stu had called.

Later, when Stu entered the bar area of the inn, sure enough, there were the two young men playing backgammon. One of them spotted him and called out, "You going to play?"

Stu said, "Well, I hate to barge in on your game. Okay if I just watch for awhile?"

They said, "No, no, no. We want you to play."

Shaking his head, Stu agreed, saying, "Boys, I just flew back in today. I've been on the move ever since I left town. I'll play, but only five games. How much do you play for?"

The two looked at each other and said, "How about twenty dollars a point?"

Stu said he thought that was a little steep, but he said he would agree, as long as the loser would pay off after each game. Stu suspected they might not be able to cover their losses if he waited until the end to collect.

The young men rolled the dice to see who would get to play Stu first.

Jeff, the first player, gained an early advantage and doubled Stu. Stu went into a back game defense. In doing so, he was able to block Jeff and regain the advantage. Then, once he was confident of his position, he doubled Jeff. All of a sudden, Jeff was playing an eighty dollar game, and losing. When the game was over, John took his seat, as Jeff threw down eighty dollars on the board.

During the next game, Stu managed to get an early advantage on John and turned the cube to double. John stood up and laid twenty dollars on the board, saying he wouldn't take the double.

Jeff told John to play him again. He wanted to sit out the next round.

As the next game turned out, John lost eighty dollars, too. John flipped eighty dollars on the board and said he had had enough.

Jeff said he didn't want to play either.

Then Stu surprised them both. He handed them back their money and said, "Next time, be a little more careful when gambling with strangers."

They took the money back, but didn't know what to say.

Stu turned and walked out.

Chapter 21

Stu had breakfast at the inn before he checked out. He wanted to get to the boatyard early. There certainly was activity around his boat. The yard owner spotted him and walked over to report on the progress.

Stu asked, "Now that you've gotten to know a little about my boat, do you have any suggestions of things to do?"

The yard owner said, "Well, if it was my boat, I would paint the hull. Most of the top-of-the-line boats are coming from the factory already painted."

He showed Stu some of the boats in the yard they had recently painted.

Stu said, "Do it."

Then he said, "Next I would put a stainless steel rubrail over the edge of that gunnel."

Stu again said, "Do it."

Still making suggestions, he said, "We have had a few boats like yours in here, where the owners have cut a small opening in back of the helm seat, about twenty by ten inches. They then seal it off with a teak door. It makes a great place to hang your dock lines."

Again, Stu said, "Do it."

Stu asked if he had any guess about when the boat would be finished.

He said, "My guess is another five days. Mr. Vogel, do you mind if I ask you a personal question?"

Stu looked at him and said, "I would rather you didn't."

Agreeing, he said, "Understood."

Stu still had plenty of time before he was to meet Larry. He stopped at the marine store in Bradenton and purchased some boating books to study. Chapman's was recommended by one of the store clerks.

The clerk said, "There is more in that book than you will ever want to know."

He also picked up a *Cruising Guide to the Bahamas*. He had five days with nothing special to do, so he figured he might be able to learn a few things that could help him later.

The Sarasota Yacht Club is actually on an island directly west of the city. It, of course, is on the east side of the island which offers protection from the Gulf. Stu was still too early when he drove to the yacht club. He decided to drive on past and see if he could find a nice lodging on the Gulf of Mexico for the next few days.

He found a beautiful spot on the south end of the island overlooking the Gulf. When Stu checked in, he was surprised to find that all of the units were little efficiency apartments. They came furnished with everything. He told the girl at the desk that he was planning on staying five or six nights.

The view from his room was magnificent. It overlooked the gorgeous sand beach and the blue water of the Gulf of Mexico.

Life was now being good to Stu, but he missed his friend, Nick. He didn't know if a winter sailing trip would end up just being a lonely adventure or not. Bob had promised that Stu would enjoy every day of it.

The drive from his hotel back to the yacht club was less than five minutes. Larry and his young lawyer were already seated. From the drift of the conversation, Stu was able to pick up that someone wanted to purchase one of Larry's properties.

Larry explained a little of what was going on. "I don't like to sell to speculators. If I own property next to someone's business and he is trying to expand or needs more parking, I will sell every time."

Larry instructed his lawyer to find out the potential buyers' intentions.

When they finished lunch, the lawyer reached over and shook hands with Stu and wished him good luck.

Larry said that before they went to the game room, he would like to sit in a corner of the lounge and hear Stu's story. "I know it couldn't have been much more than a nightmare, but I would like to hear whatever you will share with me."

Stu explained about how he got caught as a stepping stone for John Wathen. "He needed a major conviction to start his career, and I was it." Stu didn't go into the details of just how everything happened. He did mention that Kelly, the head of the FBI, was an ex-Marine.

He talked a little about his sailboat and the trip that he was planning on making to the Bahamas. He even told about the two hot shots he had played backgammon with the past evening at the Inn. "After three games, they had had enough. I gave them their money back and told them to be careful in the future."

Larry said he should be staying at one of the beach hotels.

"Actually, I just rented a place on the beach before I came here."

"Where?"

"A nice place on the north end of the island called The Gulf View."

"I know the place."

Larry suggested that they go out to dinner at one of the other clubs. "You get to drive. I don't drive at night anymore." He then suggested that they just play ten games of backgammon and quit for the day. If they were going out, he wanted to get in a little nap.

Once they were in the game room and sitting at the board, Larry suggested that they play for fifty dollars a point, which they did. The game this time attracted a few onlookers.

Larry paid twelve hundred dollars to Stu at the end of the session. As Stu was pocketing the money, Larry asked, "Aren't you going to give it back?"

"I will, if you want it," said Stu, as he started pulling the money out of his pocket. This was too much for the onlookers.

Larry quickly responded, "No, no, no!" He then explained to the onlookers that Stu had played a couple of hot shots last night and had then given them their money back.

On the drive back to The Gulf View, Stu stopped at a small grocery to purchase a few provisions. He also had to purchase a necktie, because Larry said it was required at the club where they would be dining.

St. Armen's Circle, just three city blocks from the yacht club, is nothing but high end shops. It was easy for Stu to find a shop with a nautical tie, which would go well with his blue blazer.

Stu picked up Larry at his condo building, located next to the Sarasota Yacht Club. Larry commented on Stu's Volvo and asked if it was new.

He told him the history of the car and how much he liked it.

Larry, in turn, told him a little of the history of their destination, The Field Club. Prior to its becoming a yacht club, it had been a winter home for some of the Marshall Field family. They owned a large department store in Chicago. The yacht club setting was very elegant.

After they had parked the Volvo, Larry spotted a large yacht on the visitor's dock. They walked down to the dock so Larry could see it up close. Larry knew his yachts, but he didn't seem to recognize it. He paced off the distance and guessed it was a sixty-footer. He looked at the stern to see where it was from.

Oklahoma City.

Stu then asked Larry if the boat had actually come from Oklahoma City.

Larry said, "No, that would just be the owners' hometown."

Larry was curious if the people on the Oklahoma yacht were in the dining room. He asked the waitress and she didn't know.

Later, the waitress came back and reported that the people from Oklahoma City were not dining at the club. She mentioned that they had been there the night before and that the boat had been there for three days.

Larry commented that they must be waiting for someone or they were not in a hurry.

During dinner, Larry asked Stu if he would be joining him for lunch the next day.

Stu said, "No, I want to spend a little time studying some books I purchased."

Larry then said, "Well, I hope you're not going to back out on dinner tomorrow night. You might have guessed I need a driver."

Stu said, "Larry, I would be more than pleased to dine with you tomorrow."

Larry said, "Okay, I'll make reservations at the Bird Key Club tomorrow."

The next morning, Stu stayed in his room until noon. The book he was reading on seamanship held his interest. He was a little surprised about how much he had already learned. Bringing the boat down the Mississippi had been a major training experience.

Stu planned to have lunch at the poolside. There were a dozen tables, shaded with large umbrellas. The weather was just perfect. Stu sat there, wearing a pair of his new sailing shorts, a light cotton pullover and boat shoes with no socks. He looked sporty and he felt it.

A waitress asked if he was having lunch.

Stu asked, "Could I just start with a beer and then order a little later?"

She said, "Of course. No problem. What kind of beer?"

He replied, "Just whatever you have on tap."

He was busy, studying, when a lady sat at the next table. He didn't look up or take notice of her presence.

She said, "Hello."

He didn't seem to notice or hear her.

Again, she said, "I said hello!"

Stu looked up, a little embarrassed, and said, "Oh, hello. I'm sorry I didn't hear you at first."

She said, "Well, that was pretty obvious." She was in a talkative mood.

Stu didn't want to seem unfriendly, but he was interested in his studies. She wasn't going to let go and asked him where he was from.

He replied that he didn't feel he was from anywhere because he had been in prison for the last twenty-five years.

She asked, "My word, what were you in prison for?"

With a smile, Stu said, "Actually, I killed my wife."

She was quick to say, "Ha Ha. What am I to say? 'Oh, you're single then?'"

Stu smiled and asked if she would care to join him for lunch.

She asked, "Are you sure? I can't say I would feel too safe." However she didn't waste time pulling her chair up to his table. She was from Cincinnati and said her name was Carol Burger. She couldn't wait to tell everything she ever thought she knew.

He just let her talk. He actually didn't feel he could talk about himself. She was very content just to talk about herself.

Finally she said, "Enough of me talking about myself. Let's talk about you. What do you think of me?"

He picked up the menu. "Let's order."

As they were finishing their lunch, Stu explained that he needed to continue his studies that afternoon. However, he and a friend were going to dinner that evening and asked if she would like to join them.

She asked, "Another wife killer?"

Stu said, "No, he's 'Ice Pick Larry'."

She said, "Sounds safe enough to me. What time?"

They agreed to meet in the lobby at six.

He spent the afternoon in his room, reading and napping. He hadn't bothered to tell Larry that they had an addition to their table.

Six o'clock came up pretty fast. Stu was a few minutes late in getting to the lobby. Carol was waiting, but didn't seem upset that he was a little late. She was surprised to see he was wearing a coat and tie.

He said, "We are going to pick up Ice Pick, so I hope you don't mind riding in the back seat."

Larry was standing outside, in front of the building, talking to his lawyer. As he was getting out of his car, Stu could hear Larry say in a loud voice, "I don't care how much they want to pay, I don't sell to speculators."

Stu asked if he needed to drive around the block a few times.

Larry said, "No." He shook hands with his lawyer, saying, "Don't come back with any more offers from these people."

Stu surprised Larry when he pointed out that they had an additional dinner guest. The drive to the Bird Key Club was only about a mile. The club had valet parking. As Stu was turning the keys over to the young attendant, he pointed out that the car was stick shift.

The young man said he had never driven a stick shift and it might work better if Stu parked his own car.

While Carol and Larry were waiting, Carol tried to get Larry to make some comments about Stu.

Larry said, "Stu and I don't discuss each other's business. But, I can tell you he has never been married."

While they were dining, several members stopped at their table to say hello to Larry. Larry introduced Carol and Stu to everyone who had stopped. He mentioned that Stu was a member of the Bradenton club. Carol wasn't too sure where Bradenton was, but assumed it was somewhere in Florida.

After dinner, Larry wasn't quite ready to go home, so he suggested that they sit in the bar area and have an after-dinner drink.

Stu started to get the idea that maybe Larry didn't get out much, at least not past the Sarasota Club. There was a piano player in the lounge. He had a very good singing voice and knew most of the members in the lounge by name.

After two rounds of drinks, Stu decided it was time to take Larry home. Remembering Bruce's advise to stay out of trouble, he had not kept up with Carol and Larry on the drinking. He was the driver and he was sober.

When they returned to their resort, there was music coming from the lounge. Carol suggested that they go in and dance.

Stu shook his head, saying he hadn't danced with anyone since high school.

Pulling him into the dance area, she said, "You lie more than a used car salesman."

He really hadn't danced since high school, but he did manage not to step on her feet. She really was starting to show that she had had too much to drink.

Leaving the lounge, he stopped at the desk and asked the lady clerk to help him. He held up a twenty dollar bill. That did the trick.

They got Carol to her room, put her to bed, fully clothed, and only took off her shoes. The clerk was wearing a name tag, *Peggy*, on her uniform. Stu wrote down her name and the time that they had taken her to her room. He just had a feeling something might go wrong.

The next morning, he had breakfast in the coffee shop. He guessed that Carol was suffering from last night's binge. He went out to the pool area with his book. He felt that sooner or later, Carol would show up. As it turned out, it was later. Almost noon. She spotted Stu where he was sitting in the shade.

Still showing the effects of the night before, she sat in the lounge chair next to him and said, "I don't remember getting in bed."

Stu said, "Peggy, the night clerk helped. You were completely out of it."

She said, "Sorry," and got up and walked away without saying another word.

He called Larry to see about lunch. He wasn't very comfortable around Carol and didn't want to see her anytime soon. He took some of his reading material when he went to the yacht club.

During lunch, Larry wanted to hear about Stu's boat and his upcoming trip to the Bahamas.

Stu said, "I feel it is going to be an adventure that has to happen a day at a time. I have no idea as to how far south I will go. Right now I don't plan on going any further south than the Bahamas. When I return, I'm sure I will want to find a place to settle down; someplace with a garage. I'm thinking about heading west in the Volvo in the late spring. I just want to be able to call someplace home."

Larry said, "You know, Carol probably feels like shit about now. Stu, I think you should call her and invite her to go to dinner again tonight. There is a great seafood restaurant out on Longboat Key and I haven't been there in a year."

Without saying another word to Stu, he told the waiter to bring him a phone. It surprised Stu how Larry was able to dial the Inn without looking up the number. Larry asked the inn operator to ring Carole's room. He handed the phone to Stu while it was still ringing.

Carol wasn't expecting a call and answered the phone with a questioning "Hello?" She hadn't expected Stu to call, and even much less, to get invited out to dinner again.

They would be going casual tonight. Same time, same lobby.

She said, "Thank you very much. Yes, I'll be ready at six."

Larry then said, "Now that I have us a date for tonight, play me some backgammon. I still don't think you are as good as you think you are."

Stu said, "Five games."

Stu again won four out of five games. He decided to return to the Inn and study some more. Also, he needed to check in with the boatyard, and let them know where he was staying. They reported that the work on the boat was progressing and said that if they didn't have any major last minute problems, they expected to have the boat back in the water in three days.

After meeting Carol in the lobby, she again apologized for last night.

"I've been taking an antidepressant. Maybe my drinking wasn't a very good idea. Anyway, thanks for asking me out again."

Stu agreed, "I kind of guessed it was something other than the booze."

Larry was again waiting outside of his condo building entrance. The drive to the restaurant was a good six miles on a narrow road. The parking lot was packed and there were thirty or forty customers waiting for a table. Larry told Stu to park in front of a dumpster. There was a big "No Parking" sign right where he told Stu to park. Larry led them in through the kitchen door.

One of the fry cooks recognized Larry and called him by name. "I'll tell Mr. Mark that you are here."

Mark seemed very pleased to see Larry and greeted him like a long-lost cousin.

Larry introduced Carol and Stu.

Mark said, "Follow me. I've just cleared a table by the water."

After they were seated, Larry explained that he always entered through the kitchen. "You have people that have been waiting thirty or forty minutes for a table. I can't just walk up and get the next table without causing a riot."

Stu ask, "What's with Mark? He owe you money or something?"

Larry said, "He pays rent once a month."

Carol was starting to wonder just who these nice men were that were taking her to dinner. They really hadn't talked about themselves. She asked Stu what he had retired from. Larry was wondering how Stu would answer her question.

Stu said, "I don't know that I am retired. If not having a job is being retired, I would qualify. But my case is a little different. Actually, I have been in prison for twenty-five years. If you had been reading the papers lately, you might remember the news story about Senator Wathen."

She said, "Oh! I saw that on the news. You poor man. I never would have guessed. You certainly don't act like someone who's been in prison, but hell, I've never met anyone who has been in prison."

Stu said, "Well it's nothing that I am ashamed of, or proud of either. It was just a big part of my life. So far, I've done a pretty fair job of putting it all behind me. I have answered your question, so now let's change the subject."

"Okay, but I heard you talk about a boat and you're also staying at a fairly expensive resort. How can you manage all of that?"

Stu explained, "It's unbelievable, but a friend gave me the boat. The State of Kentucky offered me a settlement for my false imprisonment, and I took it. Just that simple."

She looked at Larry. "Do I dare ask about you?"

Larry said, "I've been in Florida real estate for the last forty years. My wife died several years ago. We weren't fortunate enough to have had children. As a result, I look at Sarasota as my child. I have helped her grow and do my very best to protect her."

She asked, "How did you two manage to become friends, or is this something that goes way back?"

Larry laughed. "I'm not too sure we are friends. He beats me like a stepchild at backgammon. That's how we met, playing backgammon."

The restaurant offered a great selection of seafood. Carol and Stu agreed it might be smart to just let Larry do the ordering.

Mark came to their table, just as a waitress appeared. He told her that these were very special people and said that she should take special care of them.

Larry reached up and grabbed Mark by the sleeve. "Wait, don't go away. My friends here pushed the responsibility of ordering in my lap. Seeing as I haven't raised your rent in the last twenty years, you might want to accept my offer of letting you be in charge of the ordering."

Mark said, "Tradition. Having the same rent is a tradition. I'm a strong believer in tradition and I certainly wouldn't want to break tradition. Is anyone allergic to anything like shellfish?"

The waitress asked about drinks.

Three draft beers. It really didn't make any difference what brand.

When the waitress returned with the beer, another waitress came and placed a crab cake in front of each of them. Next came the salad. After the salad they were served charcoal-grilled grouper with a baked potato. The meal was topped off with key lime pie.

Larry didn't bother asking for the check, but he did give each of the waitresses a fifty dollar tip.

Mark came to the table as they were leaving and thanked everyone for coming in. He was very genuine. Stu guessed that they both had enjoyed a very profitable relationship.

They left the same way they had come in, through the kitchen. Larry stopped and talked to the fry cook and gave him a twenty dollar tip, too.

Driving back, Stu asked Larry how he could come out ahead without raising Mark's rent in twenty years.

Larry said, "Very simple. The rent is tied to a percentage of sales. If he has a bad year, I have a bad year. However, he's never had a bad year."

Stu told Larry that he was going to save him some money tomorrow. He announced that he wanted to drive up to check on the boat.

Larry said, "Call me when you get back. I would like to have dinner with you two at the Inn where you are staying."

After they had dropped off Larry and were driving to the Inn, Carol asked if she could ride along with him tomorrow.

Although Stu said he would be glad to have her company, he wasn't so sure. They agreed to meet in the coffee shop at eight in the morning.

As they were entering the Inn, Carol asked if he wanted to stop by her room for awhile.

"This might sound a little strange, but I went twenty-five years without even seeing a woman, except for the prison nurse, and you had to be sick to see her. Now I'm planning on spending two or three months, mainly alone, on a sailboat. My best friend just died last week and I have his ashes in the trunk. I'm going to spread them in the ocean on the way to the Bahamas. I don't know if I'm a romantic or just someone who is twenty-five years behind in time."

He walked her to her room and, as he was leaving, she grabbed him and kissed him. He kissed her back, said good night again, and walked away. He just wasn't ready for another Vickie.

Chapter 22

At breakfast, Stu said he wanted to drive up through Longboat Key towards Bradenton. They could come back the other way, on highway 41. He was just interested in seeing a little more of the area.

The work on the boat had progressed to the point where the owner of the boatyard said they would have him back in the water late the next day. Carol thought the boat was fantastic. She asked, "Do I get to go with you?"

In reply, Stu asked, "Do you have a passport?"

She said, "No."

Stu said, "Well, there's your answer."

The thought of having someone else aboard got him thinking. He asked the boatyard owner if he could make a long distance call.

He said, "Certainly."

Stu excused himself from Carol, and walked to the yard office and called Henry at his home in Evansville.

Patrish answered. She was excited to hear from him. She said that Henry was getting along very well.

Stu asked, "Well enough to be on the boat for a few days?"

Patrish said, "I know he would love it. Here, I'll let you talk to him."

Stu explained that he was about three days away from starting his trip across Florida and wanted to invite him to come along if he felt up to it. Stu said, "We should be able to get in a little sailing and visit several of the Florida yacht clubs."

Henry said he could be down to Florida in three days.

"That would be perfect. I'll call you tomorrow and get your flight information."

After leaving the boatyard, Stu took Carol to lunch at the Bradenton Yacht Club. Carol had become very quiet and was not her talkative self. As they were finishing their lunch, she asked Stu if she would ever see him again after tomorrow.

"That's a hard question to answer. I think I'll be in the islands two or three months. After that, I have no idea what I want to do for the rest of my life."

When they returned to the Inn, they each had a message from Larry, stating that he would meet them in the lounge at six o'clock.

They were all on time for the six o'clock rendezvous.

When they all ordered a drink, Larry instructed the waiter to bring the drinks in plastic cups to the beach area. "We will be watching the sunset."

"Yes sir, Mr. McConnel," replied the waiter.

Walking to the beach, Stu asked Larry if everyone in Sarasota knew him.

Larry said, "Hardly. Just the ones that work for me."

Stu asked, "Then you're saying that you own this place, too?"

Larry nodded his head and said, "Correct."

It was a beautiful evening and there were fifty or sixty people on the beach to see the sunset. Just as the sun disappeared into the Gulf of Mexico, everyone clapped just like they had seen a great performance.

Walking back toward the dining room, Larry asked how the work on the boat was moving along.

Stu said, "Great! They expect to have me back in the water after tomorrow."

Larry asked, "Do I ever get to see your boat?"

Stu answered, "Certainly. I'll stop here on my first stop after I leave Bradenton."

The next morning, Stu was up early. He removed his bike from the rack and pumped up the tires. It was a beautiful morning for a ride. He had planned on calling Carol when he returned.

When he did return, there was a note that had been placed under his room door. It was from Carol, thanking him for all of his kindness. She had taken the shuttle to the airport and was flying back to Cincinnati. The note said, "If you are ever looking for a crewmember, call. Thank Larry for everything." She left her phone number and address.

He met Larry for lunch and showed him the note. He went on to explain that he had lived twenty-five years without any female contact, so he guessed he was a little behind the times when it came to women.

Larry said, "Well, let me know if you ever figure women out."

They drove down to the Venice Yacht Club that evening for dinner. They were having their bingo buffet. They stayed and played bingo. Larry won seventy-five dollars right off the bat. He was ready to leave after collecting his winnings.

He said, "I always say, quit while you're ahead."

The next morning, Stu found a Laundromat and took care of his laundry. He stopped by a liquor store and purchased an assortment of liquors to have on the boat. He really didn't know brand names, so he just made sure it was expensive.

He checked out of the Inn and found out that Larry had taken care of his bill. He stopped by Larry's club and had lunch with him and his lawyer. He thanked Larry for taking care of his lodgings.

Larry mentioned that he had taken care of Carol's too.

Stu left for the boat after lunch. They had his boat on the travel lift and were moving it to the slip where they lowered boats into the water. He got there just in time to see the action. Once the boat was in the water, the workers from the yard moved it to another slip.

Stu knew the next thing he had to do was settle up with the yard office. As he had told them earlier, he paid the balance in cash.

Next, he drove to the yacht club and made arrangements with the dock master for a place to keep his boat for the next few days. He paid the dock master twenty dollars to drive him back to the boatyard. He thanked the yard owner and told him that he would be moving out, shortly.

The diesel engine started on the first try. He untied all of the lines and proceeded to motor to the yacht club. Even though the run to the club was less than a mile, it was special. He was at the helm of his own boat.

When he got there, the dock master was waiting to help him secure the boat.

He phoned Bob and LuSue to report that he had his boat in the water. LuSue said she had made up a list of provisions that he would need to purchase. She said she would fax it to the yacht club. She was sorry, but she was too busy at her office to take the time out to help him shop.

Chapter 23

When it came time to pick up Henry, Stu had the boat fully provisioned. Henry was walking with a cane. Other than the cane, he seemed to be in fairly good shape. Henry was very impressed with all of the improvements to the boat.

Stu was anxious to get underway. He called Larry and told him that they would stop at his club in time for dinner. His Volvo was safely tucked away in a storage locker.

They motored away from the Bradenton Yacht Club. Stu didn't want to pass through Sarasota without Larry getting a chance to meet Henry and also to see his boat. He had radioed the Sarasota dock master when they got close, so Larry was on the dock to greet them.

During dinner, they talked a little about Carol. They had both enjoyed her company. Hutch said he had almost forgotten to tell Stu about Vickie. She had called several times, since reading about him in the papers. "She wants you to call her."

"There have been so many people that I have met since I have left Eddyville. You, for one. I needed the trust that they all had in me. Joe, Tom Lavery and even the President, have helped me so much. Vickie didn't make the list."

Larry looked up at the mention of the President. "You haven't told me about the President!"

Larry said, "That's correct and I'm not going to."

They got away from Sarasota early the next morning and actually sailed further than Stu had planned. They anchored inside of the Boca Grande inlet.

The next day, they sailed and motored and planned to stop early at the Royal Palm Yacht Club on the Caloosahatchee River. Stu could see that Henry was a little worn down from the long day they had put in sailing the day before. Today would mark the end to their sailing because the rest of the trip across Florida would mainly be by motor.

As they approached the channel going into the club, they had to wait for a large motor yacht that was in the process of leaving. As it turned out, it was the same yacht he had seen at the Field Club in Sarasota. Stu stopped at the fuel dock first to top off his fuel tank.

The dock master commented that Stu was getting off easy. "That yacht you saw when you were coming in took over five hundred gallons of fuel."

After they had the boat secured in a slip, they walked up to the clubhouse for lunch. There wasn't much going on, so the waitress visited with them and suggested that they tour the Thomas Edison home that adjoined the club property.

They agreed that it would be a good idea, but waited until a little later in the day before taking the tour.

The next morning, they were away from the dock early and motored up the Caloosahatchee River. It was a very restful day. Stu allowed the autopilot to do most of the steering. They made it all of the way to Moore Haven and tied up to a dock that the city provided for visiting boaters. Stu cooked dinner on the boat and they retired early.

The next morning, they were again on the move early. They had passed through two locks the day before and had one more to go before they entered Lake Okeechobee. It was after three in the afternoon when they cleared the lock on the east side of the lake. They stopped at the Indian Town Marina a little before five. It looked like another dine-aboard night. Tomorrow would be their last day of travel before reaching the other coast.

Stu placed the scotch bottle out and was filling their glasses when, suddenly, their boat rocked.

Hutch said, "It looks like we have company."

It is very unusual for anyone to step on a boat without first asking permission. Stu and Henry looked at each other with a puzzled look.

Suddenly, a man appeared in their companionway holding a pistol.

He said, "Put your hands on the table where I can see them. I'm coming down."

Henry was visibly shaken, but Stu just sat there, unshaken and very calm.

The man told them he had just escaped from the local Florida State prison.

He yelled, "I want you to get this boat out of here, NOW!"

Stu, still very calm, asked, "Just where do you want to go?"

The man pointed the gun at Stu. "I said out of here. NOW!"

Stu just looked at him and grinned. "Well, let me tell you something you don't know. First we can't go anywhere. If we get back on that river, there is a government lock that is closed for the night. If we go the other direction, there is a railroad bridge that is also closed for the night. So, mister dumb-ass, we would look awfully stupid sitting out there in the river."

Henry couldn't believe Stu was talking this way to someone holding a pistol pointed his way.

Stu said, "Now, sit your ass down. My buddy and I were just getting ready to have some scotch when you joined us. You're more than welcome to join us, but I want to tell you who we are."

The man motioned with the gun and told Stu to pour.

Stu poured them all a drink and then proceeded to talk.

Stu said, "Twenty-five years ago, my buddy and I were bank robbers. I got caught by the police, but my buddy here never did. I was released a short while back from the Eddyville prison in Kentucky after serving twenty-five years. Now, when we leave here tomorrow, we are not stopping until we get to the Bahamas. You're more than welcome to join us. I'm going to fix dinner here, shortly, but I need to check the engine oil first."

The man with the gun gave Stu the okay to check the engine, but told him not try any tricks. Henry sat there drinking his scotch, wondering what the hell Stu was up to. Stu had to open the front of the engine cover, which was also the stairway out of the boat.

Turning to the man he said, "I'm going to open this drawer and get out my flashlight. Nothing else is coming out of that drawer. I'll do it with one hand, so you can watch me. Okay?"

The man holding the gun said, "Okay."

Stu tore off some paper towels and got down on his knees to check the engine oil. "Goddammit. This fucking flashlight isn't working. It must be the bulb; the fucking batteries are new."

Stu unscrewed the front cover to the flashlight and left it on the floor when he stood up.

"Don't worry. I'm just going to do a little bulb snatching. There was a bright red EPIRB mounted on the bulkhead. He unscrewed the red lens that covered a small bulb. Removing the bulb, he proceeded to make the bulb exchange.

Henry finally had an idea of what Stu was up to. He knew that the flashlight and the EPIRB didn't use the same type of bulb. The EPIRB is a radio distress signal that broadcasts a radio signal of your location and is only used if you are in dire distress. It is activated when turned over. Normally, the red light on the top would flash also, but without a bulb it wouldn't be flashing.

Back on the floor, Stu faked the bulb replacement and proceeded to check the engine oil. When he got back up, he threw the paper towel and the EPIRB bulb in the trash. Turning to their unwelcome visitor, he announced that he was going to place the flashlight back in the drawer. He then took the EPIRB off from the bulkhead and proceeded to replace the lens. As he remounted it to the bulkhead, he turned it over, which, in turn, activated the radio signal.

Stu then said, "Now, if it's okay with you, I'm going to fix us supper."

The man with the gun had already poured himself a second drink.

Henry said he was ready for another drink.

Stu poured them both another.

Henry complained, saying Stu was holding a back a little on the pour.

"Fuck you both." Stu then proceed to add more scotch to both of their glasses.

While Stu was cooking, Henry joined into the game and proceeded to show the man with the gun the maps of the Bahamas. Henry asked him his name.

"Jeff."

Stu told Jeff that he hoped he like fried chicken because that was what he was fixing. Stu held his glass up for Henry to top it off a little.

Henry poured Jeff a little more at the same time. Jeff was starting to slur his words and they were both wondering how much longer it would be before he would be in la-la land.

Just as Jeff's head fell to his chest, the boat listed as the SWAT team came aboard. They called for everyone to come out with their hands up.

Stu called back that their man had just passed out and said that they now had his gun. Stu said, "I'm going to hand up his gun first and then I want you guys to come down and get this bastard off my boat."

Two SWAT team members climbed down into Stu's boat. They cuffed Jeff, first thing, and then lifted him out of the boat, with help from the others who were topside. Once they had Jeff off the boat, a police officer came aboard with another officer to ask questions.

The officers reported that they really weren't too sure how Jeff had managed his escape. They suspected it involved a propane truck that had made a delivery to the prison around noon. Jeff didn't show up missing until an hour after the truck had left the area. He had, apparently, broken into a farmhouse six miles from the prison. He had raped, and nearly killed, an elderly lady living in the house. They didn't know he had a gun, but they suspected it had been stolen from the farmhouse. There was an old bike missing from the barn and they believed that was how he had managed to make it so far.

One of the officers said, "I don't think we would have found him tonight without getting your EPIRB signal."

"Well, the bastard drank almost a full bottle of good scotch, or I should say we poured a good bottle of scotch down him. You were going to have him one way or another."

The officer then asked for their ID's.

Looking at Stu's passport, he commented on the fact that it was a recent issue. "Where have I heard your name before?"

Stu said, "It's a long story. I'm sure you have read about me somewhere. So as not to confuse you, I'm going to give you the private phone number of Kenny Dillman. He is the current director of the FBI. I want you to call him now and tell him what has just happened. I don't want to sit here and have to make something different out of what has happened here this evening. He will tell you not to worry yourself trying to check us out. We have performed a service, capturing a very dangerous escaped criminal. Let's leave it at that. Keep our names out of your records. We don't want to read about ourselves in the newspapers."

At that, the officer pulled out a small hand-held radio and called his station office. He started telling the station radio operator that he wanted her to make a phone call and then plug it through to his radio.

"WAIT!" yelled Stu. "You sure as hell are not going to give the private phone number of the head of the FBI out on that radio. I'm sure there are at least a hundred people listening to your radio calls tonight. Now, I am in the process of cooking supper and I would like for you to get off my boat. Make your phone call and then lose that number. I mean, never use it again or let it fall into anyone's hands. And don't come back here, unless it's to deliver a bottle of very good scotch."

The police captain was more than just a little upset that Stu had put him down in front of one of his officers. One thing was for sure. Stu wasn't afraid of him and the officer knew it. He was glad they could claim credit for Jeff's capture, without having to mention Stu and Henry's part. The captain also knew one thing for sure. They were getting off of Stu's boat. The police captain had never had anyone talk to him the way Stu had in all of his years of police work.

After they were off the boat, the captain's assistant asked if the captain was going to make the call to the FBI.

The police captain said, "I have just had my head handed to me by that son-of-a-bitch. I don't know who he is, but he sure as hell has no fear. No, I'm not making the call and I'm tearing that phone number up now. And, if I ever hear one word of what took place on that boat tonight, you will be looking for a job."

The officer said, "Yes, sir. Understood."

The captain said, "Now, I want you to find the best bottle of scotch at Joe's Liquor Store and take it back with my compliments."

Back on the boat, Henry said that he would sure have some good stories to tell his wife when he gets back home. "How you managed to set off the EPIRB without Jeff knowing what was going on was great. Chances are that he would have killed the two of us. I was scared shitless and you were as calm as someone sitting in church."

Stu said, "Henry, you have to understand that I lived with assholes like Jeff for twenty-five years. If they think you are afraid of them, they will only push the button harder. I didn't make enemies or friends while I was in prison. My cellmate was the only exception."

Hutch asked, "Why did you come down so hard on the police officer?"

Stu replied, "Well, the way things were going, it wasn't going to be very long before he found out that I am an ex-con. He would have taken my ass downtown, most likely. I'm sure they would have pushed me around a little and I have already had twenty-five years of that shit."

Just as Stu was cleaning the galley, after their fried chicken dinner, someone knocked on their boat.

Stu looked out the companionway.

There was the captain's deputy, holding a bottle of scotch.

Stu climbed up to the deck and the deputy handed him the bottle and said, "Captain said to thank you both for your help tonight and, for the record, your names will not be any part of the official reports."

Henry had another question for Stu. "Why did you want our names kept secret?"

Stu said, "Guys like Jeff have friends and family. We could wake up dead some morning as payback for our capturing Jeff. Actually, he won't remember much other than our scotch bottle, so let's leave it that way."

Chapter 24

They were both up early the next morning. Stu washed the boat down and filled the water tank. They pulled the boat around to the fuel dock and took on twenty gallons of diesel.

Stu laughed, "I guess I don't need to check the engine oil. I seem to remember doing that last night."

They only had a half of a day's run on the St. Lucie River before docking at the Harbour Ridge Yacht Club. This was the last stop for Henry because Stu's next docking would be in the Bahamas.

During dinner at the club, Henry asked Stu if he thought the police captain had placed the call to Kenny Dillman.

Stu said, "No, I think he got the message without getting caught up in some political stink."

Because it was the custom of the yacht clubs to supply the visiting yachts with the morning paper, they read with great interest the story of the capture of an escaped convict. Nothing was mentioned about their part in the capture.

Henry said that if Stu didn't mind, he would like to take the newspaper article with him.

Hutch departed after breakfast, via taxi, to the West Palm Airport. He thanked Stu for the trip and hoped he would get invited back. Hutch said, "So far, all of my trips with you have always had a little sideshow going on and they have been full of adventure."

In talking with the dock master about his trip to the Bahamas, the dock master suggested that Stu should motor down to Lake Worth in North Palm Beach. He said that he could either anchor there or dock at a marina close to the Lake Worth inlet. He added that the Lake Worth inlet would be a good place to depart from.

Following the dock master's suggestion, he motored down the

Intracoastal Waterway to the marina. He stopped at the fuel dock and again topped off his fuel tank. Stu told the dock master at Lake Worth that he would be departing at first light in the morning.

At the first sign of light the next morning, he was away from Lake Worth and setting sail to the Bahamas. Stu was able to turn the steering over to the autopilot. His wind generator was working, so the batteries had plenty of juice for the autopilot. It was a beautiful day for the crossing. There wasn't another boat to be seen in any direction. The wind was out of the south, which helped keep the sea calm.

It was a little after four in the afternoon when he arrived at West End in the Bahamas. Stu was able to clear customs and immigration. The immigration officer's main concern was if he had a gun aboard.

Stu reported that he only had the flare gun.

The custom's officer wasn't busy and said he wanted to check out Stu's boat for contraband.

As it turned out the officer was more interested in a tip. The officer picked up the bottle of 12 year old scotch that had been presented to him at Indian Town. "I've never had any of this before."

Stu reached over and took the bottle from him saying, "Most likely you never will."

The officer said, "Man, you not being friendly!"

Stu said, "I can be friendly. Come back later and I'll buy dinner."

The officer was quick to say, "Now, that's being friendly!"

The officer came back later and Stu invited him to have a drink before they left. Stu opened the scotch and poured it over ice and added a little water.

The officer said his name was Sonny Joe.

After they downed their drinks, Stu got the impression that Sonny Joe wanted another, but that wasn't going to happen.

They drove in a golf cart to a small native restaurant, less than a quarter of a mile away.

Sonny Joe suggested that Stu should order the fried conch.

Stu did, and it was great.

Sonny Joe said, "When you get down to Nassau, don't bother ordering fried conch. Man, you will think you are eating a rubber tire. Only the out-island people know how to fix conch."

There was a large chart of the Bahamas on the restaurant wall.

Sonny Joe pointed out Great Sail Cay. "That's got to be your first stopping point. It's a good anchorage and there just isn't no other place to stop."

Stu had already determined he would be sailing to Great Sail Cay next, from the guidebook he had purchased.

On the ride back, Sonny Joe commented that Stu was the only white man in the restaurant. "It doesn't seem to bother you."

Stu said, "Maybe I didn't notice. I'm used to sitting with blacks, but if I had noticed, it wouldn't have bothered me."

Sonny Joe said, "You different, man."

Back aboard his boat, he was busy making up his bunk for the night, when he realized that they had failed to unload Nick's ashes in the Gulf Stream. Not a disaster. He could do that later.

The next morning was a day like no other. The weather was great and there was a nice breeze from out of the south. Leaving the marina was no problem. Stu now had his small Bahamian flag flying from his rigging, which showed he was a visiting yacht and had cleared customs. As he entered the area north of West End, the water turned from a deep blue to a bright turquoise. The entire area was very shallow, with a bright sand bottom. The first three miles of the trip were well-marked and after that it would be clear sailing.

He waited until after he had cleared the marked area before he raised sail. The sail across the North Bahamas Bank was extremely smooth. Once under sail, Stu again engaged the autopilot. This freed him and allowed him more time to be checking his position.

Later in the day, as he spotted Great Sail Cay, he saw what he first thought was a large, white house on the island. After sighting it through his field glasses, he realized it was a large yacht.

Stu secured his sails before motoring into the anchorage area.

The yacht was the same one he had seen twice before; first, at the Field Club, and then again, in Fort Myers. He headed into the wind and stopped his boat. He ran forward and started lowering his anchor. The anchor chain made a loud rattle as it was lowered. This announced his presence in the area. He had arrived unnoticed up until that time.

A lady was sunbathing on the front deck. Stu hadn't noticed her, prior to dropping the anchor. She stood to see what was going on, not realizing that she was completely naked. When Stu realized that she was watching him, he raised his hand and gave her a little wave. At this point, she realized she was missing something and reached down to pick up a large beach towel to cover herself. Then, she retreated into the interior of the vessel.

Stu had wanted a cold beer all day, but he had waited until he anchored before he popped the cap. He was below deck when he heard the putter of a small outboard motor. Someone was calling him from the approaching dinghy.

Stu stuck his head out the companionway.

"Hello there, I'm your neighbor off of the Dry Hole. We have a little problem with where you have anchored."

Stu asked, "How's that?"

"We check the radius of our anchor swing and when the wind changes directions later tonight we are going to be on top of you. If it's okay with you, I'll help you anchor off our stern."

Stu agreed and the man came aboard to help him.

"Name's Peter. We have been here for two days. It's a great area to spear Bahamian lobster. I've managed to just about get our freezer full."

After they had finished anchoring the boat, Stu invited Peter to have a beer.

They sat in the cockpit of Stu's boat, enjoying their beer. Peter said that they were just cruising, with no time schedule or set destination.

"Sounds a little like what I'm trying to do."

There were just three of them on the boat; Peter and his wife, Mary, and the owner's niece, Megan.

"Megan's the redhead," he laughed. "I think you might have already seen her."

Stu said, "I guess I took her by surprise."

Peter reported that he and Mary had taken care of the yacht for several years. "There were years when we never left the dock in St. Petersburg. Two weeks ago, we were told to get the boat ready for this cruise. I had to get the boat down to Fort Myers and wait for Megan to show up. Before this trip we really didn't know Megan Fitzgerald even existed, nor did we know anything about her. Mary has been able to pick up a little from her about who she is and where she's been.

"Apparently, Megan was engaged to get married to a young Marine officer that was killed in Vietnam. Sometime after that, she retreated into a convent and became a nun. She was a nun for over ten years. Her uncle arranged this trip as a halfway cruise. Kind of like a halfway house for Megan coming out of the convent."

Peter then invited Stu to have a lobster dinner aboard the Dry Hole.

Stu accepted his offer, but said he would need to shower first.

Peter said that he would come back for him in about an hour, if that would be okay. As he shoved off in his dingy he said, "See you in an hour, Vogel."

Vogel! Stu didn't remember telling Peter his full name. Maybe he had; he just didn't remember.

The hot shower on his boat revived him.

Peter showed up as expected.

Both Mary and Megan were on the aft deck to greet Peter as they arrived. Mary and Megan were barefoot and wore full-length cotton chambray dresses. Megan was a redhead and Mary a blond.

Peter introduced everyone to each other.

Mary announced that she and Megan had started a bottle of white wine in Peter's short absence and asked if Stu would care to join them.

They sat on the rear deck of the yacht, enjoying their wine and watching Peter start the charcoal fire in the grill. Mary had made a pasta salad that was to be served with their meal and had already had it placed on the dining table.

Megan was extremely pleasant. She asked Stu if he had been in the military.

Stu said, "Yes, I was in the Marines for awhile."

She asked, "Vietnam?"

Stu said, "No, I was in Korea. Different war, different year."

She kept pumping him. "Do you have a family?"

Stu replied, "Just a sister and two nieces."

She wanted to know, "Have you done much cruising in the Bahamas before?"

Stu answered, "No, this is my first trip to the Bahamas."

Stu sat there, answering Megan's questions as fast as she could come up with them. Stu didn't feel like he needed to ask Megan anything because Peter had already done a pretty good job of filling him in.

Peter joined them, once he had gotten the fire started. He had poured a little scotch over some ice. He showed Stu what he had used to spear the lobster. "It's called a Hawaiian Sling." Peter pointed out that spear guns were illegal in the Bahamas, but these slings were legal to use. "If you would like, I'll take you out in the morning and show you how it's done."

Stu agreed, saying that would be great.

The dinner was wonderful. Throughout dinner, Megan continued asking Stu questions. She wanted to know if he was married or had ever been.

Stu felt that it was show and tell time. "Let me tell you a little about myself and then you won't have to ask so many questions. You might have even read about me in the papers recently."

Stu went through the whole ordeal of his being in prison and ended his story with Senator Wathen's arrest.

Megan said she remembered reading the story in the Wall Street Journal. "My Uncle Charlie showed it to me when I was in his office. Uncle Charlie is the one that owns this boat, I think. Charlie and my dad were both brothers and partners, so now I'm Charlie's partner. Most likely this boat belongs to one of our holdings."

Peter was a little surprised when Megan started talking about herself. Up to this time, she had been very much to herself during the cruise. All that Peter knew was what Uncle Charlie had told him.

After dinner, Mary played some soft island music on their CD player. Megan asked Stu if he would dance with her.

He jumped to his feet. She was very soft to touch. They danced slowly.

"I want to apologize for startling you with my nudity this afternoon. You really caught me by surprise. We had been here for two days, and I was beginning to think it was my private world."

Stu laughed, "Actually, I didn't mind it at all."

She gave him a little squeeze and said he was a little bit of a devil.

Mary brought out some homemade ice cream she had made earlier. They sat and gazed at a sky full of stars, while enjoying Mary's ice cream. Stu kissed both of the girls on the cheek before departing.

Mary suggested that if they were going lobster spearing in the morning, Stu should join them for breakfast.

Stu had no trouble accepting the invitation.

Back on his boat, lying in his bunk, his thoughts were of Megan. Do people just fall in love that quickly? There was just something about her. He had never been in love and wasn't too sure about his attraction to her. When he left The Dry Hole, it had seemed as if she wanted him to stay.

Peter had said he would pick up Stu early the next morning so they could all have breakfast on the rear deck of The Dry Hole.

Stu was still asleep when Peter knocked on the side of his boat. He told Peter to give him a few minutes. In short time, he was riding back with Peter, very anxious to see Megan again.

Stu was dressed in his bathing suit and grey sweatshirt. He hadn't shaved and was barefoot. Megan was there to greet them as they arrived. Mary was in the galley, dishing up their breakfast. Megan bent over, holding out her hand to help Stu come aboard. As he stepped on the deck, she gave him a surprise kiss on the lips. His heart sped up. He was thrilled. What an exciting woman.

Breakfast was a fresh melon, followed by an omelet with toast and coffee.

After breakfast, Peter gathered all the gear that they would need for their morning excursion.

Megan asked Peter if she could ride along.

He responded, "No, Mary wouldn't be safe being left by herself."

Megan understood.

Stu caught on to the spearing of lobster. Peter carried a net bag, where he placed their catch. Back in the dinghy, he cut the tails away from the rest of the lobster. Peter threw the tails in a bucket of ice and then motored to another location. They repeated the process several times before returning to The Dry Hole.

It was still early in the day. Stu had no idea as to what he wanted to do. He didn't want to lose contact with Megan. He asked, "Where are you guys headed next?"

Peter said he was thinking about pulling his anchor up and heading to Green Turtle.

Stu said, "Well, I'll do the same and maybe we can meet up again."

Megan spoke up, "I've never been sailing. Could I ride with you, Stu?"

Stu was caught by surprise, but it seemed like a great idea to him, too.

Peter suggested an anchorage where they could meet later. It was thirty miles east of where they were. Peter and Mary would take *The Dry Hole* there ahead of them and have dinner ready when they arrived.

Megan was very excited to be on Stu's boat. She wanted to know what she could do to help.

Stu said, "Give me a few minutes to study the charts and plan our course. Then we can raise anchor and get underway."

Peter and Mary had pulled out of the anchorage ahead of them. Once Stu reached the point where he could safely clear the island and head east, he set the autopilot. Megan followed him forward and watched him raise the mainsail.

After he had unfurled the headsail, he turned off the engine and set the sails. It was another perfect day for sailing. Megan kissed Stu on his cheek and thanked him for allowing her to sail with him.

As lunchtime approached, they both agreed that they weren't hungry.

Later in the day, Stu checked their progress. He hadn't spotted the Dry Hole yet, but he figured that it should appear on the horizon soon. He was able to reach the Dry Hole by marine radio.

Peter reported that Mary was busy in the galley and that they were going to have spaghetti for dinner.

Stu reported back that spaghetti sounded great and mentioned that he had some very good red wine to add to the meal. "This wine has a story attached to it and I think you will enjoy the story almost as much as the wine."

Chapter 25

When they finally reached the anchorage, Peter radioed that Stu should raft alongside of the Dry Hole. He was already prepared for their arrival and had several large fenders hanging over the side of the Dry Hole. The fenders were like large cushions that would prevent the boats from rubbing against each other. Peter also had mooring lines ready and Stu was able to secure his boat without any problems.

Megan was quick to report to Peter how much she had enjoyed the day of sailing. "I hope he will let me sign on to crew for him again tomorrow."

Stu said, "Well, I was kind of expecting to meet up with a mermaid, but it looks like she isn't going to show. So, yes, I would enjoy having you aboard tomorrow, too."

Peter had lowered a swim ladder over the side of the Dry Hole. His deck was a good four feet higher than Stu's boat.

Stu handed Peter two bottles of Chianti that had been given to him in New Orleans. Stu said, "Give these a little chill while I'm sprucing myself up."

After he had showered, Stu dressed for dinner, which was nothing more than clean white shorts and a dark blue t-shirt. No shoes. After all, they were in the Bahamas.

Peter, Mary and Megan were all sitting on the rear deck by the time Stu climbed aboard. Megan stood and greeted him with a kiss. Mary had prepared some hors d'oeuvres. Peter said he was having a scotch on the rocks, and the girls were enjoying gin and tonics.

Stu said, "I'll try some of your rotgut scotch with a little water."

Peter said, "Good. I wouldn't want to waste any of my good stuff on a motley sailor."

Megan was thrilled with her first sailing experience and told about everything she could recall of her day.

Stu agreed it had been a perfect day for sailing.

As Peter was opening the wine bottles for dinner, he turned to Stu and said, "Okay, you said there was a story that went with the wine. Let's hear it."

Stu went through the whole story of how he and Henry had met up with Les and then rescued Millie. "Getting the wine was a reward."

Peter commented that that was a pretty exciting story.

"You think that was exciting, wait until I tell you about the most recent experience Henry and I had, moving the boat across Florida. This was a couple of days after we had seen your boat leaving out of the Royal Palm Yacht Club in Fort Myers."

Stu told the story of the visitor who had come aboard their boat at Indian Town. "Henry was scared shitless, but I knew we weren't going to have any problems once we got him drinking our scotch." Stu didn't mention anything about his dealing with the local police chief.

The dinner was terrific and the wine fit in nicely.

After dinner, Megan asked if Stu would like to have a tour of the Dry Hole.

"Yes, I've got no idea what a yacht like this has. She walked him through the main salon and then the pilot steering station. She explained all of the electronics. "Everything here is duplicated topside, on the flying bridge location."

Stu was impressed.

Next, he followed her down a stairway into the kitchen area. It had everything, including a booth that would seat four crew members.

Megan explained that the boat had two generators and both were located beneath where they were standing. "They only use the large generator when using the air conditioner or the heat."

They walked through a long companionway. The large diesel engines were housed on both sides. She opened one of the doors so he could see. The engines still hadn't cooled down from the day's run.

Next she showed him the sleeping accommodations. There were three staterooms, each with its own private bath. She explained that there was another area forward, with accommodations for two crew members, along with an additional bath.

As they were in the process of returning topside, Megan stopped and turned toward Stu. She kissed him and said how much she had loved being with him today. He held her in his arms and kissed her again.

"I hope you want to repeat crewing for me again tomorrow."

After they had returned to the rear deck where Mary and Peter were sitting, Megan announced that she wanted to sail again tomorrow. She said, "We could get an earlier start and meet up again later."

Peter pulled the charts out and found a suitable anchorage. It would be a full day of sailing for Stu to reach the anchorage before dark. It was agreed that he and Megan would get an early start.

With the early starting time, Stu said he had better turn in a little early. Stu thanked everyone for such a lovely evening. Megan followed him to the boarding ladder and kissed him good night.

Stu climbed down the ladder into his boat. Once he was again bedded down in his boat for the night, his thoughts turned to Megan.

Stu was up early and stuck his head out to see the dawn starting to burn off the darkness of the night. He was in the process of fixing his breakfast when he heard Megan come aboard.

Megan said, "You said you wanted to get an early start, so here I am."

They kissed again. Stu wasn't too sure if he wanted to finish fixing breakfast or just stand there and continue to kiss Megan. The coffee was already perking, so he was able to pour them each a full mug. He scrambled some eggs and made toast on the propane stove. After their breakfast, the sun was starting to peek over the horizon. It was indeed a beautiful sight.

Stu started the diesel engine and they untied the lines from the Dry Hole. They motored away without seeing any sign of Mary or Peter. Once clear of the anchorage, they set sail. It was almost three hours before the Dry Hole caught up to them.

Peter called them on the marine radio and reported that there was a tropical storm that was going to hit them later in the evening. He wanted Megan to return to the Dry Hole so he could make it to Green Turtle Harbor before the storm hit. Peter didn't want to meet up with the storm while at anchor.

Megan announced that she wanted to stay aboard Stu's boat.

Peter wasn't very happy with the idea of leaving her, but felt he had no choice. He knew he would be looking for a new job if anything happened to Megan. The best he could do was to explain to Stu that he should go about finding an anchorage, in preparation for the storm. Peter said, "I hope you have two anchors and plenty of anchor line."

Later in the day, the wind was starting to freshen a little, but not enough to make them reduce sail. They followed Peter's instructions about anchoring. As they were anchoring, the rains started and both were soaked through to the skin before they had finished. When they were able to get below, Megan turned to Stu and asked what he could offer in the way of dry clothing.

Stu suggested that she start with a warm shower. He gave her his bathrobe and an extra large white t-shirt. He was able to get out of his wet clothing and into some dry shorts and another t-shirt.

By the time Megan returned after her shower, she was wearing just the t-shirt. It was almost like a dress on her.

Stu turned to Megan and laughed, "I guess you will be spending the night."

Megan said, "Actually I had other plans, but I guess I could change them."

The wind had picked up and was blowing pretty hard. The boat rocked a little.

Megan said she wasn't a scotch drinker, but maybe tonight she should start.

They both had a scotch on the rocks. They hadn't even thought about supper. They started kissing and food was the last thing on their minds. Stu started feeling her breast. It wasn't too much longer before she removed the t-shirt and suggested that they go to the forward bunk. He kissed her, while holding her very close. Then she proceeded to the forward sleeping area. It only took Stu a few seconds to rid himself of his garments and join her.

Stu told her he had never been in love before, but even not having known real love, he knew he loved her.

Megan said she didn't know just when it hit her that she was in love with him, but she knew last night when she went to bed that she wanted him for the rest of her life.

They kissed. He kissed her breasts.

She whispered, "I want you in me now, and hurry!"

Stu was barely in her before she screamed with excitement. When he finally climaxed, she said, "Yes, yes, yes. Oh God, that's wonderful."

Stu pulled a sheet up over them and they lay in each other's arms until they fell asleep. They awoke four hours later and again made love.

"I've heard of people trying to live on love, but I think we should have a little late-night snack," said Stu.

Stu fixed grilled cheese sandwiches and poured them each a glass of milk.

In the morning, Stu showered and Megan cleaned up the galley area.

While Megan showered, Stu fixed some toast, a pot of coffee, and poured two glasses of orange juice.

During their breakfast, he commented that if he had gone to prison, knowing her love, he never would have lasted twenty-five years.

She asked, "Okay, now, when are we going to get married?"

Stu said, "Well, we could get married here in the Bahamas or go back to Oklahoma City. It may surprise you that, for someone who only recently left Eddyville Prison, I have managed to make some very good friends and I might want them to come to our wedding."

Megan said, "Tell me about them."

Stu went through the whole list, including Bob, Catherine, Susan's family, Bruce, Joe, General Lavery, Sergeant Major, Larry, Fred and Henry. He told of his relationship with each.

She said, "Thank you, Uncle Charlie."

Stu asked, "What are you saying?"

Megan said, "We have been set up by my Uncle Charlie. My Uncle Charlie is my father's brother. Fitzgerald Enterprises has always been just the two of them. Now, it's just Uncle Charlie and me."

Stu said, "So, what are you talking about, being set up?"

She said, "Uncle Charlie and Marie never had children. I am the heir to everything. When I went into the convent, Charlie went into depression. He needed me to hold together what he and my father had spent a lifetime building."

Stu said, "I still don't get just what you're talking about."

Megan said, "You will, once I tell you that your good friend, Larry

McConnel, is Uncle Charlie's brother-in-law. Those old foxes set the whole thing up. Charlie flew me down here, saying that a cruise on The Dry Hole would be great for me. He said he would join me later. Peter had us waiting at Great Sail, knowing you would be anchoring there. Now, how does that make you feel?"

Stu said, "Well, I don't know whether to thank Uncle Charlie or Larry McConnel. We'll let them keep their little secret, for now."

She said, "Well, what next?"

Stu suggested that they have their honeymoon right away and then fly back to Oklahoma City for their wedding.

Megan said, "Sounds good to me."

He kissed her and they were back in the sack doing what comes naturally.

They stayed in the anchorage the entire day. The worst of the storm had passed through, but there were a few rain showers that followed.

Their second night at anchor, Stu held a burial service for Nick's ashes. He told of their years together at Eddy. Megan joined in prayer as Nick's ashes were poured into the sea. They lit a small candle, mounted it onto a small piece of Styrofoam and then watched it drift away with the ashes.

They were able to stay in contact with the Dry Hole via the marine radio. Peter was relieved to know they were okay.

Peter informed Stu that he had a boat slip reserved for him at the Green Turtle Club. "Give me a call when you're coming in and I will be down on the dock to help you."

After their arrival at Green Turtle, Peter announced that they had dinner reservations at the Green Turtle Club.

Megan told Stu that she would have to get on The Dry Hole to get dressed for dinner, but she was planning on him staying on The Dry Hole, or she would be staying with him on his boat.

Peter and Mary were having as much fun as anyone. They had been stuck in St. Petersburg for quite some time, and making the trip to the Bahamas was a real treat for them, too.

During dinner at the Green Turtle Club, Stu told Megan that he thought it might be best if he stayed on his boat by himself tonight. She looked at him with a very questionable look.

Stu said, "I'm sorry, but I think there might be some trouble." Stu went on to explain that the man who had been sitting at one of the other tables was Les. Stu reminded them of the story that went with the wine that they had a few nights back.

Peter suggested that it might be a better idea for all of them to stay on the Dry Hole.

Stu said, "No I'll be ready for Les, if he tries anything."

Megan was really worried and didn't want Stu to stay by himself.

"Please, trust me. I have taken care of Les in the past and I can do it again. Just stay away from my boat tonight."

Later, after Stu had returned to his boat, he found the box of small tacks that Lu Sue had made him purchase. He scattered them over the deck, outside the entrance to his companionway. Next, he removed the flare gun from its storage. He closed down his companionway, so it could not be entered from the outside.

It was after one o'clock in the morning when Les came aboard Stu's boat. He had jumped down into the area where the tacks were scattered, with two bare feet. Les yelled out with the pain he was having.

Stu opened his forward hatch and pointed his flare gun at Les. He called to Les, telling him to drop the pistol he was holding.

Les fired toward Stu and missed.

Stu shot Les with the flair and hit his right shoulder. Les went down with a serious burn. He fell on even more tacks, and at this point, was in dire need of help.

The two shots awoke everyone in the area and it wasn't long before a large black man appeared and announced that he was the local constable. Les was still lying in pain on Stu's deck.

Stu explained, the best he could, what had taken place.

The constable radioed for more help and they moved Les to the island jail. The island nurse had to come from the other end of the island.

Les was put into a one man jail cell. The constable explained that Les would be moved to Nassau and held for trial there. After the incident, the constable had found copies of the customs papers that Les had filled out when he entered the Bahamas. Les had signed a statement stating that he did not have gun.

The constable told Stu that he had been sitting on the rear deck of The Dry Hole when the shooting started. Peter had hired his guard services for the entire night.

The next morning, Stu went to where Les was being held. Les was not happy to see him, but was willing to talk.

Les told him about what happened to him in New Orleans. He was drugged and taken to a small room where someone cut off his testicles. Les said that it was eight days before he was taken back to his boat. Les was told never to return to New Orleans. Les wanted to know who these people were.

Stu told him, "They are the same people who will most likely kill you if you ever do return there. Les, I would say you have had a bad run of luck, but I'm sure you were lucky that the father of your fifteen-year-old girlfriend never got ahold of you."

Les shouted, "Fifteen! Millie told me she was nineteen. Shit!"

The constable had Stu make a statement, which was then typed and given to him to sign.

Stu was informed that Les would most likely have to spend five years in the Nassau jail. The constable said, "If he lives that long, he will be free to leave the islands."

Megan was glad to have Les back, safe and sound. She said, "He could have killed you."

Stu said, "Believe me, I've had closer calls than that. Les wasn't experienced at shooting a gun. Ready, shoot, aim isn't the way you do it. I never pulled a trigger until I was sure I would hit the intended target.

After spending two nights at Green Turtle, both boats moved south to Guana Cay. They anchored offshore and all rode in the dinghy, with Peter at the helm. They had heard about a bar, Nippers, which overlooked the Atlantic Ocean on the other side of the island.

It was a very short walk. The view was awesome. The bar sat on the edge of a cliff with miles of beach in both directions.

After a couple of drinks, they walked to a beachfront restaurant, where they dined.

Their next island visit was the Hope Town Harbor. Peter was able to place a phone call to Uncle Charlie from there. Peter was informed that Megan needed to fly home for a funeral.

Uncle Charlie said that he would have the company plane at the

Marsh Harbor airport by noon the next day. Her mother's sister's third husband had died. Megan didn't really know him, since he had married into the family while she was in the convent. Aunt Mabel was kind of the black sheep of the family.

Peter said, "I told Mr. Fitzgerald that you had a friend that might want to make the trip too. He said any friend of Megan's was a friend of his."

They made arrangements to leave Stu's boat on a rented mooring.

The next morning, they took the water taxi to Marsh Harbor. The sleek Fitzgerald jet was waiting for them when they arrived at the airport.

While in flight, Stu announced that he didn't have much in the way of dress clothes.

She had the co-pilot come back and write down all of Stu's sizes, including shoes. He, in turn, made a radio telephone call back to Oklahoma.

They were able to clear customs and immigration when they landed in Oklahoma City. They were met at the airport by Karl. He and his wife, Alberta, had worked for Megan's family for over forty years. Karl looked after the family's automobiles and drove, when needed. Alberta took care of the inside jobs. They both had additional help, when needed. Karl didn't do any of the yard work and Alberta didn't do any of the cleaning. During most of the time that Megan was in the convent, they were nothing but caretakers, living in the estate home, by themselves. Megan's parents had both died during the first five years she was in the convent.

Karl was driving a twenty year old Lincoln that looked like it had just come out of a new car showroom.

When they reached the Fitzgerald home, Alberta was there to greet them. She announced that some clothes had been delivered earlier and were hanging in one of the guest bedrooms.

Megan looked at Alberta and said, "Would you move Mr. Vogel's things into my room?"

Alberta had changed Megan's diapers when she was a baby, and she knew one thing for sure, and that was to do as told and not to show any surprise at anything.

Megan suggested that they go for a swim, have an early dinner and then meet what little family she had at the funeral home. She had talked to her Uncle Charlie, from the car phone, while they were driving in from the airport. He had pretty much given her a schedule of events.

Uncle Charlie said, "I understand that you have a new friend. I look forward to meeting him."

The pool was enclosed in a glass dome that opened and closed, depending on the season. It was, indeed, very private. They spent more time kissing and touching than they did swimming.

The poolside phone rang and Megan answered it. It was Alberta, wanting to know what they would like for dinner. She said she had the following items she could prepare: sea bass, lobster, fried chicken, steak or barbecued ribs. They both agreed on the sea bass and asked for it to be fixed on the charcoal grill. Megan said they would be down for dinner at 5:30. She said it, more or less, so that Alberta knew they were not to be disturbed.

They showered together before getting into Megan's bed. Stu had noticed a picture of a Marine officer on the night stand next to the bed, earlier, but it had somehow disappeared.

Dressing for the evening, Stu found that he had quite a selection of things to wear.

After dinner, Karl drove them to the funeral home and waited outside. Uncle Charlie was there and very anxious to meet Stu. They visited for awhile. Uncle Charlie wanted to know about their trip in the Bahamas, but he really didn't ask Stu anything about himself. Stu guessed that Uncle Charlie knew most everything that there was to know about him.

The funeral was to be in the morning, with the bishop saying the Mass. They had a luncheon planned at their country club, for after the funeral.

Later that evening, when they were back in her family home, Megan commented that she really didn't like the bishop. "My father was very opposed to my going into the convent. He left his estate in a trust that could never pass on to me, as long as I remained a nun. The bishop was after the Fitzgerald money, and was consistent in his efforts to break my father's trust."

Stu said, "Let's find a jewelry store that is open, to see about getting you a ring before the funeral."

Megan said, "I don't want a diamond. I just want a pretty gold ring. Nothing flashy. I'm going to call Mr. Silverman and have him meet us at his store at eight in the morning. We will have plenty of time to get back here and dress for the funeral."

Stu asked, "Do you think he will agree to meet us that early?"

She said, "I think he won't be able to sleep tonight thinking he might be selling the biggest diamond in his store."

She called Karl and said that they needed him to drive them at 7:45 in the morning.

Karl answered, "Yes, Miss Megan. The car will be waiting at the front door."

Stu purchased a beautiful gold ring that was to serve as both an engagement ring, and later, a wedding ring. Anyone seeing it would most likely assume that it was a wedding ring.

After the funeral, during the luncheon at the country club, the bishop noticed Megan's gold ring. "Sister Megan, is that a wedding ring I see on your finger?"

"I'm not Sister Megan, but Miss Fitzgerald. And, no, it is not a wedding ring, but it will be shortly."

Needless to say, the bishop did not like the manner in which Megan spoke to him. She had no fear of him or his church. She had been an insider and knew a few things he wouldn't care to discuss.

Aunt Mabel heard something said about a ring and rushed over to see. "Well, bless you child. Now that leaves the rest of the field open for me."

"Aunt Mabel, don't tell me you're already looking for another man!"

"Yep, and I want a young one this time. I am tired of stains on ties and flies."

Uncle Charlie was very pleased to see the ring. He looked at it with pride, feeling he had pulled off a major coup. And, maybe he had. He asked Stu if he would mind coming by his office in the morning and staying through lunch. "It looks like you're going to be one of us."

Stu said, "I'm going to be married to Megan and her name will be Vogel after the wedding."

The next morning, in his office, Charlie explained that he had had to carry the ball ever since Megan's father died. "We were great together. We started as roughnecks working on oil wells, and then we started cementing wells. We started and built one of the largest service companies to the oil industry. We drilled our own wells and had great success there, too. Later, we created a marine division and built offshore oil platforms. We drilled our own wells offshore, too. Somewhere along the line, we got into banking. We have the controlling interest in the largest bank in the state. We also have a real estate holding company that owns several large properties, both here, and in Tulsa. Every division has an operating manager, but somehow all of the big problems come right back to this office."

Stu said, "I can understand that. So, what are your big problems today?"

Charlie said, "Well, we have a major construction site, south of New Orleans, where we build the offshore rigs. There is a gang of rednecks down there that has been vandalizing our work. They are trying to sell us protection."

Stu spoke up, "This may seem strange, but I may be able to help you with that one. Let me borrow your phone."

He went through his billfold and found the phone number that Tony Mandolino had given him in New Orleans.

After dialing the phone, a soft voice answered, "Yes."

Stu said, "May I speak to Tony Mandolino?"

The voice on the other end said, "Who's calling?"

Stu said, "Stewart Vogel. I helped a friend of Tony's daughter a few months ago. He might remember."

After a short pause, Tony said, "I remember, Mr. Vogel. What can I do for you?"

Stu told Tony, "There is a group south of New Orleans that has been giving Fitzgerald Marine Construction some problems with vandalism, while trying to sell them protection."

Tony asked, "How do you fit in with Fitzgerald?"

Stu replied, "Family."

Tony said, "I'll send Sammy and Oil down to take care of it for you this afternoon."

"Thank you very much," said Stu. "I really appreciate your help."

Tony commented, "Call me anytime. I enjoyed reading about you in the newspapers."

Stu said, "I also need to tell you about Les. I met up with him last week in the Bahamas." Stu then proceeded to tell him the whole story of the events at Green Turtle.

After getting off the phone, Stu said, "Okay, Uncle Charlie. I just fixed your problem."

"Well, I doubt you could help me very much on this one. The president, and CEO, of our bank has cancer and has taken a leave of absence. He won't be coming back. There just isn't anyone in the bank capable of filling his shoes. All we have is a bunch of young kids farting through silk underwear, thinking they know everything. They are so impressed with their golf scores, that nothing else matters."

Stu surprised Charlie when he said, "Maybe I can help there, too."

Charlie said, "Now you're a banker?" Charlie was just a little put out, knowing most of Stu's background.

Stu said, "Let me ask you a question. Did you learn from your mistakes or didn't you ever make any?"

Charlie thought that was a funny question and was wondering where Stu was going with it. "Hell yes! I made more than my share of mistakes. It was a hard way to learn, but I did learn."

Stu said, "There is a guy selling used cars here in town that you might want to consider."

Charlie responded, saying, "That's the nuttiest thing I've ever heard; a used car salesman being CEO of a half-billion dollar bank."

Stu asked, "Do you know Tony Luci?"

Charlie said, "Hell, everyone knows Tony. He's one sharp cookie. Got ruined in the downturn of the oil industry. I haven't heard anything about him since his bank folded. His home was down the street from where I live. I know it's been sold. I heard he lost everything. Haven't heard about him lately, though."

Stu asked, "Do you think he has what it would take to run your bank?"

Charlie said, "I hadn't thought of him, but yes, he could be real good. How do you happen to know Tony?"

Stu said, "I don't, but I would like to talk to him, if you are interested."

Charlie said, "Okay. Go find him and bring him back here. I'm more than interested."

Stu needed the local telephone operator to get Tony's new home phone number. Stu talked to his wife and found out where the used car lot was where Tony was working.

Karl was waiting down in the lobby entrance. Stu gave him the address of the used car lot.

When they pulled onto the lot, Tony came out of the little, white-framed office building. He looked at the shiny old Lincoln, with Karl sitting behind the steering wheel, wearing his black chauffeur's cap. He guessed that Stu was another ex-oilman looking to unload a big piece of iron. Stu was out of the car and headed towards Tony.

Tony asked, "How can I help you?"

Stu asked, "Are you Tony Luci?"

Tony returned Stu's question with another question. "Are you another lawyer?"

Stu replied, "No!"

Tony asked, "Do you work for a collection agency?"

Again, Stu said, "No."

"Okay, you know who I am," Tony said. "What's your business?"

"Let's go in your office," Stu suggested. "It's a little warm, standing here in the sun."

Once they were both seated, Stu said he wanted to find out if Tony had any interest in getting back into banking.

Tony answered, "Yeah, like I'd rather be selling used cars. What bank and what kind of position?"

"How would being CEO of Fitzgerald's bank sound to you?" asked Stu.

Tony asked, "What's with Tommy Marshall? He can't be wanting to retire."

"Health," Stu answered.

"Did Tommy send you to talk to me?" asked Tony.

Stu said, "No."

"Whose idea was it to talk to me?" asked Tony.

Stu said, "Mine."

"Who the hell are you?" asked Tony. "I don't think you told me your name."

"Stewart Vogel. I am a good friend of Bob Henderson."

Tony said, "Well, I don't understand. Why would a good friend of Henderson want to help me?"

Stu spoke up, saying, "Actually, I don't give a shit about you, but I suspect you might be a good man for the job. My interest is Bob's boys. I want you to consider making sure Bob gets to know his sons. If you cannot agree to that, well, you can just keep on selling used cars."

Tony said, "No problem there."

"Okay," Stu said. "Lock this place up and let's go have lunch with Charlie Fitzgerald."

Tony said, "I can't believe this is happening."

They climbed into the back of the Lincoln and then headed back to Charlie's office.

Everything went well between Charlie and Tony. They went to lunch at the local Petroleum Club. Several of the members came to the table to say hello to Tony. These were the same people that wouldn't have given him the time of day, earlier. The fact that he was sitting with Charlie Fitzgerald changed things. No one paid any attention to Stu. Charlie tried to introduce him a couple of times, but everyone was most interested in shaking Tony's hand. If any of the Petroleum Club members had any idea that Stu was soon to be Megan's husband, they would have worn him out, shaking his hand.

It was agreed, over lunch, that Tony would start at the bank in ten days.

Charlie said he would give Tony a fifty thousand dollar advance, so he could start getting his feet back on the ground. He asked Tony for his card and said, "You can expect my check this afternoon. I'll need you to come into my office in a few days. I'll give you a call."

Stu rode back to Charlie's office with Charlie, and Karl took Tony back to the car lot.

Charlie said, "Well, I have accomplished more than normal today, or should I say, we have. Someone told me that you are also a damned good backgammon player. My brother and I used to play backgammon every afternoon. Megan's father really liked to win."

"I guess if I helped solve your problems, we could find time to play," Stu said.

"You have been a great help today, but the problems in the oil industry are ruining the entire industry," Charlie replied. "Foreign oil is coming in here so cheaply, it has run the price down to under twelve dollars a barrel."

Stu asked, "So, what's the answer?"

Charlie said, "Twenty-two dollar a barrel oil."

Stu asked, "How can that happen?"

"We need an import tax on foreign oil that would target a twenty-two dollar minimum," Charlie replied. "Fitzgerald has three full time lobbyists working in Washington, and so far, they haven't been able to get anyone's attention."

Stu wanted to know if Charlie had talked to the President about his suggestion.

"No, but I have prayed to God," he answered. "I have a better chance of Him listening."

Stu asked, "Would it help if you could talk to the President?"

Charlie said, "It certainly wouldn't hurt. Don't tell me you can arrange that too."

Stu said he could give it a try. He then picked up the telephone and called Sergeant Major.

When he got off the phone, he announced that they would be meeting with the President and one of his advisors at eleven o'clock the next morning and then they would be having lunch at the White House, before flying back.

They played a few games of backgammon. Uncle Charlie talked while they were playing. He mentioned that Megan was the only heir to Fitzgerald Enterprises.

Stu commented that he didn't know what real wealth was. He knew that nothing happened without investments and hard work. "It looks like you and Megan's father had the formula for both. From the little I was able to pick up from you today, it's my guess that Fitzgerald Enterprises is worth over a billion dollars, maybe even two billion. I'm almost past middle age myself. I'm not making any announcement, but Megan is young enough that she could still have a child. So, there could be another heir. I don't feel that I would ever want to be at the helm of such a large enterprise. I'm sure I would be more than capable of making major mistakes that could affect the lives of thousands of people. What were your plans if Megan stayed in the convent?"

"Actually, Megan's father and I were talking about turning the whole company into a charitable trust," Charlie said.

"Charlie, let's think about maybe doing that anyway," Stu said. "Think of the good we could do."

When he returned to Megan's home, he asked if she would be interested in meeting the President. "Your Uncle Charlie and I are flying up to Washington in the morning. Why don't you come along?"

Megan said, "Well, thanks for the short notice. Of course I'll go, but not to see the President. I just want to be with you."

The plane lifted off at five thirty CST. They were going to be very early.

Stu asked if they could pick up two friends on the way.

He phoned Catherine and General Tom Lavery. It was seven o'clock their time.

Stu said, "If you guys can high-tail it out to the airfield, we will pick you up and take you to the White House for lunch."

They both agreed. The plane was barely on the ground at the Paris Island Marine Base before they had boarded.

When they landed, Sergeant Major was waiting with a White House limo. It had been a few weeks since Stu had seen the General.

Stu introduced Megan and Uncle Charlie.

They had a motorcycle escort to the White House.

Megan leaned over and whispered in Stu's ear that she would rather be back in the Bahamas with just him.

Sergeant Major suggested that he arrange a private tour of the White House, while Charlie had his meeting in the Oval Office. They would all get to meet the President during lunch.

Megan was impressed and asked, "How do you know all of these people?"

"It's a long story that I'm saving for a cold, rainy night," Stu replied.

Charlie's meeting with the President had gone well. They had come to some kind of plan. The President was happy to see everyone, especially Stu. During lunch, the President asked Megan when she and Stu were getting married.

Stu spoke up before Megan had a chance to answer, "As soon as possible."

The President said, "I'm sure you remember the Attorney General. I could arrange for him to marry you in the Oval Office after lunch."

Stu looked at Megan. "It's up to you. What do you think?"

She answered, "Let's go for it."

Sergeant Major jumped up and left the room to start making the arrangements.

Catherine was Megan's maid of honor and Sergeant Major was Stu's best man. Stu had asked the Attorney General to make a few remarks, saying that he and Megan wanted to thank Larry McConnel and Charlie Fitzgerald for making this day possible.

Charlie's expression was like a little kid, caught with his hand in the candy jar.

After the short service, they were ushered into another room where there was a small wedding cake and champagne glasses being filled, as they entered the room.

Sergeant Major rode in the limo with them to the airport. He thanked Stu for bringing Charlie in and said, "I feel that both the nation and the oil industry profited from this meeting."

Catherine and Megan had become friends. Charlie was happy. Megan was married. It was just a good day all around.

After they had dropped off Catherine and the General, Charlie announced that he wanted to talk a little business with the two of them. "First of all, Stu, the President understood what I was saying about the oil industry, but he didn't feel he could get Congress to go along with the tax. Your friend, Sergeant Major, came up with an idea, but I'm not free to talk about it. Now, let's talk about family business."

Charlie said, "Megan, when you entered the convent, both your father and I were concerned about the future of Fitzgerald Enterprises. We had a plan to convert it into a charitable trust. Stu and I had a little visit yesterday. I feel that the two of you could do a wonderful job of putting Fitzgerald money where it could do the most good. I'm willing to spin off everything but the oil. It will give the trust some income for over a hundred years. This cannot happen overnight, but I can start the wheels in motion, starting tomorrow. I think it would only be fair to turn over some of our interest to all of our employees, past and present."

Megan agreed.

Charlie told Megan, "You don't have to worry about going broke, because you still have thirty million in your name, outside of Fitzgerald Enterprises."

As the plane landed and taxied to the hangar, she said, "There are two things I want to say."

They both looked at her.

"First, we want to fly back to the Bahamas tomorrow," Megan said, smiling. "I'm pregnant."

Epilogue

Five years later, the Vogel twin boys are now four years old. Stu has been elected as a Congressman from Oklahoma and is learning about Washington politics. During most of the year, Megan and Stu live in Georgetown. They keep Stu's sailboat on the Chesapeake Bay so they can sail with their boys on weekends. Sergeant Major is working in Stu's Washington office as his aide. Senator Wathen was released from prison after serving three years. He is now living in Europe. Margaret Dunn is still in prison.

Acknowledgements

A special thanks to Ann Korb and Martha Mehringer for their editing and proofreading. I would also like to again thank the many veterans that shared their wartime stories with me. Front cover photograph credit goes to Terri Sauer. The picture of the author was taken by his wife, Rebecca Manion.